KEVIN HASLAM

The Cotton Candy Machine

First published by Calling Field Press 2026

Copyright © 2026 by Kevin Haslam

All rights reserved. No part of this publication may be reproduced, stored, or transmitted in any form or by any means, electronic, mechanical, photocopying, recording, scanning, or otherwise without written permission from the publisher. It is illegal to copy this book, post it to a website, or distribute it by any other means without permission.

This novel is entirely a work of fiction. The names, characters, and incidents portrayed in it are the work of the author's imagination. Any resemblance to actual persons, living or dead, events, or localities is entirely coincidental.

Kevin Haslam asserts the moral right to be identified as the author of this work.

Kevin Haslam has no responsibility for the persistence or accuracy of URLs for external or third-party Internet Websites referred to in this publication and does not guarantee that any content on such Websites is, or will remain, accurate or appropriate.

Designations used by companies to distinguish their products are often claimed as trademarks. All brand names and product names used in this book and on its cover are trade names, service marks, trademarks, and registered trademarks of their respective owners. The publishers and the book are not associated with any product or vendor mentioned in this book. None of the companies referenced within the book have endorsed the book.

First edition

ISBN: 978-1-7323668-7-9

Cover art by Yoonie Co.

This book was professionally typeset on Reedsy.
Find out more at reedsy.com

For Daisy Buchanan—our beloved Saint Bernard, gentle giant and patron saint of puddles and porcelain—who treated the bathtub like a throne and turned even the loudest days into something softer.

Cotton candy is a soft thing made by force—
sugar spun until it forgets it is sugar.
A man can do that too:
spin himself into ease,
and call it "fine."

—Richard Twister, "Dissolve"

Preface

There is a kind of work no one puts on a résumé.

It happens before the day "starts," in the soft hours when the house is still negotiating itself into wakefulness: a lunchbox built from whatever is left, a permission slip found under a receipt, a small person's socks treated like moral pairs, a dog's quiet supervision, the tiny treaties you sign without ink because there's no time to draft a constitution every morning. Then you drive to the place where you are paid, and everyone agrees to call that "work," as if the first part were merely love, and love were free.

This book begins inside that seam—between what counts and what costs.

It is not a book about the big, cinematic disasters. No burning buildings. No courtroom revelations. No villains with theme music. The threats here arrive in the modern way: a short email with no greeting; a door that is always half closed; a meeting stacked on top of another meeting like pancakes made of dread. A man whose power is expressed through implication, through questions that aren't questions, through a smile that denies responsibility while it rearranges the air. A culture that calls your humanity "emotional," your boundaries "rigidity," your exhaustion "a performance issue." The violence is polite. The lighting is fluorescent. The damage is cumulative.

If you've lived long enough in rooms like that, you learn something. You learn that language can be both shelter and trap. You learn that

"How are things?" can be a setup. You learn to provide the right amount of information—enough to seem cooperative, not enough to be used. You learn to confess preemptively, to offer your own weakness like a peace offering, because you hope it will make the knives put themselves away. And then, if you're unlucky, you take that training home. You bring it into your kitchen. You let it sit at the table with your child.

Declan Burke is not a monster. He is not an angel. He is a person whose nervous system has become a kind of second job.

He is a husband, a father, an employee, a son—roles that are supposed to coexist inside one body, as if one body can hold all that without friction. He tries to do the right things. He tries to be kind. He tries to be calm. He tries to be the bigger person. Those are all good intentions. They are also, sometimes, camouflage.

There is a particular species of self-deception that thrives in adulthood: the belief that avoidance is a personality trait rather than a pattern. Declan calls it patience. He calls it composure. He calls it strategy. He calls it "needing ten minutes." He calls it "later." And because he is intelligent, because he is articulate, because he can make a case for his own behavior with impressive precision, he almost believes himself.

The story you're about to read is, in part, about the moment when that kind of camouflage starts to fail.

It begins small—almost insultingly small. A marker line on a mug. A ritual of coffee measured not by taste but by jurisdiction: a line that says, *Here is where the day begins. Here is where I still belong to myself.* It's a domestic sacrament, not because coffee is holy, but because control is. Declan draws that line the way some people draw borders: not to expand, but to feel safe. He believes the line is structure. Sometimes it is. Sometimes it is a moat.

The trouble with moats is that they keep things out, but they also keep you in.

And the trouble with adulthood is that you can build an entire life out of postponements and call it responsibility. You can delay hard conversations because you're "tired." You can avoid conflict because you're "keeping the peace." You can let a phone ring because you're "in a meeting." You can treat love like a task you will complete when your calendar permits it. You can do this for years. You can do it so convincingly that people begin to tiptoe around the parts of you that feel brittle, the way you tiptoe around someone else's sore spot so you don't have to deal with the reaction.

What changes a person like Declan is not, usually, a lightning strike. It is a sequence of ordinary moments that finally refuse to stay ordinary.

A client who has been angry long enough to stop accepting tone as a substitute for repair.

A coworker who smiles politely while applying pressure like a thumb to a bruise.

A boss who speaks in the passive voice of power: *There's a perception. Some concerns. People notice.* A man who can say "family first" in the same breath as "how flexible is it?" and mean both, depending on which version of you is sitting in the chair.

A son who repeats adult phrases back to you without knowing what they cost.

A wife who names the thing you keep calling something else.

A dog who offers uncomplicated presence and thereby makes human complexity look like a choice.

And, eventually, a father who says "nothing big" in a voice that is older than you want it to be.

If you are looking for a story about a man becoming fearless, this is not that.

If you are looking for a story about a man becoming perfect, this is also not that.

This is a story about a man learning—slowly, clumsily, sometimes too late—that **kindness is not softness. Kindness is structure.** It is not a mood. It is not a performance. It is not a soothing tone delivered while nothing changes. It is the unromantic labor of saying what is true, in order, and then living inside the truth without demanding that everyone else make it comfortable for you.

Structure looks like a clean sentence: *Here is what I can do today. Here is what I cannot. Here is what I need from you. Here is what you can expect from me.*

Structure looks like ownership without theater: *I forgot. I'm sorry. I'll fix it.*

Structure looks like refusing to offer your throat to people who collect throats.

Structure looks like learning which silences are protection and which are punishment.

And structure—perhaps most painfully—looks like finishing the story even when the person you're reading to has fallen asleep.

Because that's where the heart of this book lives: in the tension between being witnessed and doing the work anyway. Between performance and presence. Between wanting credit and wanting contact.

There are people who can't stand children's bedtime. They find it boring, repetitive, sticky. They treat it like a hurdle before "real" life begins again. Declan, on his better nights, understands something different: bedtime is where your child hands you the most unguarded version of themselves and asks you to be steady. Not heroic. Steady. It is where you discover, in miniature, the whole problem of adulthood: how to show up in a way that isn't transactional. How to offer attention without demanding reward. How to be there even when you are tired, even when your mind is sprinting, even when you have been trained by bright rooms and unspoken hierarchies to keep your heart in a locked drawer.

The novel's world is full of sound, but it is also full of a particular kind of listening.

There are the big noises: cartoons too loud, office laughter that tries too hard, traffic, phones buzzing, the vending machine clunk of small money turned into small comfort. And then there are the noises that are not really noises at all—what Declan thinks of as the *choir of the living*: coughs wrapped in tissue, the click of a clipboard, the squeak of hospital shoes, the low murmur of a television doing its best to pretend the world is fine. These are the sounds of bodies continuing. The sounds of time moving. The sounds you hear when you stop filling every gap with explanation.

Declan is not good at gaps. His brain treats a gap as an invitation to catastrophe.

That's part of why the book returns, again and again, to what he can control: a line on a mug, a timeline in an email, the careful order of next steps. He wants the world to be sequential, because sequence is the opposite of panic. Panic is everything at once. Sequence is one thing, then the next. Sequence is the difference between drowning and swimming. Sequence is what lets you live inside a day without turning it into a trial.

And yet—sequence is also what forces him toward the things he wants to postpone.

A phone call you keep delaying does not become smaller. It becomes heavier.

A conversation you keep avoiding does not go away. It moves into the walls.

A relationship you keep "managing" with distance does not become safer. It becomes thinner.

This novel is interested in that thinning: the quiet way people disappear from one another while standing in the same kitchen. The way a marriage can become a system rather than a place. The way a family can turn into a set of roles that are executed efficiently but inhabited less and less.

It is also, stubbornly, interested in repair.

Not the kind of repair you post online, polished and inspiring. The kind of repair that looks like wiping down counters without announcing it. Like adding the appointment to your calendar without asking your partner to do it. Like calling the school instead of leaving the folder on the table as a monument to your own guilt. Like learning to say "no" without attaching an apology that makes "no" meaningless.

Repair is not a montage. It is repetition with intent.

If you've read far enough to find yourself here, you may already recognize this book's sense of humor. It is not the kind that winks at the reader and asks to be liked. It's the kind that shows up when a person is trying not to drown. A line that slips out sideways. A phrase a child says that is accidentally perfect. A small absurdity that makes you laugh and then makes you sad, because the laughter is true and the sadness is also true.

Humor is one of Declan's emergency exits. It is a good tool. It is also, sometimes, a trapdoor. The book doesn't ask you to despise that. It asks you to notice it. It asks you to watch when humor is a bridge and when it is a moat.

The same is true for "being nice."

There are people—good people—who confuse niceness with kindness. They believe kindness means keeping everything smooth. They believe a kind person is someone who never makes things awkward, never causes discomfort, never demands clarity from anyone who has the power to punish them for it. They believe kindness is a tone. They believe kindness is the absence of conflict.

This book argues, quietly, that this is how adults are trained into submission.

Sometimes the most compassionate thing you can do is make the room slightly uncomfortable by naming what is real. Sometimes the most loving thing you can do is refuse to be managed by someone else's fear. Sometimes the clean sentence is the kind sentence, even when it doesn't sound soft.

And sometimes, the cleanest sentence is simply: *I'm here.*

Not "I'm around." Not "later." Not "I'm listening" with a phone in your hand. Here—room, moment, awkwardness, work. Here.

If you've been in a relationship with someone who disappears into themselves and calls it "decompression," you know how lonely that can be. If you've been the person who disappears, you know how necessary it can feel. This book doesn't mock that need. It treats it as real. But it also asks a hard question: what happens when your coping mechanisms become your personality? What happens when your rituals begin to serve avoidance more than health? What happens when your survival skills—learned in rooms where power is predatory—start injuring the people who are not your enemies?

Declan is learning to make a distinction he should have learned long ago: **your bosses are not your family.** The strategies that protect you at work can poison you at home. Silence can be armor in one place and a weapon in another. Confession can be a trap in one room and an intimacy in another. Not everything is a courtroom. Not everything is a threat. And yet, your body doesn't always know that. Your body keeps score. Your body remembers which rooms punished you for being honest.

The novel's question is not: *How does Declan become fearless?*
It is: *How does Declan become available?*

Available to his son's odd questions and sticky cheeks, yes. Available to his wife's exhaustion, which is its own kind of truth. Available to his father, who has a lifetime of sanded-down sentences and still, sometimes, wants to hear his son's voice. Available to himself—his own limits, his own patterns, his own capacity for both kindness and cowardice in the same hour.

Availability is not a personality type. It is a practice.

This is why the book returns to "clean sentences." They are not merely stylistic choices. They are a moral technology. They are a way to live without narrating yourself into paralysis. They are a way to stop turning every moment into a referendum on your worth. They are a way to do the next right thing without demanding that the world reward you for it.

There is a moment in adulthood—sometimes late, sometimes early—when you realize something almost insulting: most days are not made of grand decisions. They are made of small ones. Whether you answer the call. Whether you apologize plainly or hide inside a performance. Whether you draw the line and why. Whether you listen without composing your defense. Whether you finish the page even when the audience is gone.

If that sounds too small to matter, it's because we are taught to look for drama as proof. We are taught that what matters must be loud. But anyone who has lived through real adulthood knows the truth: the biggest changes happen in the quiet. Not as inspiration, but as sequence. Not as transformation, but as repetition with different intent.

This is, in the end, a novel about men and the ways they are trained to disappear.

It is also a novel about what it costs to stay.

It will not offer you a neat moral. It will offer you a man learning, in painful increments, that love is not something you feel and then keep private. Love is something you do in public, in the form of responsibility. Love is structure. Love is a calendar entry you didn't leave for someone else. Love is a call you make even when you're afraid of what it will require. Love is letting the clean sentence stand without dressing it up to be palatable to the wrong people.

And if you've ever sat in a waiting room under fluorescent honesty—if you've ever listened to the choir of bodies continuing—if you've ever watched someone you love try to shrink a "big" thing into "nothing" because naming it felt like inviting it in, you will recognize what Declan is up against.

He is not fighting a dragon.

He is fighting *later*.

He is fighting the instinct to build his life out of lines and moats and postponed calls. He is fighting the urge to survive his days rather than enter them. He is fighting the inherited belief that tenderness is embarrassing, that need is weakness, that being witnessed is more important than being present.

The book does not pretend this fight is glamorous. It is not. It is daily. It is awkward. It is sometimes funny in the way a mistake is funny until you realize what the mistake protects you from. It is sometimes sad in the way a kitchen is sad when it's quiet and you can hear the refrigerator hum and nothing else.

But it is real.

And if there is any hope here—any cherry on top—it is this: a life can be rebuilt without grand gestures. A man can learn to stop confessing to people who collect confessions. A man can learn to stop punishing the people who love him with silence. A man can learn to become sequential, to do one thing, then the next, until the day is no longer merely a sentence he must serve.

So, consider this your permission slip, if you need one.

Not permission to excuse Declan. Not permission to admire him. Permission to recognize what is familiar: the tightness in the throat when the phone rings, the relief and shame of voicemail, the way a clean sentence feels like stepping into traffic the first time you say it. Permission to notice how often adults are taught to manage pain rather than repair it. Permission to see the invisible labor that holds a house together and the quiet resentments that grow when that labor is treated like air.

And if you find yourself laughing at the absurdity—at the marker line, at the phrase a child adopts like a new religion—let yourself laugh. Humor is not denial here. It is a small act of refusal. It is the proof that the mind is still alive inside the machinery.

Then turn the page.

The day is already starting.

Prologue

The phone lay on the counter face-up, bright as a small accusation.

Declan had placed it there deliberately, as if visibility could count as virtue. As if not hiding the thing was the same as doing it. The screen had dimmed, then lit again with a soft pulse—an afterglow of notification—before settling into that quiet, dead stare devices had when they were waiting to be touched.

He stood at the sink rinsing his mug, letting hot water run over the inside like he was scrubbing out a thought.

The marker line had survived the night. It hadn't run this time. It held its place along the ceramic like a border on a map—thin, black, decisive. He'd drawn it in the half-light before anyone else woke, that old, private ceremony: a man making a small law in a world that didn't ask his permission. The mark was supposed to mean something simple: *stop here*. A limit you could point to when everything else was slippery.

This morning it felt less like a limit and more like a symptom.

He ran the sponge along the inside of the cup anyway, not touching the line, careful around it, protective of it the way people were protective of quirks they pretended were principles. The water smelled faintly metallic, the way it always did in winter. The faucet hissed. The drain gurgled. The house layered its own sounds on top: a distant floorboard settling, the refrigerator humming, the heat clicking on with a small, impatient clack—brief, disconnected noises that formed a kind of domestic Morse code.

Time is already moving. Keep up.

In the doorway Daisy watched him.

She wasn't in the way. She didn't pant or beg or perform. She simply existed at the threshold—huge and quiet, a body built for rescue that had become, in this house, a kind of emotional infrastructure. Her head was slightly tilted, her eyes steady. She looked at Declan the way a good dog looked at a person who was trying to get away with something: patiently, with the polite insistence of an animal who didn't accept theater as proof.

Declan shut off the water and held the mug in both hands. Warm ceramic. Wet glaze. A small heat he could control.

The rash on his wrist tingled faintly under his sleeve, a petty little patch of red that flared and faded whenever it felt like it. It was never dramatic enough to justify the dread it triggered, which was part of the torture. If it had been a clear symptom—if it had announced itself in a way you could take seriously—he would have handled it like an adult. Instead it hovered on the edge of meaning, half real and half projection, perfectly tailored to his nervous system: the kind of signal that invited catastrophe without providing evidence.

He pressed his thumb against it once, just to check.

The itch answered, then withdrew, as if even his skin didn't want to commit.

Behind him, something thumped upstairs—Theo, moving through his room with that blunt joy of a child who didn't know the day could be used as a weapon. Then Lena's footsteps, purposeful and already mid-task, crossed the hallway above like a person walking a tightrope she'd been born on.

Declan dried the mug, set it on the rack, and checked his phone again.

He told himself he was not avoiding it. He was spacing it. He was sequencing. He was doing the next thing before the other thing. He was being responsible with his own mind, like someone managing a skittish animal.

He could call his father. He would call his father.

Just not yet.

The notification sat there anyway, patient and blunt:

Voicemail. Walt Burke.

It was the word *voicemail* that did it—old-fashioned, faintly intimate. A call you missed could be dismissed as timing. A voicemail was effort. A voicemail was a person speaking into the air because the air was all they were given.

Declan's throat tightened, the body beginning its familiar translation: *stakes → fear → delay.*

He picked up the phone and turned it over in his hand. It felt heavier than it should have. Smooth glass. Warm from the counter light. He could feel his own pulse in the heel of his palm.

He didn't press play.

He opened the calendar instead, as if paperwork could neutralize emotion.

The day appeared in clean blocks, bright and rectangular, indifferent to his inner weather: a meeting at nine, another at ten, Mitchell prep, internal check-in, a reminder to drink water that felt like a personal insult. Appointments stacked on appointments like pancakes made of dread. The calendar was not a plan; it was an indictment of anyone who believed they had time.

He scrolled down.

There it was again, the thing that had been sitting in his pocket for days without him touching it:

Walt — follow-up. 10:30 a.m.

He stared at it until his eyes stung. The entry didn't explain itself. It didn't soften. It simply existed, calm as a gravestone.

He had not added it.

That was the part that made him feel exposed—the quiet certainty that Lena had been looped in before him, that planning had happened in the room he kept walking out of, that the scaffolding was being assembled around his avoidance to keep the whole house from collapsing.

He set the phone down again, face-up. Not hiding. Just... not acting.

He drifted to the pantry, opened it, and stared at cereal boxes like a man reading legal statutes. His hand went to a box, paused, changed its mind. He wasn't hungry. He was trying to make his body do something normal so his mind would follow.

Theo's feet hammered the stairs—quick, confident, still innocent of how many ways a day could go wrong.

"DAD," Theo called, because Theo did not speak; he broadcast.

Declan turned and watched his son appear—hair sticking up in the back, pajama shirt twisted, carrying a sock in one hand like evidence.

"This one is missing its brother," Theo announced, solemn. "It's a single."

Declan blinked. "Like a song?"

Theo frowned. "No. Like lonely."

Daisy shifted slightly, as if the mention of loneliness required monitoring.

Declan knelt and took the sock, inspecting it with the seriousness of a man pretending socks were not the least of his concerns. The fabric smelled like detergent and child sweat and the soft, sweet rot of something that had been abandoned under a bed for too long.

"We'll find it," Declan said.

Theo studied his face. Sometimes Theo looked at him like he was trying to read instructions. "Are you okay?"

Declan almost laughed. Seven years old and already doing emotional triage. The household had trained the kid without meaning to.

"I'm fine," Declan said automatically.

PROLOGUE

Theo's eyes narrowed with the suspicious wisdom of someone who had heard *fine* used as a doorframe lie. "You're doing your 'fine' voice," he said.

Declan inhaled, then exhaled slowly, the way he did when he was trying to keep the day from turning into performance. "I'm okay," he corrected. "I'm just... thinking."

Theo nodded, satisfied. "Okay. New territory for you, Bucko."

Declan looked at him. "Excuse me?"

Theo grinned. He loved words the way other kids loved sugar—something sweet that made adults react. "New territory," he repeated, enjoying the rhythm. "For you. Bucko."

From upstairs, Lena's voice called, "Shoes. Backpack. Lunch."

Lena entered the kitchen a minute later already mid-motion—hair half-up, sleeves rolled, face in that morning mode that was not unkind but assembled. A person who built the day like a bridge while everyone else was still arguing about the river.

She looked at the mug. She looked at the marker line. She didn't say anything.

Then her eyes flicked to Declan's phone on the counter. The voicemail notification glowed faintly, stubborn.

"Did you call your dad back?" she asked.

Not accusatory. Not dramatic. Practical. Procedural. A gentle probe into the place he kept postponing.

Declan felt heat rise in his throat. "Not yet."

Lena nodded once, the way you nodded at a fact you'd already filed. "Don't make it weird," she said.

Then she turned to Theo, efficient and soft in the same motion: "Did you pack your folder?"

Theo froze. Then looked at Declan, eyes wide with that particular child panic that arrived when adults said the word *folder*. "I have a folder?"

5

Declan's stomach tightened—an echo of the previous week, the forgotten folder, the small failure that had cracked something in the kitchen like a hairline fracture.

"I packed it," Declan said quickly. Too quickly. "It's in your backpack."

Lena didn't look at him. That was mercy. Or fatigue. Or both.

Theo ran off to find shoes. Daisy moved with her slow gravity to stand where she could see the hallway and the kitchen at the same time, a furry checkpoint.

Declan stood at the counter and stared at his phone again.

He told himself: after drop-off. He told himself: once he was in the car. He told himself: once he had silence.

Silence, the addict's word. Silence, the drug he loved because it felt like control and acted like delay.

They got out the door with the usual choreography: coat, backpack, a last-minute bathroom emergency that could not be argued with, Lena handing Declan Theo's lunch with the same firm motion she used to shove a sandwich into a bag.

In the driveway, the cold air bit his wrist. The rash tingled. A small, unnecessary punctuation mark.

Declan drove with the radio off because sound felt like an intrusion. The world outside was damp and unfinished—gray sky, wet pavement, trees stripped down to their honest skeletons. The kind of morning that made everything look like it was waiting for permission to begin.

At a red light, he glanced at his phone in the cup holder.

No new notification. No second voicemail. No third call. Walt's name was not on the screen. That should have felt like relief.

It didn't.

It felt like waiting for a shoe to drop and realizing the shoe might already be on your throat.

Theo hummed to himself in the back seat, then abruptly asked, "Dad,

PROLOGUE

do you ever think you're going to die?"

Declan's hands tightened on the wheel. The question arrived with the casual cruelty of children, who spoke about mortality the way they spoke about snack time: as if the universe were obligated to answer them.

He glanced at Theo in the mirror. Theo's face was open, curious, not frightened. He wasn't asking because he was afraid. He was asking because his brain had just discovered the concept and wanted to touch it.

Declan heard his own voice from another night: *Yeah. All the time.*

He didn't want to put that in Theo's mouth again.

"I think about it sometimes," Declan said carefully. "But mostly I think about breakfast."

Theo seemed satisfied. Then he said, "Are you allowed to be scared?"

Declan almost smiled, then felt his throat tighten. Allowed. The language of permission threading itself into his kid. The subtle dominance of rules without reasons.

"You're allowed," Declan said. "Everyone's allowed. But scared isn't the boss. It's just a feeling."

Theo considered this with his tiny philosopher face. "Okay," he said. "New territory."

Declan dropped Theo off at school and watched him disappear into the building—small body swallowed by institutional hallways. He waited until Theo was out of sight before pulling away, because leaving too quickly always felt like a minor betrayal.

On the drive to work, he told himself again: call Walt at lunch. Call Walt between meetings. Call Walt once you have a minute.

A minute, like it was spare change.

At the office, the air hit him with its usual cocktail: copier toner, cheap citrus disinfectant, overheated printer breath. Fluorescent lights buzzed overhead with a quiet insistence. Adults moved through the hallways with careful choreography—people who did not want to meet anyone's eyes before coffee. The building vibrated with office anxiety, the communal dread of grown-ups pretending not to be scared.

Declan sat at his desk, clicked his computer awake, and watched emails populate like bacteria.

Mitchell's name appeared. His body tightened before his eyes read a word.

He clicked.

The email was almost human. A request. Specific. Reasonable. The tone of someone who had been angry long enough to become tired.

Declan felt a sad kind of pride: structure had done that. Structure made other people less feral.

He started drafting a response—clean, brief, anchored in sequence—when his phone buzzed.

He glanced down before he could stop himself.

Voicemail. Walt Burke.

Still waiting. Still there.

He could listen now. Here, in this office, where everything was already a performance. He could press play and let his father's voice enter this fluorescent room like something living.

He didn't.

He turned his phone face-down in his desk drawer, as if hiding it changed anything.

Then he wrote the Mitchell email the way he'd learned to write lately: plain, honest, unadorned. No apology that begged. No defensive paragraph that hid. Just the truth in a shape someone else could hold.

He hit send.

He stared at the screen, then leaned back, trying to breathe without making it dramatic. Air in. Air out. No story.

A Slack notification chimed. A printer groaned. Someone laughed too loudly. Keys clacked in a panic rhythm. Brief, disconnected sounds forming the office's private choir: *he is not safe here. he is not safe here.*

At 10:17, Kyle appeared at his desk holding a mug and a neutral expression so carefully constructed it looked like it had been assembled in an HR workshop.

"Got a second?" Kyle asked.

Declan heard the old reflex: smile, say yes, keep it light, be easy. The reflex that had kept him employed and exhausted.

He glanced at the calendar block for noon. Lunch. The little empty space he'd been promising to fill with his father's voice.

"Two minutes," Declan said. "Then I have to step out at lunch."

Kyle's eyebrows lifted slightly—an involuntary reaction, as if Declan had used a language Kyle didn't expect him to know. A language with edges.

"Sure," Kyle said.

Kyle talked. Malloy wanted more. Mitchell wanted faster. The timeline needed to be "aggressive." The team needed to be "aligned."

Declan listened, nodded, answered in clean sentences. He did not offer his throat. He did not confess stress. He did not hand Kyle a story Kyle could later turn into a narrative.

When Kyle walked away, Declan's hands shook slightly. Not visible. Not dramatic. Just enough to remind him his body kept score when his face lied.

At noon, Declan took his lunch outside and stood in the cold air with a sandwich he could barely taste. The traffic beyond the parking lot moved steady and indifferent. A woman ate in her car with her shoulders hunched, staring at her phone like it contained instructions for how to live. A man in a hoodie smoked near the edge of the lot, exhaling slowly, looking at nothing.

Declan pulled his phone from his pocket.

The voicemail notification stared back.

He held it in his hand and felt his mind begin rehearsing the moment the way it rehearsed every hard conversation: scripts, counter-scripts, ways to be tender without being ridiculous.

He could just press play. He didn't even have to call. He could let his father speak and simply listen. That was the low-bar version of courage.

He didn't press play.

Instead he opened messages and typed:

Hey Dad. In meetings earlier. I'll call later.

Later. The word he used to store people he couldn't afford to lose.

He hit send and immediately felt the small, sharp shame of it—like he'd put a bandage over a wound without cleaning it first.

He put the phone back in his pocket and finished his sandwich in three bites, barely chewing. The cold made his jaw ache. The cold made everything feel more real, which was the problem.

Back inside, the day continued. Mitchell. Malloy. Kyle. Emails stacking. Meetings multiplying. The urgent always grew new heads.

At 3:06, his phone buzzed again.

For a split second, his heart lifted—hope disguised as dread.

He checked.

Not Walt. Just a reminder: *Drink water.*

Declan laughed once, quietly, because the absurdity was clean. As if hydration was an exorcism. As if water fixed dread.

He drank anyway.

At 5:18, he shut down his computer and walked out to the parking lot under a gray sky that had started dimming into evening. The cold air hit him and his body loosened slightly, as if it had been holding itself together with invisible clenched muscles all day.

He got into his car and sat with his hands on the wheel, listening to the engine tick as it warmed, letting the silence settle.

In the cup holder, his phone lit up again.

Voicemail. Walt Burke.

Still.
Still waiting.
Declan stared at it.

There was a moment—always a moment—where he considered doing the one thing instead of all the other things. Where he considered not negotiating with his fear as if fear were a reasonable man.

He picked up the phone.
His thumb hovered.
He did not press play.

He set it back down, face-up, because he was honest about his avoidance even when he refused to change it.

Then he put the car in reverse and backed out carefully, as if the day might spill if he moved too fast.

Driving home, he told himself: tonight. Tonight he would listen. Tonight he would call. Tonight he would be a son.

The promises sounded clean in his head. They always did.

And somewhere—somewhere in the quiet space between roads and houses and the life he kept postponing—Declan understood, with a clarity that hurt, that his father's voice was sitting right there on his phone like a door left half-open.

A deliberate almost-welcome.

And he kept walking past it like it didn't belong to him.

⁎⁎⁎

He drew the line on the cup, still believing in borders. Not the national kind—those were mostly imaginary anyway—but the domestic kind: the thin, private demarcations that keep a household from turning into a 7:03 a.m. riot. Thick Sharpie. Black as a threat. A simple rule for a complicated mind: nobody talks to him until the coffee drops to the mark.

Declan didn't call it a rule. He called it a system. Systems sounded mature. Systems sounded like something a visionary would have—something nestled somewhere between post-basic and hipster-mythical, like a minimalist monk who owned too many sneakers. A rule was what children had, and children, famously, were ungovernable.

He held the mug up to the light and assessed the line the way a foreman assesses a beam: level, steady, nonnegotiable. The kitchen light was the wrong kind of light—too honest, too yellow in places and too white in others, making the counters look older than they were and his own hands look faintly ill. The cup was already stained from years of mornings—brown rings like tree growth, proof that time had been passing when he swore he'd been standing still. He'd drawn the line last week and redrew it every morning because marker on ceramic fades like virtue: fast, and for no good reason.

There were other rituals, too, smaller and more embarrassing. The way he rinsed the spoon before stirring, as if cleanliness could fix him. The way he clicked the kettle switch twice, superstition dressed as habit. The way he listened—briefly—for the sound of running water upstairs, because if Theo had gotten up first, the day would arrive with its shoes already on.

Behind him, the house was waking the way a ship wakes—slow creaks, distant knocks, a series of brief, disconnected sounds: a drawer's complaint, the cough of a radiator, the soft slap of a bare foot missing the rug and finding hardwood. The noises had their own personality. The fridge hummed like it was thinking. The baseboards popped like someone clearing a throat. The whole place suggested life was happening without asking his permission.

He wanted permission. He wanted structure. He wanted—if he was being honest—to be left alone long enough to become someone worth talking to.

Because the truth, the one he hated, was that he woke up already behind. Not behind on tasks—those would come later, on their little corporate stilts—but behind in himself. Behind the man he meant to be. Behind the version of fatherhood he'd pictured before the kid existed, when fatherhood was an idea and not an alarm that could speak.

The dog came first, because the dog always came first.

Daisy, a Saint Bernard with the lazy intelligence of a man who'd done his work in a previous life and retired early, appeared in the doorway like a soft verdict. Big head. Heavy eyelids. The world's gentlest bouncer. Her fur carried the smell of last night's couch—fabric warmed by bodies, a faint note of dog shampoo that had never fully done its job, and the more honest scent beneath: animal, earth, home. She moved like she had all the time in the world and was generous enough to share it.

Daisy knew the rules. She knew which hand fed. She did enough to pass. She moved through the house with the strategic compliance of someone who had survived multiple administrations. She didn't love him in an idealistic way; she loved him in a practical, infrastructural way. She followed the simple order because order kept the peace—and the peace kept the treats coming.

"Morning," Declan said, because the rule didn't apply to him talking. Obviously. That would be absurd.

Daisy blinked slowly, then padded over and pressed her shoulder against Declan's shin, not demanding, not pleading—establishing contact. A sandbag. A ballast. Her weight was gentle but undeniable, a quiet insistence that he occupy space rather than hover above it. This is where you are, her body seemed to say. In this kitchen. In this morning. In this life you keep threatening to abandon for some future one you'll finally start living.

Declan looked down at her and felt the familiar sting of shame—because Daisy, on paper, had every reason to be selfish. She was enormous. She was powerful. She could take what she wanted. And yet she had never once taken pleasure in wielding it while denying it. Daisy's power was real, but she didn't gaslight the room with it. She simply existed. If she wanted to sit, she sat. If she wanted to lean on him, she leaned. But when the humans started getting sharp, Daisy got soft.

Kindness, Declan thought, was a kind of structure. It held the place up when the beams fail.

The kettle hissed, a small angry serpent sound. He poured. The coffee bloomed, that bitter, wonderful smell—part comfort, part alarm bell. It filled the kitchen the way incense fills a church, except this church had a dish rack, a stack of kid cups, and a magnet on the fridge that said YOU GOT THIS in a font that looked like it had never met an actual human problem.

He took the first sip, too hot, because he liked pain in small doses.

※
※※

It was proof he was still here, still capable of reacting to the world instead of watching it from behind glass. The heat moved down his throat and hit his stomach like a small reprimand. Good, he thought. Something is happening. Something is real.

The line sat below the rim, a good inch and a half. A respectable amount of silence.

He took the mug to the counter like it was an offering. He studied the marker mark again. He said, softly, to no one: "Until there."

He wasn't proud of it. He was proud of the feeling it gave him—two minutes, three, sometimes five, of not being required to perform. Not being required to receive someone else's need and translate it into a face. Because he could do need. He could do emergency. He was excellent in a crisis, the way certain people are excellent on a sinking ship. What broke him was the steady pressure of ordinary life: the ongoingness. The endlessness. The daily proof that you didn't get to clock out of being a person.

From the hallway came a voice—Lena's—already moving, already doing. Her footsteps had purpose. Declan's always had anxiety.

"Do you have the forms?" she called.

The question wasn't hostile. It was a question born of the urgent—the endless procession of small responsibilities that arrive like bills and leave like smoke. School forms. Doctor forms. Insurance forms. Permission slips that made him laugh because nothing in adult life required more permission than trying to keep a child alive.

Declan stared at his cup. The line stared back.

He wasn't mad at Lena for asking. He wasn't mad at their son for existing, or at Daisy for breathing, or at the house for waking. He was mad at time for not slowing down to match the speed of his body. He was mad at his brain for insisting that everything was either trivial or catastrophic.

He always felt he was one bad night's sleep away from a devastating illness. Not a sniffle. Not a cold. A biblical plague. One restless night and the immune system would fold like a cheap chair and his body would take its revenge for all the years he'd treated it like a rental car. He could almost feel the future headline sometimes—LOCAL MAN DROPS DEAD AFTER THINKING ABOUT IT TOO MUCH—and the sick part was that his brain found it plausible.

He'd mentioned this once, casually, as a joke—the way he floated a confession into a room to see if anyone flinches. Lena hadn't laughed. She'd looked at him with an expression that wasn't pity. It was assessment. Like a person checking a bridge for stress fractures.

"You're always waiting for the collapse," she'd said. "Do you know that?"

That morning—this morning—Declan tightened his grip on the mug and tried to remember the difference between patience and being afraid of conflict. For him, there wasn't one. Patience was cowardice with better PR.

"We're not living life," he'd told a friend recently, half-drunk and over-brave. "We're just waiting it out."

His friend had nodded like that was profound. Or his friend had been tired.

Daisy lifted her head, watching him with those careful eyes—the eyes of an animal that had learned human mood the way some people learned weather. Daisy could tell when the air pressure changed. Daisy could tell when a joke was about to become a problem.

Lena's footsteps stopped at the edge of the kitchen, but she didn't enter. She understood the line, too. She'd never agreed to it—she wasn't a citizen of his little republic—but she understood it the way you understand a storm warning. You don't argue with it. You adjust.

Declan hated himself for that: for making her adjust. The selfishness of silence. The way his quiet wasn't neutral—it took up space. It was a tax.

⁂

"I put them on the table," he said, and immediately regretted it, like he'd broken his own law in public. He was allowed to speak. But speaking meant being reachable, and being reachable meant the day could touch him, and if the day touched him too soon, something in him might rash with a whisper.

Lena stepped in anyway. She moved with that infuriating competence—the kind that looked like ease but was really years of practice. She picked up the forms, glanced at them, and then looked at the mug.

"You know," she said, not unkindly, "it's impressive how you can build a whole religion out of coffee."

Declan smiled because he couldn't help it. That was the thing about Lena: she didn't destroy him to correct him. She didn't confuse criticism with cruelty. She offered structure in the form of humor, which was the only kind he could accept before 8 a.m.

"My religion says I can't do that," he said, lifting the mug slightly, like a chalice.

"Cool," Lena replied.

He waited—because this was their dance.

She nodded toward the Sharpie mark. "Your religion says I can't do that," she added, and her smile sharpened just enough to make the point. "Fuck off."

He barked a laugh—quiet, so it wouldn't wake Theo—and Daisy's tail thumped once against the cabinet, as if approving the exchange. As if Daisy, too, understood that a household needs boundaries, yes, but it also needs challenge. It needs someone willing to say: your rules are not the same as everyone's safety.

Declan took another sip. The coffee level had dropped a fraction, an imperceptible mercy. He watched it the way he watched an hourglass. He could almost feel the grains of time slipping, not dramatic enough to stop, but relentless enough to make you tired.

He drew the line anyway—slow, careful—like the marker could enforce peace. The squeak of Sharpie against ceramic made his teeth itch. Ridiculous, he knew. And yet the ridiculousness was part of the relief. If he could control this—this small, stupid thing—the rest of the day wouldn't come apart in his hands.

From upstairs came a thud, then a small voice, half-asleep and already demanding the universe.

"Dad?"

The word hit Declan like a hand on the shoulder.

He didn't move right away. He watched the coffee, then the line. He watched Daisy, who had already shifted her body toward the stairs, loyal as gravity.

"Dad," Theo said again, louder now, the patience of childhood already spent.

Declan felt it—that familiar mismatch between his ability and his ambition. He wanted to be something larger than his moods. He wanted to be the visionary and the transcendentalist, the guy who stretched toward new territory. But he was also, often, a man with a cup of coffee and a marker line trying to buy himself a little peace.

And the problem was: the peace was never just his. The peace had a cost. It always did. Somebody paid.

He took one more sip. The coffee fell, finally, brushing the mark.

He exhaled, as if stepping over a border.

"Okay," he said, and his voice was softer than he intended. "Okay. I'm coming."

Daisy went ahead, heavy and gentle, carrying the first portion of the day on her back the way saints carry burdens in old paintings.

And Declan followed—mug in hand, line behind him—trying, for once, not to wait his life out, but to enter it.

※

By the time Declan reached the top of the stairs, Theo had already escalated from Dad? to Dad!—the way a tiny person can turn a syllable into a subpoena.

The clock on the landing read 6:42. The red digital numbers looked too crisp for what they represented, like time was something clean and reasonable instead of a hand on his throat. In nineteen minutes, the school's aftercare window would start charging in half-hours, and the mortgage autopay would hit at noon whether he'd earned the day or not. Adult life ran on invisible timers: grace periods, late fees, things nobody explained until you were already failing them.

The hallway smelled like night: warm dust, dryer sheets, the faint sweetness of Theo's shampoo lingering in the bathroom like a promise the day would immediately break. The banister felt cold and slightly sticky under Declan's palm—some residue of kid hands and life, the tacky proof of living in a house with another nervous system inside it.

Daisy arrived first, of course. That was her gift: she was always early to the emotional scene, like a bouncer who also happened to be a therapist. She stood at the doorway of Theo's room and performed her usual assessment—ears slightly forward, head tilted, eyes doing the soft math of human mood.

Theo was sitting up in bed, hair in every direction, face puffy with sleep and outrage. His blanket had been thrown off like a political statement. He clutched a stuffed animal whose fur had been loved into a grayish despair.

"You didn't come," Theo said. This wasn't an observation; it was an accusation filed in triplicate.

"I'm here now," Declan said, and then, because he couldn't help it, "I didn't know you'd called a meeting."

Theo squinted, deciding whether this was funny or disrespectful. Children are born with the instinct to evaluate power. They test the room the way scientists test acids: small experiments, careful observation, a willingness to burn you if you're lying.

Declan leaned on the doorframe, still holding his mug like a shield. The coffee's heat had begun to settle, a small internal radiator. He was trying to keep his body calm, trying to keep the day from lunging at him. If he moved too quickly, he feared, something inside him would rip. A tendon. A nerve. A whole future. He hated that his body spoke in threats. He hated that he listened.

He always felt he was one bad night's sleep away from a devastating illness. Not in the way other people worried—normal people who worried about getting the flu and being annoyed for three days. He worried like the universe was due. Like the bill had been paid late too many times and the collector was finally coming.

Theo pointed at his own face. "My nose is stuffy."

Declan's mind instantly lit up, a Christmas tree of dread.

Stuffy nose.

Incubation. Fever.

Pneumonia. Hospital.

I will die in an ER chair next to a man eating Doritos and watching TikTok at full volume.

He'd learned, over time, to smile through this internal slideshow of catastrophe. He'd learned that other people did not enjoy being dragged into the theater of his worst-case imagination before sunrise.

He'd also learned that kids could smell panic like smoke. If he acted like Theo's stuffy nose mattered too much, Theo would start narrating it like a calamity, because children copy the tone even when they don't understand the words.

He walked over, sat on the edge of the bed, and put his hand on Theo's forehead. The skin was warm because skin was warm. It wasn't a symptom. It was a fact. A human fact. The texture of Theo's hair against Declan's knuckles was soft in an almost insulting way—like the body of a child hadn't yet learned what the world did to softness.

"You're okay," Declan said.

"How do you know?" Theo asked, already practicing skepticism like it was a sport.

Declan almost laughed. *Because I have anxiety and a coffee religion, son. Because I have spent a decade imagining the ambulance siren as a lullaby.*

Instead he said, "Because your forehead is not hot-hot. It's just… forehead-hot."

Theo accepted this with the solemnity of someone being briefed on military intelligence. Then he leaned forward and, without asking, started running his fingers through Declan's hair, tugging and shaping it in that oddly tender way children have—gentle until it isn't.

Declan winced when a finger snagged. "Easy," he murmured.

Theo didn't stop. He pulled again, harder this time, like he was trying to sculpt Declan into someone else.

"I let him," Declan would later tell Lena, "because he says he wants me to look like him."

Right now, he didn't say anything. He let it happen. There was a sweetness to it that made him ache—the boy's small hand, the simple desire to claim likeness, to create continuity. But it also hurt, because love, in a household, is rarely clean. It's sticky. It's fingers in his hair. It's someone he would die for accidentally hurting him because they don't know their own strength yet.

And it struck him—one of those quick, inconvenient flashes—that Theo didn't really want him to look like him. Theo wanted him to stay. To be stable. To be the same man in every room. The hair was just a handle Theo could grab, a way to say mine without knowing how to say I'm scared you won't be.

Daisy flopped down with a sigh that sounded like a retired person who'd seen every version of this morning. Her huge head hit the carpet. She watched as if this was a television show she pretended not to like but followed religiously.

Downstairs, Lena called up, "We are leaving in ten minutes."

Ten minutes. The unit of measurement used by the sane to describe manageable time.

To Declan, ten minutes was a cliff.

He glanced at Theo, whose eyes were already half-closing again, hand still messing with his hair. He looked at Daisy, who had positioned herself so her body created a barrier between the bed and the rest of the world—like: I've got this. Go do your human paperwork, you fragile idiot.

Declan stood up and immediately felt dizzy, which was not dizziness, he reminded himself. It was the normal sensation of rising too quickly after thirty-something years of thinking your thoughts at an illegal speed. His body was fine. His body was fine. His body was—his body was always the argument.

As he left the room, Theo called after him in a voice that had already softened. "Can we have pancakes?"

"We can have the concept of pancakes," Declan replied.

"What?"

"Nothing."

He walked downstairs, where the kitchen had shifted from morning quiet to morning machinery. Lena had already turned on lights, started the toaster, found socks, located a missing folder that had been missing for days until the exact moment it was required. She moved through tasks the way certain people moved through grief: briskly, not because she didn't feel it, but because if she stopped, it would swallow her.

Declan admired this about her the way a person admires a bridge: functional, strong, quietly heroic.

Also, it made him feel like a decorative plant.

The forms sat on the table. Permission slip. Field trip money. A note from the nurse. A reminder that picture day was coming, which meant there would be a day when someone looked at his child under fluorescent lighting and decided whether he was a good parent based on the cleanliness of their collar.

Lena slid Theo's folder across the table toward Declan as if she were dealing a card she was tired of holding.

"You're dropping this," she said. Not a question. A transfer of responsibility.

Declan tapped it once—checking the weight—then scooped it up and told himself he would not forget it. He took a sip of coffee. It tasted like the inside of a burned memory.

"You talked before the line," Lena said, without looking at him.

"It doesn't count if it's parenting," Declan said. "Parenting is emergency services. I'm basically first responder adjacent."

"Everything is an emergency service to you," Lena said.

Declan opened his mouth to defend himself, to produce a clever line that would make him sound both wounded and superior, but he stopped. His pattern showed up in his mouth—tongue worrying a sore tooth: make a joke, dodge the deeper thing, keep moving. Keep smiling. If you keep the surface busy enough, nobody can see the fracture.

He set the mug down and picked up the permission slip. "Where's the money?"

"In your wallet," Lena said.

"I don't have a wallet," Declan said.

"Yes you do."

"I have a card graveyard," Declan said. "A loose pile of plastic I keep in my pocket like a raccoon."

Lena finally looked at him. Her eyes weren't angry; they were tired in the way that made anger look like a luxury.

"Can you please just do it?" she said.

That sentence—Can you please do it?—held an entire relationship inside it. The request. The restraint. The fact that she wasn't saying what she could say, which was: I am not your mother. I am your partner. Stop acting like the world is happening to you.

Declan nodded. "Okay."

There was a pause, the kind of pause where the air thickens. He hated those pauses because they made room for truth. And truth, in his nervous system, registered as an attack even when it arrived gently.

"All I know," Declan said, softer now, "is that my life is better when I assume people are doing their best. It keeps me out of judgment."

Lena's face changed—not into a smile, exactly, but into something less tight.

"That's true," she said. "But sometimes it sounds like you say it so you don't have to ask anything of people."

Declan blinked. Of course she would do this. Of course she would take his one pretty philosophy and test it for weakness, like pressing on drywall to find the stud.

"What do you mean?" Declan asked, though he already knew.

Lena turned back to the counter, pulling cereal boxes out like she was dealing cards.

"I mean," she said, "assuming people are doing their best is good. But you also use it to avoid conflict. You pretend patience is a virtue when it's really fear."

Declan felt heat rise in his throat. Not anger—something closer to exposure. The sensation of being seen too clearly. Like she'd turned on a light in a room he'd kept dim on purpose.

There was no difference between patience and being afraid of conflict, for him anyway. He'd always known that. He didn't enjoy hearing it said out loud by someone who loved him enough to tell the truth and stay.

Daisy thumped her tail once, as if to say: Yep. That. That's the thing.

Upstairs, Theo started singing—one of his made-up songs that sounded like a tiny drunk poet narrating his own breakfast. Declan listened and felt that weird, fleeting joy that arrives like a bird and leaves if he look at it too hard.

They got out the door barely on time. This was the household's primary athletic event: The Morning. Shoes. Coats. Water bottles. A last-minute bathroom run that could not be argued with. Daisy watched from the threshold, calm and disappointed in the species.

"Be good," Declan said to her, which was ridiculous because Daisy was always good. Daisy's moral compass was so consistent it was boring.

Daisy blinked slowly, then nudged Declan's hand with her nose, a gesture that wasn't affection so much as instruction: Remember what matters.

Outside, the air had that damp edge that made Declan's skin feel reactive. The kind of skin that rashes with a whisper. The neighborhood looked suspended between night and day—driveway puddles catching the gray sky, bare trees clawing at nothing, the faint smell of someone's wood stove lingering like nostalgia.

Theo hopped down the front steps as if gravity was optional. Declan followed, slower, his joints negotiating with him like union reps.

At the end of the driveway, the neighbors were out, as if summoned by the idea of leaving the house.

They were an elderly couple who had lived on the street longer than anyone could remember. They were always outside at exactly the wrong moment—collecting mail, adjusting a shrub, slowly moving a trash can as if it was a sacred object. As if the street itself produced them whenever someone needed reminding what time did to bodies.

In Declan's head, he called them The Dribble and The Hip. He wasn't proud of this. But his brain made nicknames the way other brains made memories. The Dribble had incontinence issues that Declan had once overheard, accidentally, in a conversation no one wanted to have. The Hip walked with the careful, mechanical limp of someone rebuilt. Declan's mind had filed them under mortality: comic edition.

They waved.

"Morning!" The Hip called, cheerful as ever.

"Morning," Declan said, and then corrected himself mentally: You are not a monster. Say it like a human.

"Morning," he repeated, warmer.

The Dribble approached with a smile that was too big for his face, like he'd practiced it in the mirror and decided this was the best one he had.

"Big day?" The Dribble asked, eyes on Theo.

Theo waved back, already forgetting them the second his hand lowered. Children love the world the way the world deserves to be loved: briefly and completely.

"We're always late," Declan said, because honesty sometimes leaked out of him in simple forms.

The Hip laughed. "That's life."

No, Declan thought. That's your version of life. Mine is a list of urgent tasks wearing a trench coat.

He wanted to say: We're not living life, we're waiting it out. He wanted it to land the way a man says something true when he isn't sure he's allowed to.

Instead he said, "How are you guys doing?"

The Hip lifted his chin as if considering the question from a great height. "Can't complain."

The Dribble chuckled. "Even if we did, nobody'd want to hear it."

They were joking. They were always joking, these two. They had learned, over decades, that humor was a kind of social currency. You paid with it so people didn't see the cost of your pain.

Declan felt something twist in him. The softness he hated. The tenderness he didn't know what to do with.

Lena called from the car, "We have to go."

Declan nodded, waved to the couple, and herded Theo toward the passenger seat.

As he buckled him in, Theo said, "Why does that man walk like a robot?"

Declan paused, hand on the seatbelt. He felt the temptation to be clever—Because his hip is made of spaceship parts. He could also feel the moral weight of the moment: Theo was learning how to see people.

"He had surgeries," Declan said, choosing plainness. "So he has to be careful."

Theo nodded, satisfied. Then: "Can I have a robot hip when I'm big?"

"You can have two," Declan said. "We'll get you an upgrade."

They pulled away. The street receded. The couple remained in the driveway, small in the rearview mirror, still waving at a life that didn't stop long enough to wave back.

At the next light, Declan's phone buzzed in the cup holder. A notification. Another reminder. Another thing he was supposed to do.

He glanced at it and felt the familiar internal rush—his mind sprinting ahead, stacking tasks into a tower that always swayed but never fell, because the falling would be too final. He could live in the sway. He could live in the almost. The tyranny of the urgent kept him from the tyranny of the deep.

He thought, briefly, of getting high. Not because he was a stoner in a cartoon, but because his mind ran at an incredibly fast speed and weed helped him slow it down. It gave him time enough to think before he acted.

The problem was, sometimes it gave him time enough to think at all, and thinking was not always his friend.

He pictured himself, on some doomed morning, listening to Limp Bizkit at 5:58 a.m. and sincerely wondering if he liked it. The thought made him laugh—a small, involuntary burst. He didn't even like most of the music that came with being high—too many songs that tried to sound profound. But there was one exception: an old Providence College relic with a stupid name and a perfect groove. Sweet Spiral. Track one: "Dissolve," by Dick Twister & the Cotton Candy Machine— named, absurdly, after his freshman roommate Richard Twister, a lanky kid who thought the universe was funniest when it involved two dicks in the same sentence.

Lena glanced at him. "What?"

"Nothing," Declan said, still smiling.

"Tell me," Lena said.

Declan shook his head. "If I tell you, you'll think I'm insane."

"I already think you're insane," Lena said. "But I love you."

The line hit him—sharp, casual, devastating—and something in him flinched like it had a bruise. Love offered as fact, not sentiment. Love as scaffolding.

Declan cleared his throat. "I just… I feel like my ability and my ambition don't match," he said, surprising himself with the honesty.

Lena's expression softened again, but she didn't rescue him from it. She let it exist.

※

"That's most people," Lena said. "The difference is you narrate it like it's a tragedy."

Declan nodded. She was right. He narrated his life like he was both the problem and the solution, and that was exhausting.

They drove on.

Theo hummed. The world passed. The day continued its relentless forward motion, indifferent to Declan's rituals, indifferent to his fear.

And somewhere beneath the buzzing phone, beneath the forms and the schedules and the unasked questions, Declan felt a quiet, inconvenient truth: he wasn't waiting it out. Not really. He was building something—badly, clumsily, with marker and coffee and half-prayers—trying to make a life sturdy enough to hold the people he loved.

Whether his body already knew it yet or not, that was the work.

That was the structure.

⁂

Declan arrived at work with the faint sensation that he'd already been at work for three hours.

That was the trick of mornings like his: they were unpaid labor disguised as love. You'd negotiate treaties over cereal, mediate a hostage situation in the bathroom, draft and sign legal documents called permission slips, then pull yourself into traffic as if heading to your "real" responsibilities—as if the first act hadn't been the most intimate kind of governance.

The parking lot was half-full and already vibrating with office anxiety: the subtle, communal dread of adults pretending not to be scared. Cars slid into spaces with the careful choreography of people who did not want to meet anyone's eyes before coffee. Someone two rows over sat with their head tilted back against the seat, mouth open, inhaling like they were about to go underwater. A man in a fleece vest walked too fast, shoulders angled forward, as if speed could outpace the day's expectations.

Declan shut the engine off and sat there, hands still on the wheel, listening to the car tick as it cooled. The glass held the faint chill of winter. The heater's last exhale smelled like dust and the ghost of Theo's crackers ground into the floor mats. He stared at the steering wheel emblem as if it might tell him what kind of man he was supposed to be today.

※
※ ※

There was a moment—always a moment—where he considered simply going home.

Not impulsive. Not loud. Just the small fantasy of reversing out of the lot like he'd forgotten something—one sock, one spine, one alternate life.

He'd never done it, of course. He was a coward, not a criminal. Besides, the tyranny of the urgent would follow him home. It was not location-dependent. It lived in him. It had moved into his chest years ago and started charging rent.

His phone buzzed again. A calendar reminder. A meeting. Another meeting. A third meeting stacked on top of the second meeting like pancakes made of dread. He glanced at the subject lines without truly reading them, the way you glance at the ocean and understand, immediately, that it has no intention of caring about your schedule.

He'd once told a friend—half-joking, half-begging—that the older he got, the smaller the world became. The friend had nodded like it was wisdom. Maybe it was. Or it was exhaustion wearing a graduation cap.

Declan got out of the car and walked toward the building.

The office was one of those low-slung structures that looked like it had been designed by someone who hated humans but respected permits. Beige siding. Tinted windows. A landscaping strip of shrubs that looked permanently ashamed to be alive. The kind of place where ambition went to sit under fluorescent lighting until it grew bored and died.

Inside, the air smelled faintly of copier toner and cheap citrus disinfectant someone had chosen because it tested well in a focus group. The overhead lights weren't bright so much as insistent—flat illumination that made everyone look a little sick and a little guilty, like the building itself assumed you'd done something wrong and would eventually confess if given enough time.

A woman at the front desk looked up with the bright, empty cheer of someone paid to behave like she'd never had a private thought.

"Morning, Declan," she said.

"Morning," he replied, and felt, briefly, like a liar.

On his way to his desk he passed the break room, where two people were already talking about their weekend with the intensity of hostages negotiating for water. Declan nodded at them, did the thin-lipped half-smile that meant I am a person and also please don't speak to me, collected his coffee from the machine—not coffee, really, but brown liquid with a job—and continued.

At his desk he clicked his computer awake and watched emails populate like bacteria.

The first was from Mr. Malloy.

Need you in my office at 9:15.

That was it. No "good morning." No context. No subject line. The message had the lean efficiency of a threat.

Declan stared at it until his eyes burned, then looked away as if the email might infect him. He wasn't new here. His body already knew what the summons meant. Sometimes it meant nothing. Sometimes it meant everything. Mr. Malloy had a tremendous amount of power and took pleasure in simultaneously wielding it and denying it.

He would call Declan in, sit him down, and then look at him as if Declan had intruded. He would ask questions without asking them. He would hint. He would imply. He would force Declan to climb inside his own mind and turn every worry into an accusation. Then, at the end, he would say something like, *I'm not saying you did anything wrong,* which was exactly what you said when you wanted someone to feel they had.

Declan looked at the clock. 8:52.

He tried to work. He opened a file, read the same paragraph three times, and felt his mind skitter. His thoughts ran at an incredibly fast

⁂

speed, not in a fun genius way—in a way that made small tasks feel like trying to thread a needle while someone shouted directions in your ear. His jaw locked. Teeth set so hard it made his temples ache. He forced it loose. He could feel his foot bouncing under the desk. He pinned it flat, as if you could discipline your own nervous system by ordering it to behave.

He checked the clock again. 9:03.

It was always like this: the tyranny of the urgent colonized the present. He couldn't be in now because soon was always reaching forward with its greasy hands.

He leaned back in his chair and tried to do what Lena would do: focus on the next action, not the thousand possible outcomes.

Next action: walk to Mr. Malloy's office.

That was it. A simple thing. A man walking down a hallway.

He stood up, gathered a notepad he didn't need—he liked props in moments of stress, as if paper could make him look competent—and headed toward the far end of the building.

The hallway carpet was the color of stale oatmeal and had the springy give of something designed to disguise footfalls and despair. The walls were lined with framed "values" posters: teamwork, accountability, integrity. Words that meant nothing in the hands of someone who used them as camouflage.

Mr. Malloy's office door was half-closed. That was his signature posture: a deliberate almost-welcome.

Declan knocked.

"Yeah," Mr. Malloy said, as if the sound of Declan's knuckles had interrupted something sacred.

Declan opened the door.

Mr. Malloy sat behind his desk, posture perfect, wearing a navy suit that looked expensive enough to have feelings. His hair was combed in a way that suggested not vanity, but control. A photo frame sat at the corner of his desk: a smiling family in bright sunlight, the kind of family people used as evidence. Declan always noticed it the way you notice a weapon mounted on a wall. It wasn't meant to be admired. It was meant to be reassuring, which was a different kind of threat.

"Close the door," Mr. Malloy said.

Declan did, and immediately regretted it. Closing the door always made the air heavier, as if the room itself preferred privacy for whatever it did to people.

"Sit," Mr. Malloy said, gesturing to the chair across from him like a judge offering mercy.

Declan sat, placed the notepad on his lap, and waited.

Mr. Malloy looked down at his computer. He typed something slowly, deliberately, as if each keystroke had moral weight. He did this often. It was part of his theater. It made him feel like your presence required administrative processing. The click of the keys was too measured, too calm. It told Declan: *I have time. You do not.*

Finally, without looking up, Mr. Malloy said, "How are things?"

It wasn't a question. It was a setup.

"Fine," Declan said. He hated that word. It was a lie people told to get through doorways.

Mr. Malloy's eyes flicked up. "Fine," he repeated, as if tasting it for weakness. "Good. Because we've had... some concerns."

The way he said *some* made it sound like many, but also like he was doing Declan a favor by not enumerating them.

Declan felt his stomach tighten. He kept his face neutral. This was something he'd learned over the years: the body could panic, but the face had to look like it had never heard of the concept.

"Concerns?" Declan asked.

Mr. Malloy smiled a fraction too late—after the discomfort landed—like he wanted Declan to notice the bruise forming. "Nothing major," Mr. Malloy said quickly, which was an alarm bell. "Just... a couple things have come up."

Declan waited. Silence stretched. Mr. Malloy loved silence. He used it the way other people used knives.

"There's a perception," Mr. Malloy said, "that you've been... distracted lately."

There it was: the accusation delivered as gossip. Not *I think.* Not *I've noticed.* A *perception,* as if concern was a weather pattern drifting through the office.

"I don't think I've been distracted," Declan said carefully. He chose each word like he was walking across thin ice.

Mr. Malloy nodded, the way he nodded at someone he didn't believe.

"That's good," Mr. Malloy said. "Because we need people who are fully present. You understand."

Declan understood. The pattern snapped into focus: this was the kind of statement that could mean anything later if Mr. Malloy chose to use it. It could be recalled, cited, attached to a future narrative. It was a brick being placed, quietly, in a wall Declan hadn't agreed to build.

"Yes," Declan said.

Mr. Malloy's eyes moved to the notepad. "You taking notes?"

Declan glanced down. He hadn't written anything. The blank page felt humiliating, like he'd shown up to court without pants.

"Just... in case," Declan said.

Mr. Malloy gave a small laugh. "Let's not be dramatic."

Let's not be dramatic, Declan thought. Says the man staging a psychological séance in his office at nine fifteen.

Mr. Malloy tapped a pen against his desk. "We all have personal lives," he said. "I get that. Kids. Responsibilities."

Declan's throat tightened at the mention of Theo. Not because it was forbidden, but because it was being used. Mr. Malloy didn't have to raise his voice. He could touch your most tender places with a sentence and then pretend it was empathy.

"But," Mr. Malloy continued, "when those things start to affect performance... we have to address it."

"What specifically?" Declan asked, trying to hold the line. A real line, not the marker kind. An adult line.

Mr. Malloy's smile returned. "I don't want to get into specifics," he said, which was a way of making the accusation impossible to answer. "I just want you to be aware."

Aware of what, exactly? That someone somewhere might be thinking something? That reality here was malleable, dependent on the moods of powerful men?

Declan felt the old fear rise—the fear that if he pushed, he'd be labeled difficult. If he didn't push, he'd be labeled weak. Either way, the narrative would belong to someone else.

He thought of Lena that morning, cereal boxes like cards, saying: *You pretend patience is a virtue when it's fear.*

His skin prickled. The kind of skin that rashes with a whisper.

"I'm aware," Declan said, the words tasting like compromise.

Mr. Malloy nodded, satisfied. "Good. Also—" He glanced at his computer again, performing bureaucracy. "You'll be taking on the Mitchell account. Effective immediately."

Declan blinked. "I thought that was going to—"

"—go to Kyle," Mr. Malloy finished, smiling. "Yes. That was the initial plan."

"Why the change?" Declan asked.

Mr. Malloy lifted his hands slightly, palms open, the universal gesture of *I'm innocent.* "It's not a change," he said. "It's just... what's best for the team."

Declan stared at him.

This was it. This was the pleasure: wielding power and denying it. Making a decision and pretending it was a natural event, like rain.

※
※※

"The Mitchell account is…" Declan began, then stopped. He nearly said: *It's a mess.* He almost said: *It's designed to fail.* He wanted to say: *This is punishment.* He nearly said: *Just be honest with me.*

Instead he said, "A lot."

Mr. Malloy shrugged slightly. "We believe you can handle it."

There was a kindness-shaped lie in that. It sounded supportive. It wasn't.

Declan nodded again. His mind stacked futures like cheap plates—late nights, missed bedtime, Theo asleep mid-story, Lena's patience thinning until it looked a lot like grief.

"We're all stretched," Mr. Malloy added. "We do our best to do the best we can."

Declan almost laughed out loud. The phrase—one of his own internal mantras—coming from Mr. Malloy's mouth like a corporate sticker.

It landed in him like an insult.

He thought, wildly, of saying something obscene. He thought of saying: *You never truly get the taste of a priest's uninvited dick out of your mouth.* Not because it belonged here, but because it belonged to the same category of violation: the powerful taking what they wanted and calling it "best practices."

But he didn't. He nodded.

Mr. Malloy leaned forward, steepling his fingers. "I'm glad we had this talk," he said, as if Declan should be grateful for the experience.

"Me too," Declan lied.

Mr. Malloy stood, signaling the meeting was over. His body language always made it clear: he existed at his pleasure.

Declan stood too, held his notepad like a man who had attended a class, and walked toward the door.

"Oh," Mr. Malloy said, just as Declan reached for the handle.

Declan paused, hand on the knob.

"Try to get ahead of things," Mr. Malloy said. "The urgency has been… noticeable."

Declan turned back. "Meaning?"

Mr. Malloy smiled again. "You know. The scrambling. The last-minute energy. It affects the team."

Declan's jaw tightened. He wanted to ask how the scrambling was supposed to stop when Mr. Malloy's decisions were ambushes. He wanted to ask whether the team's feelings mattered when deadlines were moved like goalposts.

He almost said: *We're not living life, we're just waiting it out.* But here, in this office, "life" meant "work," and "waiting it out" meant "enduring men like you."

Instead he said, "I'll work on it."

Mr. Malloy nodded, satisfied, and Declan left.

In the hallway, the air felt different—thinner, less weaponized. He walked back to his desk with the careful calm of a man carrying a full cup he didn't want to spill.

When he sat down, his hands shook slightly. Not visibly, not dramatically. Just enough to remind him that his body kept score when his face lied.

He opened the Mitchell account file and stared at it.

Mitchell. A name that already sounded like trouble. A client who had been angry for months. A mess of emails, complaints, shifting expectations. The kind of account that could swallow your calendar and still ask for dessert.

His phone buzzed again. A text from Lena.

You dropped Theo's folder off, right?

Declan stared at the screen.

His stomach sank. The folder. The missing folder that had appeared at the last minute. The folder he'd meant to grab. The folder that was now sitting, probably, on their kitchen table like an accusation.

He pictured Lena's face when she realized. Not fury, exactly—worse. That slow tightening. That tired disappointment. The quiet that took up space.

He typed back.

I thought I did. Let me check.

He didn't know why he lied. His body already knew he hadn't. He could see the folder in his mind like a crime scene photo.

He put his phone down and stared at his computer.

This was what his life felt like: constantly one step behind a disaster he was personally scheduling.

He closed his eyes.

Daisy filled the doorway in his memory—big, soft, loyal—shoulder pressed to his shin, an anchor dragging him back into the present.

The dog's kindness was so uncomplicated it made him want to weep.

He opened his eyes and looked around the office.

Everyone was working. Everyone was typing. Everyone was pretending not to be scared. Their lives were smaller here—reduced to screens and deadlines and the polite tyranny of men like Mr. Malloy, who called it "team culture."

Declan thought, briefly, of getting high.

Not in the office. He wasn't stupid. But later. Later, when he got home. A small edible, maybe, or a pull from the pen he kept hidden like contraband. Just enough to slow his mind down and give him time enough to think before he acted.

The problem was, sometimes weed gave him time enough to notice what he'd been avoiding.

And what he'd been avoiding, lately, was the fact that his life was built on half-executed ideas and fragile rituals. A marker line. A coffee religion. A man convincing himself he was structured when he was controlling the one thing he could.

He glanced at the Mitchell thread again. The email chain was long.

Angry. It read like a marriage in its late stages.

He clicked open the most recent message.

THIS IS UNACCEPTABLE.

All caps. Bold. The modern equivalent of someone shouting in a hallway.

He exhaled slowly. Instinct took over: apologize until there was nothing left of him but agreement. Perform contrition. Offer softness and hope the other person would accept it as resolution.

Instead he thought of Theo's hand in his hair, pulling, shaping. *I let him, because he says he wants me to look like him.*

What did Theo see when he looked at him? A father who built rules out of coffee? A man who flinched from conflict and called it patience? A person who assumed everyone was doing their best—but sometimes used that assumption as a way to avoid asking for what he needed?

A man whose last breath would be a yawn?

No. He hated that thought. *My last breath will NOT be a yawn. My last word will NOT be a conjunction. How fucking embarrassing?*

He sat up straighter.

Maybe the smallest rebellion was not letting the day happen to him. Maybe the smallest rebellion was saying a clean sentence out loud, in a room built to make him whisper.

He opened a blank email draft to the Mitchell client. His fingers hovered over the keys.

He could hear Mr. Malloy's voice: *Let's not be dramatic.*

He could hear Lena's voice: *You pretend patience is a virtue when it's fear.*

He could hear his own voice: *We're not living life, we're waiting it out.*

Declan typed.

Not an apology that begged.

Not a defensive paragraph that hid.

A clear message. A line. Structure.

It wasn't marker on ceramic, but it was the same idea: a boundary you could point to when everything got slippery. He wrote:

I hear you. This has been handled poorly. That's on us, and I'm going to fix it. Here is what I can do today, and here is what I need from you to do it.

He paused, reread it, and felt something like relief.

It wasn't genius. It wasn't transcendentalist. It wasn't new territory. But it was honest.

And honesty, he was learning, was a kind of kindness. Not soft kindness. Structural kindness. The kind that held up a day.

His phone buzzed again.

Another notification. And, lower down, a missed call he hadn't seen—Walt Burke—from earlier, sitting there like a stone.

Walt was one of the few people left who still called him Dick. Not as a joke, exactly—more like a fossil from childhood that refused to erode. Fourth grade, some kid had decided Declan sounded like "Dick-Land," and the chant had run wild for a week. Then the week became a year. Then the name got shortened, laundered, made familiar.

Declan had never liked it. It sounded like a dare, like a headline. But when Walt used it, it landed differently: not affection, not ridicule—just history.

Declan didn't tap it. Not yet. The day already had enough ways to collapse.

Another text from Lena.

The folder is still here.

Declan closed his eyes.

There it was. The small failure. The stupid, daily crack. He typed back, this time without theater.

I'm sorry. I forgot. I'll call the school and see if I can bring it later.

He hit send before he could rephrase it into something smoother, something less blameable, something that would make him look like the victim of time.

A minute later, Lena responded.

Thank you.

Two words. Not warm, not cold. Functional. A beam placed back into the frame.

Declan stared at it until it blurred.

He opened his eyes, looked at the office around him, and felt the truth settle in his body like a weight he'd finally agreed to carry:

Kindness was not softness—it was structure.

His throat tightened as if the body wanted to argue. The words were true, but truth didn't make him calm—it just made him responsible.

Without it—without clear sentences, without ownership, without repair—everything collapsed into resentment and silence and marker lines on cups.

He glanced again at the Mitchell email. His finger hovered over "Send."

Fear rose—thin, hot, familiar—like a rash you know you're about to scratch anyway.

He could also feel the other thing: the urge to be a man who did not wait his life out.

Declan clicked "Send."

The email disappeared into the ether.

Outside his window the day moved on, indifferent and loud. Inside, something small had shifted. Not triumph. Not transformation.

Just a man choosing, in one ordinary moment, not to hide.

And down the hall, behind a half-closed door, Mr. Malloy sat in his office, perfect hair, perfect suit, smiling at the world like it belonged to him.

Declan looked at the clock.

There were still hours left in the day.

For once, that didn't feel like a sentence.

It felt like a chance.

⁂

Declan refreshed his inbox like it was a heart monitor.

He didn't pretend it was for productivity. It was for proof. Proof the message had landed. Proof it hadn't detonated. Proof that when he said a clean sentence in a dirty room, the room didn't immediately punish him for it.

Nothing.

He refreshed again. Still nothing.

His body took this personally. His jaw tightened as if his inbox had insulted him. His hand hovered over the mouse. He didn't click. Didn't breathe right. Like a man waiting for a green light that never came.

Shame snapped through him—sharp and quick—as if he'd caught himself kneeling. For a moment, he felt virtuous. *Look at me,* he thought. *Look at this responsible adult, standing up for clarity, doing structural kindness like a man with a plan.*

Then he felt ashamed for needing to feel virtuous, for needing the little internal applause. He hated how quickly his morality turned into performance in his own head. He hated that he required an audience when the only audience was him.

Across the open floor, someone laughed too loudly at something not funny. A printer groaned. A Slack notification chimed. Two desks over, a keyboard clacked in a panic rhythm. There was a series of brief, disconnected sounds, like the building itself was trying to communicate in Morse code: *he is not safe here. he is not safe here.*

Declan's phone buzzed once in his pocket. Not Lena this time. A reminder he'd set months ago and forgotten about:

Drink water.

He stared at it and felt irrationally angry. The phone didn't know him. The phone didn't know that water didn't fix dread, that hydration was not an exorcism. It was the kind of advice you gave to someone whose mind wasn't trying to turn every sensation into a terminal diagnosis.

He put the phone face-down and refreshed his inbox again.

Nothing.

He leaned back and tried to do what he'd told himself he'd do more often: breathe without making it dramatic. Just air in, air out. No story. No omen. He let his shoulders fall a fraction. He loosened his grip on the mouse. He tried to be a person instead of a surveillance system.

At 10:04, the response came.

His screen blinked. A new message. His stomach tightened before his eyes read a word, because his body had already learned this language.

Re: Mitchell / Next Steps

The email was three sentences long and each one managed to be both suspicious and offended, which was impressive.

This is the first time anyone has "heard" me in weeks.
I don't know why you're involved, but I'm not interested in excuses.
What guarantee do I have you won't do what everyone else has done?

Declan reread it and felt something settle in him. Not fear. Not anger. Respect—sharp, reluctant.

The client wasn't grateful. The client wasn't soothed by the structure Declan had offered. The client was still bleeding and wanted to know

✳
✳✳

if the person approaching with gauze was going to pat them on the head and walk away.

Clarity didn't soften them; it sharpened them. The email arrived like a bare bulb—everything visible, nothing kinder.

He began typing immediately, then stopped. His fingers hesitated over the keys.

If he answered too fast, he'd look desperate. If he answered too slow, he'd look indifferent. In his head, every action had a moral shadow, every pause a confession.

He forced himself to slow down. To write like a person. Not like a man trying to earn absolution.

He typed:

I can't offer you a guarantee. What I can offer is a plan and a timeline. If we don't meet it, you'll know quickly, and you can make a decision without being strung along.

He paused. That sentence felt dangerous. It offered the client an exit. It offered the client agency. It wasn't the kind of thing the office liked. The office preferred clients trapped in politeness—so you could keep "managing expectations" instead of delivering anything that looked like accountability.

He heard Mr. Malloy's voice in his head—*Let's not be dramatic*—as if clarity itself were an emotional outburst.

Declan kept typing:

Here's what I can do today: I can get you a status report by 3:00, and I can schedule a 15-minute call tomorrow at 9:30 or 2:00. Here's what I need from you: one point of contact and a confirmation of the main priority so we're not solving the wrong problem.

He stared at it.

It was a good email—competent, honest, slightly brave. Not poetic. Not trying to be.

And now he had to send it.

That was the thing: words didn't count until he was willing to be held to them. A sentence without consequences was just performance with punctuation.

He clicked send.

The message whooshed away, and a moment later he felt lighter and worse at the same time. Like he'd stepped off a curb and realized the street was real.

He sat there watching the inbox like a man waiting for a verdict.

A shadow fell over his desk.

"Hey," a voice said—flat, deliberate. Not friendly, not hostile. Placed.

Declan looked up.

Kyle stood there holding a mug and a neutral expression so carefully constructed it looked like it had been assembled in an HR workshop. Kyle was the kind of man who could be angry without raising his voice—polite-angry, the most dangerous kind. The kind that could ruin you and still make it sound like you'd requested it.

"Hey," Declan said.

Kyle's eyes flicked to Declan's screen. Not enough to be accusatory. Just enough to signal he was aware of everything. Kyle's whole thing was awareness. He carried it like a weapon.

"So," Kyle said. "Mitchell."

Declan nodded, like the word didn't make his throat tight. "Yeah."

Kyle took a sip of coffee. He didn't need to. It was a prop. Declan recognized the move. Two men holding props in a building full of silent threats.

"I had that," Kyle said. Still polite. Still calm. "At least, that's what I was told."

Declan felt the old instinct rise: explain yourself. Apologize. Make it smooth. Make it so the conflict never has to become real.

He wanted to say, *I didn't ask for it.* He nearly said, *Malloy did this.* He almost said, *I'm trying to survive the day without collapsing into my own nervous system.*

Instead he said, "I know."

Kyle's eyebrows lifted slightly. "And now you have it."

Declan nodded again. The space between them felt artificially calm, like the quiet you get right before someone decides whether to hit you.

He felt Lena's line from the kitchen again, sharp as a fork: *You pretend patience is a virtue when it's fear.*

There was no difference between patience and being afraid of conflict, for him anyway.

Kyle waited. That was the other thing about polite-angry: it allowed space so you could hang yourself with it. Silence as a rope. Silence as "professionalism."

Declan tried to be kind. Tried to do his new structural kindness like a man with scaffolding instead of mood.

"I'm sorry," he said. "I genuinely didn't know it was going to switch. I walked into Mr. Malloy's office and it was already done."

Kyle smiled. The smile didn't reach his eyes.

"Sure," Kyle said. "I get it. Malloy makes decisions. We adapt."

The way he said *adapt* sounded like *suffer quietly.*

Kyle leaned in slightly, lowering his voice as if sharing a secret. "Just so you know, Mitchell's a grinder. They don't want solutions, they want someone to punish. And Malloy likes to... test people."

Declan's jaw tightened. A little pulse of anger tried to rise. Not heroic anger. Just the animal kind—the kind that wants to bare teeth when it recognizes a trap.

"He didn't say it was a test," Declan said.

Kyle shrugged. "He wouldn't."

There it was—another clean sentence that made the room wobble. *He wouldn't.* Because Mr. Malloy's whole pleasure was in never admitting he was the one moving the walls.

Kyle stepped back. "Anyway. Good luck," he said, and the words sounded like a curse delivered with manners.

Then he walked away.

Declan sat in the aftermath of that exchange, his hands resting on the desk as if he needed to prove to himself he was still in one piece.

Across the office, a Slack message dinged. A printer spat paper. Someone coughed. A chair squeaked. A stapler snapped. There was that series of brief, disconnected sounds again—the office's private soundtrack of people trying not to panic in front of each other.

Declan opened the Mitchell thread and scrolled, reading the history the way you'd review a crime scene. Missed calls. Vague promises. Internal notes that said things like *client upset* and *need to manage expectations*—as if "expectations" were wild animals you could calm with the right tone.

He caught himself clenching his teeth and forced his jaw open slightly, like releasing a trap.

At 10:41, Mr. Malloy appeared.

Not in a way that required a greeting. He didn't arrive like a person. He arrived like a policy change. One moment your desk was your desk, the next moment his presence was there, taking oxygen.

"Burke," he said, already moving, his shoes quiet on the carpet like a predator designed for office environments.

"Mr. Malloy," Declan said.

Malloy didn't stop walking. He hovered. He created a moving target, so Declan never knew where to stand emotionally.

"Heard you sent a nice note to Mitchell," Mr. Malloy said, glancing at Declan's screen as if the screen belonged to him. "Stepping up. Good."

The compliment landed like a paperweight. It sounded like praise, but it carried ownership.

"Just trying to get ahead of it," Declan said.

Mr. Malloy nodded. "Exactly. We need that energy."

My energy, Declan thought, *is panic disguised as diligence.*

⁂

His palms had gone faintly slick on the mouse, like the body knew the bill was coming before the mind read the invoice.

Malloy smiled. "And just so we're clear—this isn't punishment."

Declan held his face neutral.

"It's just what the team needs," Malloy continued, as if he were describing the weather. "Your skill set. Your temperament. You can handle difficult personalities."

There it was again: the pleasure. Wielding power while denying it. Making a decision and then pretending the decision had emerged organically, like a plant. He did this to you and he didn't do this to you.

"He seems... intense," Declan said, keeping his voice calm.

Malloy laughed softly. "That's one word for it."

Declan could feel something flare in his chest—a tightness, like a small band being pulled. It wasn't pain. It wasn't not pain. It was the kind of bodily ambiguity that made his brain reach for catastrophe like a familiar jacket.

Malloy's eyes slid over him, quick and cold, evaluating what he could take. "And Burke," Malloy said, still smiling, still moving, "try not to get sucked into their drama. Keep it professional. You know how people are—everyone thinks their problem is the center of the universe."

Declan swallowed.

He wanted to say: *My son's small voice at the top of the stairs is the center of my universe.* He nearly said: *My wife's exhaustion is the axis the house spins on.* He almost said: *You don't get to call other people's pain drama when your whole leadership style is psychological theater.*

But he didn't.

He nodded. "Sure."

Malloy patted the edge of Declan's desk once—not touching him, but close enough to remind Declan whose desk it was.

Then he walked away, leaving behind a faint scent of expensive cologne and the sense that the air had been rearranged.

Declan stared at his screen and felt the anger try again, a small animal scratching at the inside of his ribs.

He opened his mouth, exhaled, closed it.

Patience. Fear. Same thing.

At 11:17, Mitchell replied again.

A call tomorrow is fine. Status report by 3:00 is fine. But I'm tired of being managed. I want accountability.

Declan read it twice.

Accountability. The word felt almost religious. The kind of word people used when they'd been hurt enough to stop accepting tone as a substitute for repair.

He started drafting the status report immediately. He made a list. He divided it into sections. He wrote in plain language. He did what he did best when he was scared: he tried to build structure out of words.

Halfway through, his wrist itched. He glanced down.

A faint red patch had appeared near the base of his thumb, right where his watch rubbed. It wasn't dramatic. It wasn't impressive. It looked like nothing.

Which meant, to Declan, it looked like everything.

Allergy. Autoimmune. Blood. Hospital.

He scratched once. The itch sharpened, like his skin had taken the hint and decided to audition for a bigger role.

He felt his pulse in his throat. He tried to focus on the screen and couldn't. His eyes skimmed the words without absorbing them. The office noises grew louder—keyboard clacks, printer groans, Slack chimes—each one a tiny needle.

There was a series of brief, disconnected sounds, and they weren't background anymore. They were a chorus. They were the building telling him, *your body is a liability.*

Declan stood up too quickly, immediately regretted it, and walked to the bathroom with the careful gait of a man trying not to reveal to strangers that he was currently losing a private war.

In the mirror, he held his wrist up like evidence. The patch stared back. Red. Mild. Almost polite.

He ran cold water over it. The relief was immediate, childish. He watched the redness soften, the itch quiet. He watched his own face in the mirror—pale under fluorescent lighting, eyes sharper than they needed to be.

He looked like someone who would say *I'm fine* and then faint in a pharmacy.

He laughed quietly, once, at himself. "Get a grip," he muttered.

Back at his desk, he forced himself to drink water. Not because it solved anything, but because doing one sensible thing felt like putting a brick back in the wall.

At noon, he took his lunch outside.

Not because he was healthy. Because he was trying to practice something—something Lena might call growth if she were in a generous mood.

He walked past the break room with its microwaved sadness and out through the glass doors into cold air that slapped him awake. The sky was a washed-out gray, the kind that made him think of unfinished projects and municipal budgets. Cars moved along the road beyond the parking lot, steady and indifferent.

Declan stood there with his cheap sandwich and watched the traffic like it was a river.

He tried to do a miniature transcendentalist move—the kind of thing he liked to imagine himself doing in theory, preferably while reading a book with a cover that looked expensive. He watched the same thing everyone else watched and tried to think something different.

Discovery consists of looking at the same thing as everyone else and thinking something different.

Fine. Discovery. Here was his discovery:

Everyone was doing their best. And everyone's best looked like coping.

The woman in the car next to him ate her lunch with her shoulders hunched, staring at her phone as if it contained instructions for how to live. A man in a hoodie smoked near the edge of the lot, exhaling slowly, looking at nothing. Two coworkers walked past laughing too hard, performing ease.

It hit him, standing there in the cold, that he did the same thing. His rituals weren't quirks. They were coping dressed as philosophy.

Coffee line. Silence. Weed. The desire to control the small, stupid things because the big things didn't negotiate.

He thought of getting high later. The thought came with a soft wave of relief. Just enough to slow down. Just enough to make the world stop sprinting.

Then he thought of Theo—hand in his hair, shaping him. He thought of Lena dealing folders across the table like she was tired of holding the whole house.

He thought of how easy it would be to sedate his life instead of living it.

He took a bite of his sandwich and tasted nothing. The air was too cold. His mind was too loud.

He went back inside.

At 2:36, he sent Mitchell the status report.

It was clean. It was honest. It admitted what was late and what was unclear and what was already in motion. It promised only what could be done. It included dates and names and next steps. It wasn't fancy.

It was structure.

A few minutes later, Mitchell replied with a single line:

This is the first thing that's made me feel like a person. Thank you.

Declan stared at it.

He didn't feel triumphant. He felt... sad. Not because it was negative, but because it was so small. How little it took to make someone feel human. How rarely people received it.

He felt the urge to screenshot the message and show Lena like a child showing a gold star. *Look. I did structural kindness. I did it right.*

He didn't. He let it be what it was: one beam set in place.

At 3:48, his phone buzzed again.

Lena, earlier, had texted: *the folder is still here.* Declan had said he'd call the school.

He hadn't yet.

He stared at the phone, then at the clock, then at the Mitchell thread, then at the clock again.

The urgent always wanted more. The urgent always grew new heads.

Declan stood up, headed to the small conference room at the end of the hall, closed the door, and called the school.

A woman answered with the tired brightness of someone who had spent her entire day being asked to solve other people's small emergencies.

"Hi," Declan said. "This is Theo Burke's dad. I forgot his folder this morning. Is it still okay if I bring it later today, or tomorrow morning?"

There. A clean sentence. Ownership. No theater.

A pause. Keyboard tapping on her end—brief, disconnected sounds.

"Tomorrow morning is fine," she said. "Just send it in with him."

"Thank you," Declan said. And meant it.

When he hung up, he sat for a moment in the quiet of the small room. No Slack chimes. No printer groans. No Malloy moving through the air like a policy.

Just him.

It hit him how rare it was to end a day without performing—without the little internal monologue narrating every act as either failure or virtue.

Maybe the trick wasn't to become calm.

Maybe the trick was to become sequential.

Structure isn't speed; it's sequence.

At 5:12, he shut down his computer.

He walked out of the building with his coat in his hand, phone buzzing with reminders and emails and the world insisting it existed. He stepped into the cold air and felt his body loosen slightly, as if it had been holding itself together with invisible clenched muscles all day.

In the parking lot, he paused by his car and looked at the sky.

Gray. Ordinary. Unmoved by his bravery.

He got into the car, started the engine, and sat for one moment before pulling out—hands on the wheel, listening to the tick of the heater.

His phone buzzed again.

He didn't check it.

Not yet.

He put the car in reverse and backed out carefully, as if the day might spill if he moved too fast.

Driving home, he tried not to sprint mentally ahead of his body. Tried not to imagine the next failure before it happened. Tried, for a few minutes, to live in the space between events.

He didn't succeed perfectly.

But he noticed the attempt.

And for Declan, lately, noticing was its own kind of progress—quiet, unglamorous, structural.

※

Declan pulled into the driveway like a man returning from the front.

Not the heroic front. The modern kind—email battles, fluorescent lighting, the soft tyranny of people who never raised their voices but still got their way. He shut the engine off and sat for a beat with his hands on the wheel, letting the quiet settle, letting his body unclench in small, grudging increments. The heater clicked as it cooled. Outside, the early evening had that bluish, in-between light that made everything look slightly unreal, like a set built to resemble a life.

The house sat behind the windshield—windows dimming into evening, the porch light starting to matter. The place looked calm from the outside, which was always the funniest lie. The lawn was neatly cut, the shutters intact, the kind of suburban shell that implied stability. Declan knew better. Stability here was not a state—it was a series of small repairs no one got credit for.

Then Daisy appeared in the front window.

Not barking. Not greeting. Just… present. A huge white-and-brown head drifting into view like a benevolent surveillance camera.

Declan opened the door and stepped out, and the front door swung inward before he touched the knob.

Daisy stood there in the entryway, filling it, her tail moving once, slow and deliberate. She didn't rush him. She didn't jump. She didn't perform joy like a small dog. She simply looked at him with the steady attention of a judge who was also merciful.

So, her eyes said. You survived the day. Welcome to the next one.

The air inside smelled like dinner and crayons and the faint detergent sweetness of someone doing laundry in the background. The house breathed "shift change." Declan felt it in his bones: work ending doesn't mean work ends. It just changes uniforms. The soundscape changed, too—the low murmur of a TV somewhere, the rhythmic thump of something being put away, the faint clink of a spoon against a bowl. A home did not announce itself with a bell. A home just kept asking.

He hung his coat, bent to scratch Daisy behind the ear, and she leaned into his hand with slow certainty, like she was accepting a payment.

"Hey," he murmured.

Daisy blinked, then turned her head slightly toward the kitchen, as if to say: Your wife is in there. Her mood is currently somewhere between capable and one inconvenience away from arson. Proceed accordingly.

Declan followed her into the kitchen.

Lena was at the counter chopping something with brisk competence. The knife made that clean, efficient sound that said: *I am doing this because no one else is doing it.* She didn't turn around immediately, which told Declan more than any greeting could. The back of her shoulders looked tired. Not slumped—Lena didn't slouch when she was tired. She tightened. She became smaller and harder at the same time.

Theo was at the table with a snack that appeared to have started as something simple and become an art project. There were cracker crumbs on his shirt, on the table, possibly in his hair. His backpack was open on the floor like it had been attacked by raccoons—papers half-hanging out, a water bottle on its side, a lone sock that didn't belong to anyone.

Theo looked up and shouted, "DAD!" with the same volume he might use if he saw a fire truck explode.

"Hey, buddy," Declan said, forcing warmth into his voice. He wanted to be present. He wanted to be the guy who walked into his own home like it was the center of his life, not the place where his real life interrupted him.

Theo launched himself out of the chair and collided with Declan's legs in a hug that was more physics than affection. Declan wrapped an arm around him and felt the boy's sticky cheek press against his shirt.

Sticky. Always sticky.

In the corner of his mind, a small irrational thought rose: *What if that's a symptom?* Then he hated himself for it, because the kid had just eaten crackers and probably licked a marker. Theo was fine. Theo was a kid. Declan's brain, however, treated every bodily sensation like a press conference.

Daisy sat down nearby, not begging, not hovering—stationed. Her head turned slightly from Theo to Lena to Declan, like a weather vane with fur. She tracked moods the way sailors tracked wind.

Declan watched her, briefly jealous.

Daisy followed rules not because she was obedient, but because she was relational. She knew which hand fed, sure, but she also knew which voice cracked first, which silence meant danger, which laugh meant the fight was over for now. She did enough to pass, and then some. She had figured out how to be lazy and attached at the same time—how to conserve energy without withholding love.

There was something almost spiritual about it. Daisy didn't overthink. She didn't narrate. She didn't turn every moment into a referendum on her worth. She observed and adjusted, compassionate, loyal, gentle, too keen on reading the emotions of others.

She was the household's infrastructure with a heartbeat.

Lena glanced over her shoulder. "Hi."

It wasn't cold. It wasn't warm. It was a receipt.

"Hi," Declan said.

Theo climbed back onto the chair and immediately began talking at a speed that made Declan's brain feel slow, like his kid had woken up with fresh batteries while Declan was still operating on the dregs of a system.

"Today we had snack but then Carter said my crackers were baby crackers and I said they're not baby crackers they're normal crackers and then Ms. Ridley said we have to use kind words but Carter wasn't using kind words and then I made a spaceship with my crackers but it broke because it was too crunchy—"

"That's tragic," Declan said. "A crunchy spaceship. History is full of those."

Theo nodded solemnly, as if Declan had validated a war story.

Lena slid a plate in front of Theo. "Eat," she said. It was not a suggestion. It was an attempt to stabilize the atmosphere with carbohydrates.

Declan glanced at the counter. The cutting board was damp. Onion skin or pepper stem or something small had been flicked aside with the ruthless efficiency of someone who didn't have time to be delicate. His phone buzzed in his pocket, and he ignored it, then hated himself for ignoring it, then hated himself for hating himself. The day was still on him like a smell.

Theo pointed at Declan's wrist. "What's that?"

Declan looked down. The faint red patch was still there. It had faded a little, which should have comforted him. Instead it annoyed him. Even his symptoms couldn't commit.

"Nothing," Declan said.

Theo's eyes narrowed. "It's not nothing. It's red."

"It's a tiny rash," Declan said. "My skin is dramatic."

Lena cut in, still chopping. "He's been stressed."

Declan felt a flare of irritation. Not at Lena being wrong—she wasn't. At Lena saying it out loud in front of Theo, in front of Daisy, in front of the kitchen itself. Like his interior life had been announced over a loudspeaker.

"I'm not stressed," Declan said automatically, which was the kind of lie that made everyone in the room silently agree he was.

Theo took a bite, chewed, and then asked, without looking up, "Dad, do you ever think you're going to die?"

Declan froze.

There it was. The weird philosophical question. Children asked things like they were asking for ketchup.

Lena stopped chopping for half a second. Even Daisy's ears shifted slightly, alert.

Declan felt his mind sprint.

Do I lie? Do I tell the truth? Do I tell the kid I spend half my time convinced my organs are plotting against me? Do I pretend to be a calm father? Do I become the calm father?

He chose the wrong option: honesty.

"Yeah," he said. "All the time."

Theo looked up, interested. "Why?"

Declan opened his mouth and almost said, Because I'm one bad night's sleep away from a devastating illness. He almost said, Because my brain is a doomsday machine. He almost said, Because I'm fairly intelligent but intellectually restless and dissatisfied with my life and my body seems eager to teach me humility.

Instead he said, "Because I love you."

Theo blinked, processing. That answer landed somewhere inside him in a way Declan couldn't see.

Lena turned back to the cutting board and resumed chopping, harder now. The knife sounded louder than it needed to. A clean, repetitive sound—control masquerading as dinner prep.

Theo swallowed and said, "So... you're going to die because you love me?"

Declan laughed once, a sharp burst. "No. I'm going to die because I have organs. The love just makes me notice."

Theo accepted this like it was science. Then he went back to eating, satisfied.

Declan, however, was not satisfied. He could feel Lena's silent disapproval hovering near the ceiling. Not anger. Something more parental than romantic: *Why would you say that to him?*

Declan wanted to make a joke. Humor was his emergency exit. Humor was the little trapdoor he pulled when the room got too real.

He turned to Lena. "So. How was your day?"

Lena didn't look up. "Fine."

Declan flinched. That word again. Fine. A lie people told to get through doorways.

Theo asked, "Mom, why do you always say fine when you're not fine?"

Declan looked at the boy. Then at Lena. Then at Daisy, who looked mildly impressed, as if Theo had learned a new technique.

Lena exhaled slowly. "Because if I start describing it, I won't stop," she said.

Declan nodded, trying to look empathetic. Trying to look like a man who wasn't already reaching for a moat.

He glanced at the clock. He glanced at the phone in his pocket, buzzing again.

Mitchell. Malloy. Tomorrow. The folder. The call he hadn't returned. The missed call from Walt that sat in his phone like a stone.

Declan felt the familiar urge rise: *I need ten minutes.*

※※

Not because he was evil. Because he was overloaded. Because his mind ran at an illegal speed and he needed time to come down to the human limit.

He cleared his throat. "I'm going to just... decompress for a second."

Lena's eyes flicked to him. "Decompress how?"

Declan hated that she asked. He wanted the request to pass unexamined, to be granted like a small personal entitlement.

"Just... quiet," he said. "Ten minutes. I just need ten minutes."

Lena stared at him. Not harshly. Accurately.

"You say ten minutes," she said, "but you mean a moat."

Declan's face tightened. "That's not fair."

"It is fair," Lena said. Her voice wasn't raised. That was the dangerous part. "Because the ten minutes isn't neutral. It's not self-care. It's you putting up a wall and leaving me with everything on the other side."

Declan felt heat rise in his throat. He wanted to defend himself. He wanted to say: You don't know what it's like in my head. He nearly said: I'm trying not to die. He almost said: I'm doing my best.

Instead, because he was himself, he tried humor.

"Okay," he said, "but to be fair, I'm also leaving you with Theo, and he just asked me about death like it was ketchup."

Lena didn't laugh.

Theo, sensing tension, took another bite and chewed loudly, as if noise could fill a room the way drywall did.

Daisy shifted her body slightly closer to Lena. Not choosing sides. Just... calibrating.

Lena set the knife down and turned fully toward Declan. "This is what I mean," she said. "You call it patience. You call it calm. You call it being the 'bigger person.' But it's fear and avoidance."

Declan's jaw clenched. The words landed in his chest like nails—each one small, precise, impossible to unfeel.

"And it makes me do all the emotional labor," Lena continued.

"Because when you go quiet, I have to hold everything. Theo's mood. Your mood. The house. Dinner. Bedtime. I have to hold it because you refuse to."

Declan wanted to interrupt. He wanted to offer a counterargument. He wanted to point out the ways he contributed. He wanted to say: I work. I provide. I show up. I'm here right now, aren't I?

But something in Lena's face stopped him. Not her anger. Her exhaustion. Exhaustion was more convincing than rage.

Declan swallowed. "I'm not refusing," he said. "I'm just trying not to explode."

Lena nodded once, as if she'd been waiting for that line. "Okay," she said. "But you're not the only one trying not to explode."

Theo looked between them, eyes wide. Declan felt immediate guilt—the kind that arrived late, after damage was already done.

He softened his voice. "Theo, can you go play for a few minutes?"

Theo hesitated. "Are you mad at Mom?"

"No," Declan said quickly. Too quickly. "Nobody's mad. We're… talking."

Theo looked skeptical. "It doesn't sound like talking. It sounds like… slow yelling."

Lena almost smiled at that. Almost.

Theo slid off the chair and dragged his snack plate with him like a security blanket, leaving crumbs behind like a trail. He disappeared into the living room, where the sound of cartoons turned on at a volume that felt like a defensive maneuver.

The kitchen got quieter.

Declan heard the refrigerator hum. The dishwasher gurgle. The faint tick of the wall clock measuring his failure in real time.

He rubbed his wrist. The rash itched again, like his body was reminding him: This isn't in your head.

Lena watched him do it. "What happened at work?"

Declan shrugged. "Nothing."

Lena raised an eyebrow. The expression said: Try again.

Declan exhaled. "Malloy gave me a nightmare account," he said. "Mitchell."

Lena nodded. "You told me about Mitchell."

"Yeah," Declan said "And Kyle's pissed. And Malloy is… Malloy."

He almost said: *He had a tremendous amount of power and took pleasure in simultaneously wielding it and denying it.* But he didn't. He didn't want to drag Malloy into their kitchen. Their kitchen had enough tyrants.

Lena leaned against the counter. "Did you handle it?"

Declan hesitated. "I sent an email."

Lena's eyes narrowed. "A good email?"

Declan couldn't help it—he smiled. A little. The pride he hated.

"A good email," he admitted.

Lena nodded. "Okay. That's good."

Then, as if the world couldn't stand a moment of peace, Declan's phone buzzed again.

He pulled it out. A notification. Another email. Another reminder that the day wasn't done with him.

Also—a message from a group chat he barely participated in. Someone had shared a video. The preview image loaded: a woman in a tight dress, filmed without her knowledge, walking down a city street. The caption was something like God's favorite creation with a string of emojis.

Declan's stomach turned.

He glanced at Lena. She'd seen it too. Her eyes flicked to the screen, then back to him.

Declan felt anger rise. Real anger this time—clean and hot. He looked down at the phone, typed quickly with his thumbs:

Gross. Don't send this shit.

He hit send, then immediately felt his heart race.

Conflict. He'd invited conflict. Even in a group chat, conflict felt like stepping into traffic.

He set the phone down.

Lena stared at him. "Good," she said. Not impressed. Just acknowledging the beam placed back into the frame.

Declan swallowed. "I have a passing interest in beauty," he said, because it was a line he'd loved the moment he first thought it, "but a passion for my wife."

Lena looked at him for a long second.

Then she said, quietly, "Then show it. Don't just say the pretty line."

The words weren't cruel. They were devastating in their accuracy.

Declan nodded. His throat felt tight.

From the living room, Theo shouted, "Dad! The dog is being weird!"

Declan glanced toward the doorway. Daisy was standing near the hall, ears up, looking toward the living room with that alert stillness.

"She's not being weird," Declan said, half to Lena, half to himself. "She's… monitoring."

Lena's mouth twitched. "Must be nice," she said. "To have someone monitoring."

Declan felt the accusation, but he also felt the truth inside it. He walked into the living room.

Theo was sprawled on the rug, cartoon noise blasting. Daisy stood between Theo and the hallway like a sentry. Her eyes were on Declan, then on Theo, then back on Declan. Always tracking.

Theo pointed at Daisy. "She keeps looking at me like she knows I'm going to do something."

Daisy blinked slowly, which in her language meant: Correct.

Declan sat on the couch and felt his mind reach automatically for escape.

The thought came like a soft offer: *You could get high. Just a little.*

Slow down. Stop feeling like your brain is on fire.

He almost laughed at how quickly he reached for it.

He stood up and walked toward the kitchen again, where his bag sat near the counter. Inside it, his body already knew, was the little pen he kept hidden like contraband.

His phone was on the counter. The screen still showed the last thing he'd played—Sweet Spiral, paused mid-track. "Dissolve," by Dick Twister & the Cotton Candy Machine, sat there like an instruction. He stared at the pen in his hand and felt the old college joke rise up— Richard Twister, laughing too hard at nothing, calling him Dick-Land until it stuck.

He found himself in the doorway between rooms—the threshold space, the place where choices lived.

Lena looked at him. She didn't ask. She didn't have to. She knew his patterns the way Daisy knew weather.

Declan cleared his throat. "I'm just going to—" He meant to say: grab my charger. He meant to say: check the mail. He meant to say: take the trash out.

Instead his brain, in its own effort to sabotage him, produced a different verb entirely.

"I'm just going to think before I cat," Declan said.

Silence.

Theo turned down the cartoon, confused. "What?"

Declan froze. Then laughed—harder than the moment warranted, because the mistake was so stupid and so perfect.

"Act," he corrected, wiping at his eye. "Think before I act. I wrote that once. And I wrote cat. Because apparently my brain is—"

"A cat?" Theo offered.

"A disaster," Declan said, still laughing. "A caffeinated raccoon in a trench coat."

Theo laughed too. That was the dangerous part: how quickly humor could repair the surface while the deeper crack stayed.

Lena didn't laugh. Not yet. She watched him with the same steady attention Daisy used. Not judging. Tracking.

Declan's laughter faded. The temptation remained.

He could feel how weed would help him slow down. He could feel how it would make the room softer, make the conflict feel less sharp.

He could also feel, faintly, how it would make him less available. How it would become another ritual—a quieter marker line drawn in the evening air: Do not speak to me until I have dulled myself.

He swallowed. "I'm going to take Daisy out," he said instead.

Daisy's ears perked. Her tail thumped once. She liked clear tasks. She liked sequence.

Declan clipped the leash on and stepped outside with her into the cold night air. The stars were faint, swallowed by suburban light. The street was quiet. Somewhere down the road, a car door slammed. A dog barked once. Then nothing.

Declan walked Daisy to the edge of the yard, and she did her slow, deliberate sniffing—another kind of ritual, another kind of structure.

His phone buzzed in his pocket again. He ignored it.

Then he didn't.

He pulled it out and saw the name: Walt Burke.

Not a missed call this time. A voicemail notification from earlier, finally surfacing like a body in water.

Declan stared at it.

The world narrowed in an instant—work, marriage, Theo, Mitchell, Malloy, the group chat, the rash, the coffee line—everything collapsing into one thing: his father, waiting on the other end of the phone.

The older you get, the smaller the world becomes. Not smaller in miles. Smaller in people. Smaller in who mattered enough to hurt you.

Declan put the phone back in his pocket without listening.

Not yet, he told himself. Not in the cold. Not right now. Not when he didn't have the bandwidth.

His body already knew the lie in that. His body already knew it the way his body already knew the coffee line was a lie: a structure built to delay contact with reality.

Daisy finished her business and looked up at him, patient. Loyal. Gentle. Too keen on reading him.

"Yeah," Declan murmured to her. "I know."

They went back inside.

The living room had dimmed into evening softness. Theo was half-asleep on the couch, cartoon still murmuring, one hand holding a snack that had become a crumb sculpture. His head lolled to the side, mouth slightly open, the innocent exhaustion of a child who had spent the entire day being new.

Lena was in the kitchen wiping down counters, moving in quiet loops. Not angry. Not forgiving. Maintaining.

Daisy walked in and immediately stationed herself between Theo and Lena, like a mediator assigned by nature. She lay down with her head on her paws, eyes open, watching both directions.

Declan stood in the doorway and watched them: his son asleep, his wife cleaning, his dog guarding.

The house ran on invisible scaffolding. It ran on small repairs. It ran on people doing their best to do the best they could without being applauded for it.

Declan realized he'd been treating that scaffolding like air—something that simply existed, something he could ignore until it failed.

He walked to the couch, gently took the snack from Theo's hand, and brushed crumbs off his shirt.

Theo didn't wake.

Declan glanced toward the kitchen. Lena didn't look up.

He cleaned something that was already clean. He performed a gesture without demanding a response from it. He didn't apologize out loud, because sometimes apology was just another way to make his feelings someone else's job.

He looked at Daisy, who blinked slowly, as if to say: You can still do the next right thing.

Declan didn't know what the next right thing was yet.

But for the first time all day, he didn't try to perform not knowing.

He stood there—present, imperfect, awake—while the house held itself together around him.

⁎⁎⁎

Bedtime was not a routine in the Burke house. Bedtime was a negotiation conducted by a small, hungry lawyer with no respect for precedent.

"Two minutes," Declan said, standing at the bathroom sink with Theo. "Just brush. That's it. Two minutes and we're done."

Theo stared into the mirror like he was evaluating his own future. He moved the toothbrush around his mouth with the casual boredom of someone doing community service, doing the minimum required to keep the parole officer from showing up.

Declan watched the foam gather at the corners of Theo's lips and felt the familiar fatigue creep in—not the physical kind alone, but the psychic kind. The kind that made every small request feel like lifting a couch by yourself. The bathroom light was too bright for nighttime. It made Theo's cheeks look extra flushed, made Declan's own under-eyes look like bruises.

"Can I have water after?" Theo asked, as if water were a rare privilege.

"Yes," Declan said. "You can have water after. You can have an ocean after. You can have a hose directly to the face. Brush."

Theo brushed. Barely.

Declan tried to be patient and realized he wasn't practicing patience. He was bargaining with his own exhaustion. Every time he said "okay," he felt something in him give way, a tiny surrender. He could almost feel the future version of himself tallying it—how many minutes did you trade away tonight, Dad? How many boundaries did you soften until they weren't boundaries, just vibes?

Theo spit with unnecessary drama, rinsed, and then immediately asked, "Can I wear the dinosaur pajamas?"

"You are already wearing the dinosaur pajamas."

Theo looked down at himself, surprised, like he'd been given a gift and forgotten. "Oh."

Declan guided him down the hallway toward Theo's room. The house had quieted into that late-evening hush where the appliances sounded like they were whispering. The fridge hummed with a steady confidence. The heat kicked on with a soft click. Somewhere, a pipe ticked in complaint. It was the same series of brief, disconnected sounds he'd heard all day—only here they felt less like warning and more like a house settling into itself.

In the living room, Lena's voice floated faintly—she was on the phone with someone, soft and low, the way she spoke when she was trying not to wake the whole house with her own life. Declan couldn't make out the words, only the tone: tired, competent, present. The way a person sounded when they didn't get to disappear into rituals.

Daisy lay in the hallway, head up, eyes open. A sentry. An old soul in a dog body. She watched them pass, then stood slowly—slow enough to communicate that she was not excited, she was simply moving with purpose—and followed at a distance.

Theo climbed into bed and immediately began rearranging himself like he was preparing for a long flight. Blanket up, blanket down. Pillow adjusted. A stuffed animal placed with careful ceremony at the crook of his arm. His movements had the seriousness of ritual: as if correct positioning could protect him from the dark.

Declan sat on the edge of the bed and waited for the final demand, because there's always a final demand. Bedtime did not end because the clock said it did. Bedtime ended when Theo decided the contract was acceptable.

Theo looked at him. "Story."

Declan nodded. "Story."

Theo pointed. "The bridge one."

Declan reached to the nightstand, where a small stack of books lived like a ritual altar. He chose one with a cover that showed a river and a simple arched bridge—illustrations soft, the kind meant to soothe a child into believing the world was sturdy.

He opened it.

The first pages were gentle—an animal walking, a river, a bridge being built plank by plank. A story about connection disguised as a bedtime book. Declan began reading, letting his voice slow down, flatten into calm. He could feel his own speech changing him, too—cadence as medicine. The same man who had spent all day reacting to other people's urgency now had to become a metronome.

Theo scooted closer, his head settling against Declan's side. His small hand reached up automatically and found Declan's hair, fingers threading through it with the tender possessiveness of a child falling asleep.

Declan exhaled.

Theo's fingers tugged, shaped, pulled, as if he were sculpting Declan into someone else.

Declan winced when a finger snagged. "Easy," he whispered.

Theo didn't stop. He pulled again, harder, seeking a shape. Declan let him.

He let him because Theo claimed he wanted him to look like him. And because Declan, in a way he didn't like to admit, wanted that too. Wanted resemblance. Wanted proof that he belonged to someone, that he was not just a man running at illegal speed through a life he kept calling "urgent."

But it hurt more tonight. Declan felt raw, like the skin of his mind had been rubbed thin all day by emails and restraint and the slow, polite violence of Mr. Malloy's office. The tug in his hair became symbolic too quickly: love that asked without knowing it asked.

Theo murmured, "You have good hair."

Declan almost laughed. "Thank you. I've worked hard on it."

Theo tugged again. "I want you to have hair like mine."

"Like a helmet?" Declan asked.

Theo giggled, then yawned mid-giggle, the sound breaking open into something softer. His fingers slowed.

Declan kept reading.

A bridge was built. A river was crossed. Someone arrived safely at the other side. Declan heard himself saying the words and felt the absurd comfort of them: in a children's book, structures worked. In a children's book, someone could build something and it would hold.

Theo's breathing changed. That subtle shift. The drop into sleep that always looked like surrender and felt, to Declan, like abandonment.

Theo's hand remained in Declan's hair, but the grip loosened. His fingers went slack. His mouth opened slightly. His eyes closed.

Declan stopped reading mid-sentence. He stared at the page, then at Theo's face.

And something ugly rose in him—fast, irrational anger, like a door closing in his face.

It wasn't anger at Theo. It was anger at the moment. At the way Theo always fell asleep before the end, as if Declan's effort didn't matter enough to witness. As if Declan was performing a small act of devotion and the recipient kept leaving the room.

Declan felt it in his chest like a hot flash: *Stay awake. Let me finish. Be here for this.*

Then, immediately, the shame. Sharp, nauseating.

※

He looked at Theo—his son, asleep, innocent—and hated himself for the anger, hated that the first feeling was not tenderness but wounded pride.

He recognized it. That was the worst part. This was inherited.

A memory surfaced, not gently. It arrived like a hard object dropped on a table.

Declan was small again, in a different room, in a different house. The wallpaper older. The air smelling faintly of aftershave and dust. Walt Burke sitting on the edge of a bed, book open in his hands, reading with a kind of stern devotion. Walt didn't read the way Lena read. Lena read like the story was a gift. Walt read like the story was a job he was determined to do correctly.

He pronounced every word. He didn't do voices. He didn't skip pages. He didn't let Declan drift without noticing.

Declan remembered the warmth of the blanket, the weight of sleep pressing down like a hand. He remembered fighting it—not because he wanted to hear the ending, but because he sensed that falling asleep would disappoint his father in a way he didn't understand yet. He remembered his own small panic: the feeling that love was a test you could fail simply by being tired.

And then he did. He fell.

A few pages later, Walt stopped reading.

Declan remembered waking to silence and the sudden sharpness in the room. Walt's face in the dim light. Not furious. Something worse: wounded.

"You fell asleep," Walt said.

Declan blinked. "Sorry."

Walt closed the book with a controlled motion, like shutting a door.

"I was doing something here," Walt said, and there was a tremor underneath it he never acknowledged. "And you left."

Declan had never understood it then. He'd thought his father was angry because he wanted obedience. He hadn't considered that Walt wanted company. That the reading wasn't for the kid—it was for the man trying, awkwardly, to be close without knowing how.

Declan remembered how guilt had flooded him. How he'd wanted to be awake for his father the way you want to be good for someone you fear losing. He'd promised himself, silently, that he would do better. That next time he would stay awake. That he would be present. That he would not abandon the moment.

And then, of course, the next time came, and sleep came, and life continued doing what it did—swapping roles, stealing endings.

The memory faded, leaving Declan back in Theo's room, book open, words halted mid-bridge.

Theo breathed softly, his face slack with trust. His hand slipped from Declan's hair and fell onto the blanket.

Declan felt the anger dissolve into something else. Something heavier. Something like grief for his own childish need to be witnessed.

He looked down at the page.

And he kept reading.

Quietly.

He finished the sentence. He finished the paragraph. He finished the chapter though Theo was asleep, though no one was watching, though there would be no applause and no proof it mattered.

He read like he was finishing a prayer.

We do our best to do the best we can.

The line came to him without sarcasm tonight. Not corporate. Not Malloy. Not a sticker.

Just a plain truth: you keep building when the person you're building for can't see it yet. You keep placing beams because the point isn't recognition—the point is that the structure holds.

Declan closed the book gently and set it back on the nightstand.

He sat for a moment longer, watching Theo sleep, feeling the strange ache of loving someone so much it frightened him. Loving someone so much it made his body look for disasters. Loving someone so much it made him angry when the love didn't look back.

From the hallway came Daisy's soft nails on the floor—click, click—then her large shape appeared at the door, patient, calm. She looked in once, as if verifying that the world was still intact, then lay down in the hall where she could guard both Theo's room and the rest of the house.

Declan stood slowly, careful not to creak the bed.

He left Theo's room and closed the door until it was almost shut—Theo liked it that way, a deliberate almost-welcome. The same posture as Mr. Malloy's office, but here it meant safety.

In the hallway, Declan paused over Daisy and scratched her head once. Daisy didn't move. Her eyes stayed open, vigilant, making the quiet feel supervised.

Declan walked to the kitchen.

The house was quieter now. Lena's voice was gone—off the phone. The counters were clean. The sink empty. She'd done the invisible work, again, without needing a trophy.

Declan's phone sat where he'd left it. He picked it up.

The voicemail notification from Walt was still there, waiting. He stared at the name like it could change if he stared long enough.

He pressed play.

Walt's voice filled the kitchen—older than Declan wanted it to be. Casual, clipped, as if every emotional sentence had been sanded down before speaking.

"Hey, Dick," Walt said.

A pause. A faint cough that sounded like it came from deeper than it should have. In the background, the murmur of a television—sports or news, impossible to tell. The creak of a chair. A small exhale. There was a series of brief, disconnected sounds that made Declan's stomach tighten because bodies made those sounds when they were tired.

"Just... call me when you get a chance," Walt said.

Another pause. "Nothing big. Just wanted to hear your voice."

He cleared his throat again. "Alright. Talk soon."

The message ended with a soft click.

From the stairs, Theo's voice drifted down—sleepy, curious, too loud for a house trying to stay calm.

"Why does Grandpa call you Dick?"

Declan didn't answer right away. His face warmed with a small, irrational embarrassment—the kind that came from being seen in a childhood costume you hadn't asked to wear.

"Because he's stubborn," Declan said. "And because kids are cruel and adults are lazy. Go back upstairs."

Theo giggled once—like the word itself was a prank—and padded away.

Declan stood there holding the phone like it was hot.

Nothing big.

That phrase—nothing big—was the exact kind of phrase men used when something was, in fact, big. Or when the possibility of big was hovering nearby and nobody wanted to invite it in by naming it.

Declan put the phone down.

He stared at the dark window above the sink. His own reflection stared back—tired eyes, tense jaw, a man caught between roles.

He thought of his earlier grand, stupid vow: *My last breath will NOT be a yawn. My last word will NOT be a conjunction.* How fucking embarrassing?

It sounded childish now. Not because the fear was childish, but because the bravado was. The fear beneath it was real: the fear of leaving without finishing the sentence, the fear of being mid-story and having the book shut on you.

Declan picked up the phone again and hovered over "Call."

He could do it. He could call. It would take two minutes. He could be an adult son instead of a boy avoiding the dark.

His thumb hovered.

His mind started drafting the call like a script. Hey Dad. Sorry I missed you. Everything okay? How are you feeling? Do you need anything?

Each question felt like opening a door he didn't know how to close again.

He heard Lena's voice from earlier: *You call it calm. You call it patience. But it's fear and avoidance.*

He felt it now. The familiar stall. The delay disguised as timing.

Not tonight, he told himself. He's probably asleep.

Not tonight, he told himself. I don't have the bandwidth.

Not tonight, he told himself, like repeating it could make it kind.

He set the phone down again, face-up this time, as if honesty about postponement made postponement less cowardly.

He turned off the kitchen light and stood for a moment in the dimness, listening to the house.

The refrigerator hummed. The heat clicked on. Somewhere a floorboard settled. A living house, holding its breath.

He walked back down the hall.

Daisy lay where she'd been, eyes open, guarding. Declan stepped over her carefully, as if stepping over a threshold in his own mind.

Theo's door was almost closed. A line of light from the hallway cut across the carpet inside the room like a pale ribbon.

Declan stopped in the doorway and looked in.

Theo was asleep on his side, mouth open slightly, hair flattened in a way that made him look younger than he already was. One hand rested near the book's edge on the nightstand, as if he'd fallen asleep reaching for it.

Declan held the book in his mind—the bridge, the river, the

crossing—and felt the two fathers inside him like weights balanced on either side.

Walt, reading with stern devotion, wounded by a child's sleep.

Declan, reading into silence, trying not to be wounded by the same thing.

Time, quietly, was already swapping the roles. Already teaching Declan what it meant to stand at the edge of a bed and realize the person you love might not be awake for the ending.

Declan stayed there a moment longer, book still open in his mind, heart doing its quiet, exhausted work.

Then he let the door drift almost shut. Not a wall. Not a moat.

Just a deliberate almost-welcome.

And in the hallway, Daisy's eyes followed him as if to say: You can still call tomorrow.

Declan didn't answer.

He walked back toward his own room, carrying the unfinished call like a stone, and trying—clumsily, sincerely—to become the kind of man who didn't wait his life out, but entered it while it was still here.

※

He redrew the line the way some men redrew boundaries after losing a war.

Same mug. Same marker. Same stubborn little ceremony performed in the half-light of a kitchen that had seen enough mornings to know none of them were miracles—just repetitions with slightly different weather.

Declan held the cup up and watched the black mark catch the light. It looked cleaner than yesterday's, darker, more decisive, as if he could will himself into steadiness by making the line more convincing. The ceramic was warm from the dishwasher, heat seeping into his palm like borrowed confidence.

But the line didn't feel like comfort today. It felt like a symptom.

He turned his wrist and saw the faint red patch again—still there, still petty, still capable of turning his brain into a courtroom. It sat on his skin like a small accusation: *Look how easily you flare. Look how quickly your body votes against your peace.*

The kind of skin that rashes with a whisper.

He dragged his thumb across it once, gentle, testing. It itched, then stopped. Like everything else in him lately—never fully committing to disaster, never fully letting him relax. He could almost hear the thought forming before it became words: *You're fine. Until you're not.*

Daisy watched from the doorway, huge and quiet, her face set in that slow, benevolent seriousness she wore when she was doing her real job: emotional foreman, household inspector, living beam. Her eyes tracked him the way weather tracked a coastline—patient, certain, without judgment. She didn't look at him like an animal wanting something. She looked at him like a coworker clocking in.

Declan poured coffee, listened to it bloom—dark, bitter, alive—and took a sip too hot because he liked pain in controlled doses. He liked the clean sting that came with rules. He liked the way heat made his brain briefly stop narrating itself. The coffee tasted like roasted inevitability.

He tried to pretend the day hadn't already started drafting its demands.

Then Theo yelled from upstairs. "Dad! Where are my other socks?"

The *other socks*. As if socks came in moral pairs. As if the universe owed him symmetry.

Declan looked down at the mug. The line stared back. He'd hoped, stupidly, for an uninterrupted span of quiet big enough to crawl inside. The little republic of "me" he tried to create each morning was already under siege by wardrobe logistics.

Daisy's eyes shifted toward the stairs.

Proceed, she seemed to say. The meeting has been called.

Declan sighed and took another sip. The coffee lowered a fraction, the line moving closer like a deadline.

"Coming," he called, and tried to say it like a man who wasn't always bracing.

From the hallway came Lena's footsteps—purposeful, already mid-task. She appeared at the edge of the kitchen with her hair half-up and her face in that mode she had in the mornings: not unkind, not soft, assembled. A person who had already built the bridge while everyone else was still arguing about the river. She smelled faintly of shampoo and that neutral laundry scent of someone who did not get to have

⁎⁎⁎

rituals—only requirements.

She looked at the cup, then at the line, then at him. She didn't comment. She didn't need to. They had an entire vocabulary now made of objects.

"Did you call your dad back?" she asked.

She asked the way you ask about the trash—practical, procedural—sliding a finger under the loose edge of what he kept postponing.

Declan's mouth tightened. Two words arrived in his throat like weights.

"Not yet."

Lena nodded once, as if noting a fact in a ledger. 'Don't make it weird," she said.

Then she turned away, already reaching for something else—Theo's lunch, the forms, the day's scaffolding. Plastic baggies whispered. A drawer opened and shut with the quiet impatience of routine.

Don't make it weird.

It was exactly what made it weird. Like telling someone not to think about their tongue.

Declan stared at his cup and felt something twist in him—guilt, yes, but also something more specific: the irritation of being seen. Not caught. Just… located. Lena had an infuriating precision that required no raised voice. She could name his avoidance like she was pointing at a coat on a chair: *that, again.*

He took another sip. The coffee hit the line faster than it should have.

He pulled his phone out, opened Walt's contact, hovered, then closed it. Then opened it again. Dialed. Hung up before it rang. A rehearsed failure. A private practice of refusal.

The empty space in his day felt shaped like Walt's voice.

Theo thundered down the stairs wearing a shirt inside out and holding one sock like evidence. His hair stood up in sleepy tufts, as if his head had been in a minor fight with the pillow.

"This one is missing its brother," Theo said, solemn. "It's a single."

"Like a song?" Declan offered.

Theo frowned. "No. Like... lonely."

Declan almost laughed. He wanted to tell Theo the world was full of lonely things. He wanted to tell him how the older you got, the smaller the world became—not smaller in space, smaller in who you spoke to. Smaller in who you could afford to lose. He wanted to explain how loneliness sometimes disguised itself as independence and got applauded for it.

Instead he said, "We'll find it," and watched Daisy drift behind Theo with her slow gravity, as if the dog could keep him from spinning off.

They got out the door with the usual mix of timing and chaos. Lena did the last-minute checks—permission slip, lunch, backpack, shoes, coat, the daily audit. Declan pretended he wasn't counting his internal failures like beads.

In the driveway, the cold air bit his wrist and the red patch tingled again, faintly, as if the skin had opinions about seasons. The sky was a pale, reluctant gray. The neighborhood looked damp and half-awake. A garbage truck groaned somewhere down the street, its mechanical swallowing sound like a metaphor nobody needed.

He drove to work with the radio off, because silence felt like a small rebellion. But silence also made room for thoughts, and thoughts—his thoughts—were not gentle guests. They came in running and started rearranging furniture.

At a red light, he glanced at his phone sitting face-down in the cup holder.

Walt's name wasn't there. That should have made him feel relieved. It didn't.

It made him feel like he was waiting for a shoe to call.

At his desk, the office greeted him with its usual liturgy: citrus disinfectant, the hum of fluorescent lights, the brief, disconnected sounds of machines and humans performing competence in small bursts. The building had its own mood—sterile and mildly hostile. Even the carpet felt disapproving.

He logged in, opened his inbox, and immediately saw Mitchell's name.

His stomach tightened before he clicked. His body was so trained now it could anticipate dread the way Daisy anticipated footsteps.

Mitchell's email was short and sharp, the kind that arrived like a knuckle rap.

I reviewed your report. It's helpful.
Now I need a revised timeline by end of day.
Also: I want the vendor on the call tomorrow. Confirm.

Declan stared.

End of day.

The phrase didn't mean "by five." It meant "by the time you stop being a person." It meant "rearrange your life and pretend you're grateful." It meant: *Your calendar is not real. Only ours is.*

He could do it fast—dash out something vague, buy time, toss the timeline like a bone. He could feed urgency and hope it stayed fed.

Or he could do it right—call the vendor, verify dates, risk saying no to the client's urgency to save them from a different kind of failure later. The kind where the lie collapses publicly and you're blamed for not predicting physics.

He read the email again, then checked the clock. 8:43.

He felt the tyrannical part of him—the part trained by bosses and fear—lean toward speed. Give them something. Feed the beast.

Then he felt the newer part—the part he'd been trying to grow—lean toward structure.

Kindness, he reminded himself, was not softness. Kindness was sequence. It was not promising what you couldn't deliver. It was the unsexy work of naming reality before reality named you.

He opened a document and started building the timeline the hard way.

He called the vendor. He left a message.

He called again.

He wrote a note to himself that said: **Do not lie to buy peace.**

The minutes bled. His throat went dry. People moved around him like he'd become furniture, and he stayed there anyway—visible. He could feel his shoulders inching up toward his ears, tension gathering like static.

Across the office, Kyle's voice floated from somewhere behind him, laughing at something that didn't sound funny. Declan's skin prickled. Kyle's laugh had a way of making the room feel smaller, like the air belonged to someone else.

Declan kept working.

At 9:22, the vendor called back. Declan took notes. He asked questions. He didn't apologize for asking them. He didn't preface with *sorry* the way he'd been trained to do—like facts were rude.

The timeline took shape: dates that could hold weight. Dependencies. Risk points. Actual facts. It was boring and beautiful, in the way a properly laid foundation was beautiful if you'd ever lived in a house that shifted.

At 10:05, Kyle appeared at his desk like a man arriving to collect a debt.

"Mitchell's got you jumping," Kyle said, smiling.

The smile was polite enough to pass in public. Up close it looked like teeth hiding behind a closed door.

Declan's instinct was to soften, to deflect with humor, to make the moment airy so it couldn't hurt. To perform "easygoing" and hope it bought him safety.

He looked at Kyle and tried, for once, to be direct without being cruel.

"Yeah," he said. "They're... a lot. But I'm getting it under control."

Kyle nodded slowly, as if Declan had claimed he could tame a tornado.

"Malloy likes people who don't make waves," Kyle said.

It was phrased like advice. It landed like a threat.

Declan felt anger flicker. Then fear. Then the familiar collapse into politeness—because politeness was the socially acceptable form of surrender.

"Yeah," Declan said. "I'm not trying to make waves."

Kyle leaned in slightly. His cologne was too fresh, too confident. "Good," he said. "Because the last thing you want is to look... emotional. You know how it is."

Declan stared at him.

This was the sickness, he thought. Not Mitchell. Not even Malloy. This subtle doctrine that said your feelings were liabilities and your boundaries were "drama" and your humanity was unprofessional. A culture where "calm" meant "quiet enough to exploit."

He thought of Lena in the kitchen telling him his silence wasn't neutral. He thought of Theo asking if he was going to die and accepting the answer like it was math.

Kindness without boundaries becomes appeasement, it hit him.

Self-erasure with manners.

Kyle smiled again. "Anyway," he said. "Good luck."

Then he walked away, leaving Declan with that familiar aftertaste: the sense that he'd been sized up by a man who enjoyed keeping the tape measure.

Declan turned back to his screen. His wrists itched—not the rash, but the impulse to scratch at the whole day until it bled into something honest.

He finished the timeline. He triple-checked it. He included the vendor. He wrote the email Mitchell would not love but would need. A message shaped by reality instead of fear.

He was hovering over Send when a shadow fell across his desk.

Mr. Malloy, of course.

The man appeared the way storms appeared—quietly, with pressure. The air shifted around him, as if the office had been designed to make room for his presence.

"Burke," Malloy said, looking at the screen without asking permission. "Mitchell's happy."

Declan didn't trust compliments from Malloy. Compliments were ropes disguised as ribbons.

"That's good," Declan said.

Malloy nodded, like he'd issued a reward. "Don't get used to it," Malloy added.

There it was. The blade inside the praise.

Declan kept his face neutral. He didn't ask what Malloy meant. He did know. Malloy liked to remind people that stability was a privilege he could revoke.

"We may have other opportunities coming up," Malloy said casually, as if tossing crumbs to a starving animal. "If you keep this up. People notice."

People notice.

Not *I notice*. Not *I'm impressed*.

People—the anonymous committee of invisible judgment Malloy used like a religion. Declan felt his jaw tighten. He was tired of being managed by a phantom audience.

Malloy continued, "I'm not saying you're... on thin ice." He smiled. "Just... stay sharp."

Wielding power and denying it. A man who could imply consequences without ever stating them, so you couldn't defend yourself without looking paranoid.

※※

Declan swallowed. "Understood."

Malloy's eyes flicked to Declan's wrist. "What's that?" Malloy asked, voice light.

Declan glanced down. The red patch seemed brighter now, as if it had heard its name.

"Nothing," Declan said automatically.

Malloy chuckled, a small sound that felt like amusement at the idea of Declan having a body. "Try not to let stress get to you," he said. "Would hate to see you… unravel."

Then Malloy walked away, already moving, never fully present, leaving behind that faint scent of expensive cologne and the unmistakable impression of having been touched without being touched.

Declan stared at his screen.

Unravel.

He imagined his life as a sweater tugged from one loose thread: Mitchell, Malloy, Kyle, the rash, the folder, the missed call, the unmade call.

He clicked Send.

The email vanished into the ether. A clean sentence released into a dirty room.

He sat back and forced his shoulders down, as if relaxing on command could become real.

His phone buzzed.

He didn't look.

It buzzed again.

He looked.

Walt Burke. Incoming call.

Declan's chest tightened.

It wasn't fear of bad news. It was fear of being required. Fear of a conversation that might not be small. Fear of stepping onto a bridge and realizing the river underneath had been rising while he wasn't looking.

The phone rang. Once.

Twice.

He watched it. He didn't answer. Not because he didn't love Walt. Because he did. Because love made the stakes feel like glass: one wrong move and you shattered something you couldn't glue back together.

The phone stopped ringing.

A missed call notification appeared. Quiet. Efficient. Like the office. Declan stared at it until his eyes hurt.

Then he did what he always did: he chose the cleanest lie. He texted:

Can't talk—call you later.

The lie was small. The lie was tidy. The lie fit in a single line of text the way shame fit behind a smile.

He set the phone down like it was fragile.

His skin prickled. The rash itched. The office noise returned in waves—brief, disconnected sounds that felt like the building's heartbeat.

He told himself: Later. Later. Later.

Later was where he stored the people he didn't want to lose.

The parking lot wind cut straight through his coat, dragging exhaust and wet leaves across the asphalt. On the drive home, the sky was already dimming, that gray-blue shift that made everything look a little unfinished. Declan's mind replayed the missed call the way it replayed every moment of avoidance: not as a choice, but as an indictment.

In the driveway, The Dribble and The Hip were outside again, because of course they were—standing near their mailbox like they were waiting for time to come pick them up.

The Hip lifted a hand. "Hey there, Declan."

Declan forced a smile as he stepped out of his car. "Hey."

The Dribble ambled closer, cheerful in that practiced way that suggested pain was always nearby, kept politely in the other room.

"Haven't seen your dad in a bit," The Dribble said.

Declan felt the line land in his gut. A simple sentence with a hook.

"You saw him?" Declan asked, trying to sound casual.

The Hip nodded. "Few weeks back. Down at the hardware store. He looked... tired. But then again, don't we all."

The Dribble chuckled. "It goes fast, kid."

Kid.

Declan was in his thirties with a mortgage and a rash and a coffee religion, and the neighborhood elders still called him kid. Not to insult him. To remind him time didn't care about his self-image.

"It goes fast," The Hip repeated, and the phrase sounded less like small talk and more like an obituary written in advance.

Declan nodded, smile fixed. "Yeah," he said. "Yeah, it does."

He felt the bruise forming.

He waved, walked toward his front door, and felt Daisy's presence before he saw her—like the house exhaled through fur.

Daisy stood behind the glass, watching. Not greeting. Witnessing.

Declan stepped inside and Daisy moved toward him with slow certainty, leaning her massive shoulder against his leg like an anchor. She smelled like outside—cold air and dog warmth and whatever mystery she carried in her fur. The contact steadied him in a way he didn't want to admit he needed.

Shift change, the house breathed. *Work ending doesn't mean work ends.*

Theo's voice erupted from the living room. "Dad! You're home!"

Theo barreled into the entryway, sticky again, loud again, carrying the day on his face like fingerprints. Declan caught him in a hug, breathed in the smell of crayons and crackers and child sweat, and tried to let the moment be simple.

Daisy stayed close, head turning toward the kitchen—where Lena's movements sounded brisk, efficient, slightly sharper than they needed to be.

Declan walked in and saw her: hair up, sleeves rolled, the counter already half-cleaned, dinner mid-motion. The kitchen smelled like onions and dish soap and that faint heat from the oven that made a house feel like it was trying.

"Hey," he said.

"Hey," Lena replied.

Receipt language again. Not hostile. Not warm.

Theo started talking immediately, a stream of school facts and existential questions delivered in one breath. Declan nodded at the right places, tried to stay present, but his mind kept lurching toward the phone in his pocket like a tongue to a sore tooth.

Walt called.

I didn't answer.

I lied.

The rash itched. Mitchell will reply. Malloy will hover. Tomorrow will arrive.

He wanted to disappear for ten minutes. He felt the moat start building itself.

So he did the next thing instead: service.

He grabbed a dish towel. He started unloading the dishwasher. He wiped down the counter. He moved with exaggerated usefulness, like an actor playing "helpful husband."

It genuinely helped. The plates got put away. The counter got cleared. The house got a few beams reset.

But Lena watched him with that quiet clarity that made lying impossible.

After Theo was sent to wash his hands, Lena said, softly, "You're being very efficient."

Declan paused mid-plate. "Is that bad?"

"It's not bad," Lena said. "It's just... guilt."

Declan felt his face tighten. "It's not guilt. I'm just—"

"Declan," Lena said, and his name sounded like a hand on a shoulder. Not harsh. Direct. "You're doing the thing where you do a good thing so you don't have to do the hard thing."

Declan fixed on the dish in his hands. White ceramic. Clean. Simple. A task that obeyed.

"What hard thing?" he asked, and he hated the way the question sounded like a child trying to avoid consequences.

Lena nodded toward his pocket. She didn't have to say the name. The phone's glow was already living between them like a third person.

"Call your dad," Lena said. Gently.

Deadly.

Declan swallowed. "I will."

"When?" Lena asked.

"Later," Declan said, and felt the word reveal itself as the lie it was. The house had started to recognize his vocabulary: later, soon, after this, when I get a chance.

Lena held his gaze.

"Don't make it weird," she said again, and this time the phrase wasn't just practical—it was pleading disguised as calm.

Theo came back in, hands wet, asking for a snack he'd already eaten. Daisy wandered to the doorway and lay down where she could see them both.

Declan nodded as if agreement was action. He put the dish away. He wiped his hands. He smiled at Theo.

Later, he told himself again.

He would call later.

That night, after Theo finally collapsed into sleep and the house dimmed into its quieter version, Declan stood in the living room with the lights off.

The room was lit only by the phone in his hand, the screen bright against his face like confession.

Walt Burke. Missed call. Text sent.

A clean, small lie.

Declan's thumb hovered over the call button. His mind began rehearsing.

Hey Dad—sorry, work was insane. You okay?

Everything alright? What's going on?

Do you need something? Are you sick?

He felt the fear beneath the script: not fear of Walt, but fear of what the call would require of him—presence, steadiness, the ability to hold someone else's uncertainty without running.

Daisy was down the hall, her breathing slow, her body a warm anchor in the dark.

Theo slept with a child's complete trust.

Lena moved quietly in the bedroom, the sound of drawers closing, the soft private work of ending a day.

Declan stood alone in the living room, thumb hovering, rehearsing like a man about to jump while still checking the height.

He could call.

He didn't.

He set the phone down on the coffee table face-up, as if refusing to hide the postponement made it less cowardly. As if visibility was virtue.

The screen dimmed.

The room went darker.

Declan stared at the blank glass of the phone and felt the cost of avoidance settle in his chest like a weight he'd agreed to carry.

Not tonight, he told himself. Tomorrow.

Later.

He sat back on the couch, the silence thick around him, and realized—quietly, with a clarity that hurt—that he was building his life out of lines he drew and calls he didn't make.

Outside, the world kept moving.

Inside, the house held its breath.

And Declan, lit briefly by the ghost of his own screen stayed exactly where he was—thumb still hovering in his mind—practicing the one ritual he never admitted was a ritual:

waiting.

※

Small talk was the airless room adults agreed to breathe in together.

Declan stood in the school hallway with a paper cup of coffee—watery, apologetic—and tried to look like a person who belonged there. The walls were lined with children's art: bright suns, lopsided houses, stick families smiling like they'd never had to negotiate bedtime or pay a deductible. Someone had taped up a banner that said **WE LOVE OUR VOLUNTEERS!** in bubble letters. Declan read it like a warning.

The hallway smelled like floor wax and the faint sour-sweet of cafeteria fruit cups. Somewhere a door closed with an institutional thud. The fluorescent lights had that same flat honesty as the office, turning every face into a file photo. Parents clustered in loose circles, performing ease the way office people performed competence: laugh at the right volume, keep your hands busy, say the correct phrases. Everyone seemed to know the choreography. Declan felt like the one guy at a wedding who missed the rehearsal and kept turning the wrong way.

He caught fragments of conversation—soccer schedules, gluten, "crazy week," "can you believe," "we're so lucky"—the approved phrases people used to keep fear from showing through. He watched hands gesture, shoulders tilt, little social smiles assembled and deployed.

※

Lena was a few steps away, talking to Theo's teacher with her familiar calm—the kind of calm that didn't require an audience. Declan watched her, relieved and embarrassed. She made contact look easy. He made it look like strategy. Lena's voice carried that steady friendliness that said I will be polite without becoming porous.

A dad in a fleece vest leaned against the trophy case and said, "Oh, I can't do that. My religion says I can't."

He said it like a joke. He said it like charm. Like the phrase was a quirky hat he put on to make the moment cute.

A woman laughed. "Must be nice."

"Yeah," the man replied, grinning. "It is."

Declan felt his jaw tighten without asking his jaw's permission.

My religion says I can't do that, he thought, and heard Lena's voice from months ago—teasing him in their kitchen, nodding at his marker line. *My religion says I can't do that. Cool.*

But then the other version—the version that wasn't about self-restraint, but control.

My religion says *you* can't do that. Fuck off.

He didn't say it. He held his coffee and nodded at someone he didn't recognize, participating in the social ceremony the way a man held his breath underwater: tight-lipped, counting seconds. He could feel his skin buzzing, that mild panic of being watched, of being evaluated for belonging. Parent culture felt like a smaller, friendlier office—same rules, different snacks.

Theo tugged at his sleeve.

"Dad," Theo whispered, eyes wide in the fluorescent light, "Ms. Ridley said we're not allowed to run in the hallway because it's not allowed."

Declan blinked.

Not because the rule was new—the pattern snapped into focus: hallways and children and physics. Because of the phrasing.

It's not allowed.

Not "because you could bump someone." Not "because someone could get hurt." Just: it's not allowed.

Allowed by who, he wanted to ask. Allowed by what invisible authority?

He looked at Theo's face, so earnest, so ready to absorb the world's rules like gospel. He felt the protective urge rise—the urge to keep his son from learning the wrong kind of obedience. The kind that didn't come with reason, only permission.

"You can run outside," Declan said carefully. "Inside we walk so nobody gets hurt. That's all."

Theo nodded, satisfied, then added, "Also Carter said you're not allowed to say 'stupid' because it's a bad word."

"That's correct," Declan said. He tried to make his voice neutral. The rot wasn't in the rule. The rot was in how easily a child learned the language of permission without learning the language of reason. Declan felt it like a small grief: the world teaching Theo to comply before it taught him to think.

Theo looked up again. "Are you allowed to be mad?"

Declan paused.

He glanced at Lena across the hallway. She was smiling at the teacher—an adult smile, practiced but real. Declan envied her ability to hold it all without making it a trial.

"Yeah," he said to Theo. "You're allowed to be mad. You're just not allowed to hurt people with it."

Theo nodded like he'd been handed a tool.

"Okay," he said, and then—obedient to the hallway rule—walked very fast toward a table of cookies as if sugar were the true religion of childhood.

Declan exhaled slowly and felt the school's fluorescent hum inside his bones.

⁎⁎⁎

The same hum as the office.

Different building, same atmosphere: the soft dominance of rules you weren't supposed to question.

Lena returned to his side, slipping back into his orbit with quiet competence.

"You look like you're in court," she murmured.

Declan managed a thin smile. "Just enjoying the thrill of being perceived."

Lena's mouth twitched. Not a full laugh. A partial mercy. "Don't be weird," she said, and her voice was light, but the words still landed in that spot in Declan where timing and avoidance lived.

Declan nodded as if nodding was change.

Then Theo's teacher turned back to them and said something kind about Theo—how he'd been helpful, how he'd been gentle with a younger kid on the playground—and Declan felt his chest tighten with that irrational mix of pride and fear. Pride that his son was good. Fear that goodness was fragile. Fear that the world would punish him for being soft the way offices punished people for being human.

He watched Theo accept praise with that solemn seven-year-old modesty that was half sincerity and half not knowing what to do with admiration. Declan wanted to freeze the moment, save it like evidence that tenderness could survive in public.

As they left, Declan heard the fleece-vest dad again. "My religion says I can't," he said, laughing.

Declan kept walking.

Outside, the cold air felt like an honest slap. He breathed in and tried to let the world be physical instead of symbolic. The parking lot smelled like wet pavement and car exhaust. Winter had that particular clarity: everything stripped down, nothing decorative.

In the car, Theo chattered about cookies and who got stickers and how Carter was "not allowed" to have a second juice box. Declan listened and tried not to hear the permission-language threading itself into his son's brain like wires. Lena drove. Her hands were steady on the wheel, wedding ring catching light as she turned.

Declan watched the road and felt the itch on his wrist rise and fall like a tide.

At work, the air smelled faintly of citrus disinfectant and despair.

Declan sat down at his desk, opened his inbox, and immediately saw an email from Mitchell.

They wanted another update. Of course they did.

The urgent never had a bottom. The urgent was a well you poured your life into until you forgot what thirst felt like. Declan's shoulders tightened in anticipation of the day's familiar posture: leaning forward, bracing, apologizing with labor.

He started drafting a response, then stopped when a shadow fell across his screen.

Mr. Malloy.

He didn't approach like a person. He approached like a policy.

"Burke," Malloy said.

Declan looked up. "Mr. Malloy."

Malloy smiled in that controlled way that made the smile feel like a tool. "How are you holding up?" Malloy asked. "You seem… stressed."

Declan felt the trap assemble itself in real time.

It wasn't a genuine question. It was an invitation to confess. And confession, in the wrong hands, was evidence.

Declan's mind flashed through possibilities the way it did in any room with a power figure: If I say I'm stressed, he'll call me unstable. If I say I'm fine, he'll call me dishonest. If I say nothing, he'll call me evasive. If I say something small, he'll inflate it later into a narrative: Burke can't handle pressure.

Malloy waited, patient in the way predators were patient.

Declan heard Lena in his head: *You call it calm. You call it patience.*

⁂

But it's fear and avoidance.

He felt the difference now: silence could be cowardice, yes. But it could also be strategy. It could be self-defense.

"I'm good," Declan said.

Not warm. Not rude. Flat.

Malloy's eyebrows rose slightly, as if amused by the lack of performance.

"Good," Malloy said. "Because this kind of workload can… expose people. You know? Not everyone has the temperament."

Expose.

The word landed like a wet cloth.

Malloy leaned in just a fraction, lowering his voice as if they were sharing a confidence. "Mitchell's pleased," he said. "But they're demanding. Don't let it get to you. And don't… overshare."

Declan stared.

The hypocrisy of it was almost funny. Malloy inviting confession while warning against it, like a man opening a door and then blaming you for walking through.

Declan nodded once. "Understood."

Malloy smiled again. "I knew you would."

He patted the top of Declan's cubicle wall—ownership masquerading as encouragement—and moved on, already rearranging the air elsewhere.

Declan sat still for a moment, his fingers hovering over the keyboard.

Confession as a weapon, he thought.

How many times had he done it to himself—confessed his flaws in advance so nobody else could accuse him, offered up his own throat like a peace offering? How many times had he told the story of his anxiety like he was preemptively surrendering?

He forced himself back to the email. He wrote a clean sentence. He did what he could. He didn't write his fear into the margins.

The day dragged on in its usual segmented way—meetings like interruptions, emails like demands, the brief relief of finishing one task immediately replaced by the next. He watched the clock the way he watched his coffee line: as something that pretended to be neutral while quietly governing his life.

That night, the house felt smaller.

Not in square footage. In options.

Theo was in the living room building something out of blocks—bridge pieces, towers, little disasters he repaired without ceremony. Daisy lay nearby, head on her paws, eyes open, monitoring the room like she was employed.

Lena stood at the stove, stirring with that steady arm motion that always made Declan think of work—real work, the kind that didn't send you performance reviews. Dinner smelled like garlic and heat and the faint sweetness of something browning properly. The sound of the spoon against the pot had a soothing regularity: friction, circle, repeat.

Declan walked in with his coat still on, phone buzzing in his pocket like a trapped insect.

"Hey," Lena said.

"Hey," Declan replied.

He tried to kiss her cheek. She allowed it, but her body didn't lean in.

Contact offered. Contact received. Contact not returned.

He felt it and hated how quickly his mind turned it into a verdict.

Theo looked up. "Dad, are you allowed to have dessert?"

Declan barked a laugh. "What is with you and allowed today?"

Theo shrugged. "Ms. Ridley says lots of allowed."

Lena's eyes flicked to Declan.

A look that said: see?

Declan forced a smile. "Yeah, bud. I'm allowed."

Theo nodded, satisfied, and went back to his blocks, muttering rules to himself like an architect. "This one can't go there," he whispered. "That's not allowed."

Declan watched him and felt something ache. The kid was building structures. The kid was learning the language of authority. The kid was learning how the world decided who got to do what.

Declan pulled out his phone and checked his notifications. His group chat lit up with something stupid—another link, another video, another little piece of rot disguised as humor. A clip loaded: a woman filmed at the gym, framed like prey, the caption laughing about "motivation."

Declan felt a clean wave of disgust.

He typed fast: **Stop posting this. It's gross.**

He hit send.

His heart started racing immediately—the ridiculous adrenaline of conflict, even digital conflict, even anonymous conflict. His body didn't care that it was "just a chat." His body treated all confrontation like a cliff.

Lena saw the screen over his shoulder. Her expression changed—not into admiration, exactly. Into wariness.

"Good," she said quietly.

Declan looked at her. "What?"

"That you said something," Lena replied. "That you can do that."

Declan's chest tightened. "Why wouldn't I say something?"

Lena turned toward him fully, spoon in hand like a pointer. "Because you only get brave when you're angry," she said. "And then you call it principles."

Declan felt the words land hard.

"That's not fair," he said automatically.

Lena's gaze didn't waver. "It's not unfair," she said. "It's just... familiar."

Declan's jaw clenched. He could feel himself reaching for explanation—the whole self-defense lecture about his brain, his speed, his stress. The whole PowerPoint called *Reasons I'm Like This*. He could deliver it. He had slides.

"I'm stressed," he said. "Mitchell's blowing up my inbox. Malloy's hovering. Kyle's doing his whole—" He made a vague gesture, meaning politics, meaning threat. "And I'm trying. I'm trying to be clear. I'm trying to not—"

"Declan," Lena said, cutting through the speech like a clean blade. "I don't want the explanation."

He stopped.

She softened, slightly—not to coddle him, but to keep the moment from breaking.

"I want contact," she said. "I want you here. Not narrating your stress like it's a court case. Here."

Declan swallowed. The urge to retreat rose in him immediately, the old instinct: draw the moat. Go quiet. Make your silence look like self-care. Make her do the emotional labor while you pretend it's healing.

He felt the shame of it and still wanted it.

He tried a different move—one he didn't fully trust yet.

"I don't know how," he admitted.

Lena's face changed—tired, yes, but also tender in that annoyed way she got when he finally said something true.

"You do know how," she said. "You just keep choosing not to."

Declan flinched.

And then, because the house was always watching, Theo said from the living room, sleepy now, voice softened by exhaustion, "Mom?"

Lena answered immediately. "Yeah, honey?"

Theo rubbed his eyes. "Are you and Dad allowed to fight?"

Declan froze.

⁎⁎⁎

Lena closed her eyes for a second, as if the question had reached into her chest and squeezed gently.

"We're not fighting," she said.

Theo yawned. "It sounds like slow yelling."

Declan felt an almost laugh rise—Theo's perfect phrasing, his accidental wisdom.

Lena managed a small smile. "Okay," she said. "It's... intense talking."

Theo nodded, satisfied with the label, then asked, "Can Daisy have dessert?"

Daisy's head lifted slightly, as if she'd been summoned by title.

Declan exhaled. Something in the room loosened by a millimeter.

Lena looked at Declan. The wariness remained, but it wasn't closed.

"Go do bedtime," she said.

Declan nodded. "Okay."

Theo shuffled toward him, half-asleep, and Declan guided him down the hall. Daisy followed behind, nails clicking softly, the house's quiet metronome.

Bedtime went the usual way—water, a question, a last question, a renegotiation of the terms of reality. Declan got through it. Not gracefully, but present enough.

When Theo finally fell asleep, Declan stood for a moment in the doorway and felt the day's noise drop away. He wanted to stay there, in the child's room, where power meant safety and rules meant blankets and the worst thing in the world was a missing sock.

He closed the door until it was almost shut.

Not a wall.

Not a moat.

A deliberate almost-welcome.

In the kitchen later, Declan rinsed the mug.

The marker line was still there, faded at the edges from washing, blurred like virtue. He ran the sponge over it and watched the black smear slightly, a mark losing its authority.

His phone buzzed on the counter.

Walt Burke.

Voicemail. Again.

Declan's chest tightened before he touched the screen. The name itself had become a pressure point. He pressed play.

Walt's voice filled the kitchen—older, unmistakably older now, the consonants clipped, the breath a little more present than it used to be.

"Hey, Dick," Walt said.

A pause.

A cough—deep enough to make Declan's wrist itch in sympathy, which was absurd and also exactly how his brain worked.

In the background, a television murmuring. A chair creaking. A soft exhale. There was a series of brief, disconnected sounds that sounded like a body trying not to announce itself.

"I've got a... appointment next week," Walt said, and the word appointment landed like a stone in water. "Nothing major. Just... the doctor wants to run a couple things. I'm tired, that's all."

He cleared his throat again, and Declan felt it in his own throat, phantom-tight.

"Anyway," Walt continued, trying to sand down the emotion the way men did. "Call me when you get a chance. Just... when you get a minute."

Another pause—too long, too quiet.

"Alright," Walt said. "Talk soon."

Click.

Declan stood still with wet hands, staring at the mug.

Appointment.

Doctor.

Just tired.

Nothing major.

⁂

Men said "nothing major" the way they said "I'm fine": not to inform, but to control the story. To keep panic out. To keep weakness hidden.

Declan's thumb hovered over Call.

He could do it. He could call now, while the kitchen was quiet, while the house wasn't asking for anything else.

He could.

He didn't.

Not yet, his mind said, already building the moat out of timing. Lena's asleep. He might be asleep. I'll call tomorrow. I'll call at lunch. I'll call when I have bandwidth.

Bandwidth.

As if love were data and fathers were apps you could force-quit.

He set the phone down, face-up, because the lie felt heavier when hidden.

He looked at the marker line on the mug and felt the truth land, plain and unwelcome:

Confession could be a weapon in the wrong hands.

Malloy proved that every day—turning vulnerability into leverage, calling it care.

But silence could be a weapon too. In the office, silence protected him.

At home, silence punished the people who loved him.

Declan rinsed the mug until the water ran clear and the line looked faint, almost pathetic. He dried it, set it on the counter, and stood there in the dim kitchen like a man staring at a border he'd drawn and realizing borders were only useful if they protected something worth protecting.

The house was quiet. Daisy breathed down the hall. Theo slept. Lena's presence existed behind a closed door like gravity—constant, unseen, holding everything.

Declan looked at the mug, then at his phone, then at the dark window that reflected his own tired face.

And the pattern snapped into focus, with a clarity that didn't feel like progress so much as indictment:

He had been learning to survive power figures by refusing to confess.

But the people he loved weren't his bosses.

And if he kept bringing Malloy's logic home, he would turn his marriage into an office and call it "self-care."

Declan turned off the kitchen light.

He didn't call Walt.

Not tonight.

But for the first time, the postponement didn't feel like neutral delay.

It felt like a wound he was actively choosing to keep open.

※

Theo announced it over cereal like it was a medical diagnosis. "New territory for me, Bucko."

Declan lifted his eyes from his coffee—his *real* coffee, the one with the marker line and the thin illusion of jurisdiction—and stared at his son like he'd quoted Thoreau with a side of ransom note.

"What did you just say?" Declan asked.

Theo took another bite, chewing with the solemn authority of a person who believed chewing was part of a larger moral system. Milk glistened at the corner of his mouth. He didn't wipe it. He was seven. Wiping was for people who hadn't accepted chaos as a lifestyle.

"New territory," Theo repeated, slower, enjoying the way the words sounded in his mouth. "For me, Bucko."

Lena didn't look up. She was building Theo's lunch with the brisk competence of someone who could assemble a whole day out of plastic containers and willpower. The counter was a clean battlefield: a sandwich bag yawning open, a stack of napkins, a water bottle with a cap that never threaded right on the first try. The kitchen smelled like toasted bread and dish soap and that faint, warm-metal scent the radiator gave off when it decided to participate.

"Okay," Lena said carefully. "Who taught you that?"

Theo shrugged, which in child-language meant: *I don't know and I don't care and it doesn't matter because I'm already using it now.*

Declan's brain offered up the usual options: lean into humor, deflect, keep it light, keep it moving. But the phrase snagged him. Not just because it was funny—because it was his kind of funny. It had that slightly old-man cadence, that weird half-affectionate threat. It sounded like something a father said when he didn't know how to say tenderness. It sounded like Walt, if Walt had ever been the kind of man who joked on purpose.

"Bucko?" Declan repeated. He lifted the mug to his nose, inhaled. The coffee smelled right—dark, bitter, honest—like it had been made with intention rather than a machine that hated him. "That's... aggressive."

Theo's eyebrows lifted. "It's not aggressive," he said, offended at the accusation. "It's, like, cool."

Lena slid a sandwich into a bag with a firm little shove, the kind that implied: *please don't make a philosophical event out of this before eight a.m.* The bag crinkled loud in the kitchen, a tiny, plastic insistence.

"Where did you hear it?" she asked again.

Theo pointed vaguely toward the living room, toward the television, toward the general direction of modern life. "Some guy," he said. "On a show."

Some guy. Every influence in a child's world reduced to some guy: teachers, YouTubers, cartoon dads, the man at the end of the aisle in Target whispering to himself about coupons. Declan pictured Theo absorbing the universe like a sponge left too long in a sink—soaking up whatever drifted by, then wringing it out at breakfast like it was original thought.

Declan stared at his mug. The marker line on the ceramic had faded overnight and he'd redrawn it without thinking, the ritual so ingrained it barely qualified as choice anymore. Thick Sharpie. Black as a threat. Domestic borders. The republic of one. His coffee had dropped close to the mark already—time always moved faster than his agreements with it.

He felt the familiar bodily prickle, the thin skin of his nervous system reacting to a morning it hadn't finished consenting to. The house was waking—radiator cough, a drawer's complaint, a muffled thud upstairs as Theo had apparently thrown a sock at the laws of physics. Daisy's nails ticked across the hardwood like a slow metronome. There was a series of brief, disconnected sounds that suggested life was happening without asking his permission.

New territory, Declan thought, and felt the phrase settle into him with a faint edge of menace.

Because new territory meant contact. It meant stepping past the moat. It meant doing something without rehearsing it into death first. It meant answering a phone call. It meant saying a sentence that could be held against you and saying it anyway.

Theo slid off his chair, leaving a constellation of crumbs behind like evidence of a small crime. He did it with the confidence of someone who assumed the cleanup was a communal myth. Daisy appeared at the kitchen threshold, huge and gentle, her presence a quiet correction. She didn't demand. She didn't plead. She simply *was,* which—lately—felt like a moral flex Declan could barely tolerate. She looked from Theo to Lena to Declan, eyes soft but alert, as if taking attendance.

"Shoes," Lena called, already moving on, already building the next beam in the day.

They got out the door with the usual choreography: coat, backpack, a last-minute bathroom emergency that could not be argued with. Declan drove Theo to school with the radio off because silence felt like a tiny rebellion, even though silence also made space for the thoughts that sprinted ahead of him like panicked interns.

Outside, the morning looked damp and unfinished. Gray sky. Wet pavement. Trees stripped down to their honest skeletons. The air had that cold edge that made his skin feel reactive—the kind of skin that rashed with a whisper. As they idled at the curb, Theo leaned forward from the back seat and said again, like it was a catchphrase he intended to monetize, "New territory for me, Bucko."

Declan glanced at him in the mirror. Theo's eyes were bright, hair doing whatever it wanted, face open in that way children had before the world taught them self-consciousness. Declan felt the old twist in his chest: love that didn't know how to stay quiet.

"Buddy," he said. "Let's use that phrase responsibly."

Theo grinned. "No promises."

Fine, Declan thought. An honest child. The best kind.

He watched Theo disappear into the building—small body swallowed by institutional hallways—and waited until Theo was out of sight before pulling away, because leaving too quickly always felt like a minor betrayal. The building's glass doors reflected him back: tired face, coat collar up, a father watching a kid's small back like it was a fragile thing he'd been entrusted with and was not always sure he deserved.

His phone buzzed in the cup holder—another reminder, another obligation flashing its little LED teeth. He didn't look at it. Then he did. Then he wished he hadn't.

Work. Meetings. Mitchell.

New territory, he thought again, and the phrase didn't feel cute anymore. It felt like a dare.

At work, Declan walked in already feeling behind.

Not behind on tasks—behind on himself. Behind on the version of him who said clean sentences and meant them. Behind on the man who didn't use postponement as anesthesia.

The office air hit him with its usual cocktail: citrus disinfectant, stale carpet, overheated printer breath. Fluorescents buzzed overhead, a quiet electric insistence that flattened everything into the same bland emotional temperature. Somewhere a keyboard clacked in panic rhythm. Somewhere a laugh went too loud, trying to convince the room it was human. The place always felt like a museum exhibit devoted to modern adulthood: polished surfaces, controlled lighting, panic hidden behind polite fonts.

Declan sat, opened his inbox, and saw Mitchell's name.

His body braced before his mind read. He felt the familiar clench: a tightening under the ribs, a faint heat behind the eyes. He took a breath, clicked.

It wasn't an explosion.

It was a request. Specific. Reasonable. Almost… human.

Declan felt a sad kind of pride. Structure had done that. Structure made other people less feral. He had offered a beam and the other person had stopped punching the wall.

He started drafting a response—clean, brief, anchored in sequence—when Kyle appeared at his desk like a man who'd been practicing calm in the mirror.

"Got a second?" Kyle asked.

Declan heard the old temptation: say yes, smile, be easy. Be the kind of person who wasn't a problem. Be the kind of coworker who didn't make anyone feel things.

Kyle's expression was neutral, but Declan knew neutral the way Daisy knew weather. Neutral wasn't peace. Neutral was prelude. Neutral meant there was a story forming and Kyle wanted Declan to volunteer for the role of villain or idiot so Kyle could remain above it.

New territory for me, Bucko, Declan thought, and felt his heart thud once, hard.

"Two minutes," Declan said. Not apologizing. Not explaining. "Then I have to send a status update."

Kyle's eyebrows lifted slightly—an involuntary reaction, as if Declan had spoken in a language Kyle didn't expect him to know. A language with edges.

"Okay," Kyle said, still polite. "Sure."

Declan made himself finish what he'd said he'd do. He wrote the Mitchell update. He didn't over-promise. He didn't lace it with defensiveness. He hit send. The email whooshed away and his body reacted as if he'd stepped off a curb into traffic.

Then he turned back. "What's up?" he asked.

Kyle shifted his weight. "Malloy wants to know where we are with the Mitchell deliverables," he said. "He's asking for a timeline for the—"

"The additional work?" Declan asked. Kyle nodded.

Declan heard Malloy's voice in his head: *Don't overshare. Don't let it get to you.* The office's favorite fake therapy.

Declan didn't overshare. He didn't confess his stress. He didn't offer his throat.

He offered a boundary.

"I can deliver the status report and the revised scope by Friday at noon," Declan said. "I can't add the extra analysis—Kyle-with-a-plan version—without support."

Kyle blinked. "Support like—?"

Declan kept his voice flat. "Support like someone else taking a piece of it," he said. "Or support like Malloy agreeing to move another deadline. But I can't do both. Not well."

Kyle's mouth tightened. "He's gonna have feelings about that."

Declan nodded. His heart continued thudding like it was trying to convince him to retreat. "Then he can decide what he wants," Declan said. "Friday at noon for scope and report. Or more later with help. That's what's real."

Kyle stared, waiting for Declan to soften it. To add a little apology frosting. To turn the boundary into a request for permission. This was how the office kept itself comfortable: men asked for permission to protect themselves, and other men granted or denied it like weather.

Declan didn't.

Kyle gave a small, thin smile. "Okay," he said. "I'll tell him."

He walked away.

Declan's pulse climbed. His body treated clarity like danger. The body assumed consequence the way an abused dog assumed a raised hand. He sat very still and listened to the office's private soundtrack: Slack chimes, printer groans, chairs squeaking, the low murmur of meetings happening behind glass. There was a series of brief, disconnected sounds, and beneath them a single, coherent message: *you are always one mistake away from being punished here.*

Ten minutes later, Malloy appeared.

Not at Declan's desk—near it. In the aisle. Hovering. A man who never fully stopped walking because stopping would imply he was part of the same air as you.

"Burke," Malloy said, voice pleasant.

Declan stood halfway, then sat again, unsure which version of respect was safer. His body still didn't know if standing looked like readiness or guilt. "Mr. Malloy."

Malloy smiled. "Kyle tells me you're drawing lines," he said.

The word lines made Declan think of mugs. It made him think of borders. It made him think of how men like Malloy hated borders unless they were the ones drawing them.

"I'm giving you a realistic timeline," Declan said.

Malloy nodded slowly, like a man humoring a child with a science fair project. "Realistic is good," Malloy said. "But we don't always have the luxury of realistic."

Declan held his face steady, his hands still, his breathing shallow. He could feel the urge to appease rising in him like a reflex. He forced it down. The appeasement never bought safety. It only bought temporary quiet.

Malloy continued, still pleasant. "Mitchell's happy. Don't get used to it," he said, and the line landed like a pat on the head delivered with a closed fist inside it.

Then, as if granting generosity, Malloy added, "We'll see what we can do. No promises."

No promises. The office's favorite sacrament. The phrase they used when they wanted the power to say later: *you assumed.* You misread.* You should've known better.*

Malloy moved on, leaving behind expensive cologne and the sensation that the air had been rearranged to make Declan smaller.

Declan watched him go and felt the familiar anger rise—but it didn't sharpen into theater. It stayed quiet. Useful. A small animal that knew where to bite if it ever got the chance.

He turned back to his screen and kept working.

That was the part nobody put on motivational posters: kindness as infrastructure was labor. Structure wasn't serenity. Structure was effort made visible, day after day, in rooms built to reward collapse disguised as compliance.

At 11:42, an email came in from Mitchell.

This is the first week I've felt like someone here is telling me the truth.

Thank you for being direct.

Declan stared at it.

He didn't feel triumphant. He felt tired in his bones—the kind of tired that wasn't solved by sleep because it was moral fatigue. The tired of being clear. The tired of not hiding. The tired of being the person who had to put beams back into the walls other people had been quietly weakening for months.

He wanted to screenshot it and show Lena like a kid with a gold star. *Look, I did it. I did structural kindness like a grown-up.* But he didn't. He let the message sit there as proof he didn't need anyone else to witness for it to count.

※

And then—because the universe had a sense of timing—his phone buzzed.

Walt Burke.

Missed call.

Declan stared at his father's name lit up on the screen like a warning flare. The office seemed to shrink. The fluorescent hum got louder. He could feel his throat tighten, the body preparing to avoid.

New territory, Bucko, he thought.

He didn't answer. Not because he didn't want to. Because wanting to was the problem. Wanting to meant stakes. Stakes meant fear. Fear meant delay.

The call stopped. The missed call sat there like an accusation.

Declan texted, fast and cowardly: *In a meeting. Call you later.*

Later: the word he used to store people he couldn't afford to lose.

At home that evening, the house smelled like dinner and crayons and the faint laundry sweetness of a machine running in the background. The porch light had begun to matter. Daisy appeared in the front window like a benevolent surveillance camera, then met him in the entryway with that slow, steady attention that always felt like a test he didn't fully deserve.

Lena was at the counter, moving in quiet loops: wipe, rinse, chop. The kitchen had that end-of-day softness—warm light, damp dish towel, a pot lid leaning against the backsplash like a tired soldier. Theo narrated his day at a speed that made language feel like a flood. Declan tried to be present, tried to let the day end without dragging the office into the kitchen like a corpse.

His phone sat on the counter like a dormant grenade.

Lena glanced at it once. Then at him. Not accusation. Location.

"Did he call?" she asked.

Declan swallowed. "Yeah."

"And?"

"I didn't answer," Declan said, and the honesty felt like stepping onto ice.

Lena's face didn't harden. That was worse. She looked tired in a way that made anger feel like a luxury she couldn't afford.

"Declan," she said softly. "Don't make it weird."

There it was again. The phrase he hated because it was so accurate. The truth in four words: stop turning love into a situation you can manage by postponing it.

Theo asked a question about dessert. Daisy thumped her tail once, slow and forgiving. The house continued, indifferent to Declan's internal drama.

Later, after Theo was in pajamas and the living room had dimmed into evening softness, Declan stood in the kitchen with his phone in his hand and felt his world narrow—narrow down to one thing.

He could hear Theo in the living room singing nonsense to Daisy. He could hear the refrigerator hum. He could hear his own breath, too loud.

New territory, Bucko, he thought. And this time the phrase didn't feel like a joke.

Declan pressed Call.

The ringing started.

One ring.

Two.

He watched his thumb hover over End Call, the old reflex twitching like muscle memory. The reflex was polite. The reflex said: you don't have to do this now. The reflex said: later is kinder. The reflex was a liar.

He didn't press it.

Three rings.

Four.

He held his breath without meaning to.

※
※※

Five rings.

Voicemail.

Declan exhaled, half relief, half shame, and then the beep came—the small electronic demand: speak now. Be a son. Don't hide behind timing.

Declan swallowed.

"Hey, Dad," he said, and his voice sounded strange to him—too young inside his own throat. "It's… it's Declan."

A pause. He almost filled it with explanation. He almost did the thing Malloy trained him to do—offer confession in advance, apologize for existing.

He didn't.

"I got your messages," he continued, slower now. "I'm sorry I haven't called back. That's on me."

He felt Lena behind him, still, listening without hovering.

"I just wanted to hear your voice," Declan said, and the sentence surprised him as it came out—because it wasn't clever, and it wasn't defended, and it wasn't ashamed of being tender.

He cleared his throat. "Call me when you can. Tonight if you're up. Tomorrow morning Whenever."

A beat.

"Love you," Declan said.

Then he ended the call and stood there holding the phone like it was evidence.

Lena didn't speak. She stepped closer, put her hand lightly on his arm—contact, not rescue—and let the moment be what it was.

In the living room, Theo called out, "Dad? Are we having dinner or is this new territory too?"

Declan laughed—a small sound, not joy, not surrender.

"Dinner," he called back. "We're allowed dinner."

Theo cheered as if dinner were a prize.

Declan looked down at the phone in his hand and felt the smallest shift—not transformation, not triumph.

Just a man stepping over a line he'd kept redrawing.

New territory.

And, for once, he was actually in it.

⁎⁎⁎

Declan found out about the appointment the way he found out about most important things: by accident, and too late to pretend he didn't know.

His phone surfaced it while he was half-awake, thumb-scrolling through a fog of notifications like a man checking a shoreline for bodies. The calendar app—bright, cheerful, unearned—popped up a block of time that did not care whether he had planned for it:

Walt — follow-up. 10:30 a.m.

No location in the preview. No note. Just that calm, rectangular certainty.

He stared at it until his eyes watered, then blinked hard, as if blinking could demote it back into a normal Tuesday problem, like replacing a trash bag or remembering Theo's folder. He could feel his heart doing its anxious little math—counting hours, counting risks, counting the places life could tip over if it wanted to.

He tapped it.

The details loaded. There was a clinic name. There was an address. There was an alarm set for 9:15 and another for 9:30, which meant Lena had already decided this event required redundancy—multiple nets, multiple beams. The kind of planning you did when you were trying not to let the floor drop out from under a family.

Declan felt a small flare of irritation that wasn't irritation. It was exposure. It was the sensation of being known. Lena had done the quiet work—again—without asking permission, because permission was a luxury and she was building scaffolding, not aesthetics.

He set the phone down and lay there, listening to the house in its early-morning preface: heat clicking on, refrigerator humming, a floorboard settling somewhere like an old knee. There was a series of brief, disconnected sounds that might have been nothing and—to his nervous system—was always a warning.

Beside him, Lena breathed evenly, face turned toward the window. The pale morning light softened her cheek, made her look younger and steadier at the same time. She looked calm in sleep, which was unfair. Declan's sleep always looked like a person negotiating with an invisible creditor. Lena's sleep looked like trust.

He reached for his phone again and stared at the appointment card like it was a legal document.

Follow-up.

Follow-up to what?

His body already knew, of course. He'd heard it in Walt's voicemail—the cough too deep, the pause too long, the way "nothing big" carried a shadow behind it. Declan could still hear Walt's voice in the kitchen from the night before: *just wanted to hear your voice,* sanded down into something he could survive saying.

Declan sat up quietly, careful not to wake Lena, and swung his feet onto the cold floor.

The cold bit his soles. The rash on his wrist tingled faintly, as if his own body wanted to be part of the conversation. Declan rubbed it once and hated himself for immediately turning sensation into prophecy. He hated how quickly his mind recruited his skin as a witness for the prosecution.

He padded to the kitchen, moving like a thief in his own home, and made coffee. The smell bloomed—bitter, comforting, alarm-bell

⁎⁎

familiar. He watched the liquid hit the cup, watched the level rise, watched himself wait for a line he hadn't even drawn yet.

Structure, he thought. Even now.

He stood there in the dimness and felt the urge to draw the Sharpie line—*nobody talks to me until the coffee drops to here.* The ritual was so familiar it offered its own kind of mercy. But the appointment sat in his mind like a stone, and stones didn't care about rituals.

The phone buzzed again—not a call, just the quiet insistence of the calendar reminder lingering like a hand on his shoulder.

Behind him, Lena appeared in the doorway, hair messy, face still soft from sleep. She looked at him, then at the phone on the counter, then back at him.

"You saw it," she said.

Not a question. A statement of fact. Another receipt.

Declan swallowed. "Yeah."

Lena nodded once. "He didn't tell you."

Declan's jaw tightened. "No."

Lena moved into the kitchen, opened a cabinet, pulled out a mug. The ordinary motions of a person trying to keep the world from becoming mythic before coffee. The mug clinked against the counter. The sound felt louder than it should have. Everything felt louder when the subject was Walt.

"I put it on the calendar because he told me," she said. "He said he 'didn't want to worry you.'"

Declan felt the phrase land like an old bruise being pressed.

Men said that—didn't want to worry you—as if worry were the problem and not secrecy. As if you could prevent fear by withholding information, like fear wasn't already living in the walls. As if Declan wasn't already worried every day, about everything, even in rooms where nothing was happening.

"He's always been like that," Declan said.

Lena watched him over the rim of her mug. "And you've always let him."

Declan flinched—not because she was wrong, but because she said it cleanly, without cruelty, like a person pointing out a crack in a foundation. Not to shame him—so he'd stop pretending the crack was a design feature.

Declan took a sip. The coffee was too hot. He welcomed it. A small pain he could control.

"What is it?" he asked, though he knew Lena didn't know any more than the calendar said.

"Follow-up," she replied. "He said 'they want to check some things.'"

Declan stared at his cup.

Fine. Another lie people told to get through doorways.

The house woke up around them: Theo's footsteps upstairs, a drawer pulled too hard, Daisy's nails on the hardwood. Daisy ambled in like a sleepy bouncer, head low, eyes alert anyway. She paused, looked at both of them, and sat—stationed. Monitoring. Even half-asleep, Daisy behaved like a being who understood that feelings were weather and weather could turn fast.

Theo came down in dinosaur pajamas, carrying a sock like evidence of a new crime, and asked for cereal like hunger was an emergency service. He talked about school; he asked if pancakes could exist as a concept again. Declan nodded, made the motions, tried to keep the appointment from swallowing the kitchen whole.

But it sat there anyway—10:30 tomorrow—like a stone in a shoe. Every step felt it.

At the office, Declan tried to behave like nothing was different.

The building smelled like citrus disinfectant and fake calm. The fluorescent lights flattened everything into the same bland emotional temperature. People's voices were too bright, too practiced. Declan's body moved through routines while his mind kept drifting back to

⁕
⁎⁎

the calendar card like it was a song stuck in his head.

He was halfway through an email to Mitchell when Malloy summoned him.

The message was short. No greeting. No context. The lean efficiency of a threat. It made Declan's stomach do that familiar drop, like a small elevator in his chest.

Declan stood in front of Malloy's half-closed door—his signature almost-welcome—and felt the old reflex: rehearse, brace, confess nothing, volunteer less. He knocked.

"Yeah," Malloy said.

Declan stepped in.

Malloy sat behind his desk in the same immaculate suit, the same careful hair, the same expression that suggested he was always in control of the room's oxygen. There was a faint scent of expensive cologne over stale carpet, sweetness that didn't belong under fluorescent lighting.

"Close the door," Malloy said.

Declan did, and the air thickened.

Malloy glanced at his screen. Typed something slowly, performatively, as if bureaucracy itself were a moral act. Then, without looking up: "How are things?"

It wasn't a question. It was a trap with polite packaging.

"Good," Declan said.

Malloy's eyes flicked up. "Good," he echoed, tasting it for weakness. "Because Mitchell's been... vocal."

Declan's stomach tightened.

Malloy continued, "I'm hearing you've been direct with them. Setting expectations."

Declan kept his face neutral. "I'm trying to be clear."

Malloy nodded, as if approving a child's handwriting. "Clarity is great," he said. "As long as it doesn't become... rigidity."

Rigidity. Another word men used when they meant: don't draw lines I didn't draw first.

Declan's throat went dry. He could hear Lena in his head: *You call it patience. You call it calm. But it's fear and avoidance.*

He chose a clean sentence anyway.

"I'll be clear and realistic," Declan said. "That's how we keep it from getting worse."

Malloy smiled, thin. "Sure," he said, the word carrying disbelief like cologne. "Just remember: we're a service organization. We respond."

We respond, Declan thought. We scramble. We apologize. We accept whatever the powerful demand and call it culture.

Malloy leaned back. "Also," he said casually, "I'll need you available tomorrow morning."

Declan's chest tightened. He forced himself not to flinch. "Tomorrow morning?"

Malloy nodded. "Early. 10:00."

Declan felt the calendar card in his pocket like a heat source. Walt's appointment. 10:30. Follow-up.

This was the moment. The new territory.

Declan could say nothing and let it become a conflict later. He could pretend he was free and then scramble into a lie. He could do what he always did: postpone the hard thing until it wasn't a choice anymore.

Or he could speak.

"My father has a medical appointment tomorrow morning," Declan said, steadying his voice. "I need to take him."

Malloy blinked once—a small, involuntary reaction that suggested Declan had just violated an unspoken rule: do not have a life that interrupts me.

Then Malloy's face smoothed back into its usual polite mask.

"Of course," Malloy said. "Family first."

It sounded like the right phrase. It sounded like kindness. Declan didn't trust it.

Malloy added, "How flexible is it?"

Declan stared. "It's... medical."

Malloy nodded sympathetically, as if participating in the emotion without touching it. "Naturally," he said. "We'll see what we can do."

No promises.

Always no promises.

Declan left Malloy's office with his pulse high and his face calm, the familiar split between body and performance. He returned to his desk and wrote to Mitchell like nothing was happening, because that was what adults did: they carried private bombs beneath polite emails.

That afternoon, Declan drove to Walt's house.

The sky had the flat, drained look of winter light—the kind that made everything feel like it was waiting for permission to begin. Walt's neighborhood was quiet in a way Declan didn't fully trust. The houses sat back from the road like they were trying not to be involved. The lawns were brown and short. The trees looked tired.

Walt's porch creaked under Declan's weight, a sound that made Declan suddenly aware of his own body—his joints, his breath, the rash, the way his anxiety lived in his muscles like a second skeleton. He could feel his shoulders up near his ears like a defensive posture he'd never been taught to release.

He knocked.

Walt opened the door and stood there for a beat like he was deciding what kind of interaction was required.

He looked older than Declan wanted him to be. Not dramatically older. Just... slightly more fragile around the eyes. Slightly slower in the shoulders. A man whose body had begun adding small caveats to his movements.

"Hey," Walt said.

"Hey," Declan replied.

They did the awkward father-son choreography: a brief pat on the shoulder that was almost a hug, then the immediate retreat into normalcy because emotion was a room neither of them had been trained to enter without flinching.

Inside, Walt's house smelled like old coffee and dry heat and the faint metallic tang of radiator air. A television murmured from another room—sports or news, impossible to tell. The kitchen counter was cluttered with mail, rubber bands, a pen, the mundane evidence of a life continuing while the body negotiated different terms.

Walt opened the fridge and pulled out sandwich meat like food was a solution you could offer in place of language.

"You hungry?" Walt asked.

Declan almost laughed—not because it was funny, but because it was perfect. Walt's version of emotional intimacy was offering food. You could be dying, but you could still eat a sandwich, so you weren't dying.

"I'm good," Declan said.

Walt nodded once, satisfied. They stood there in the kitchen like two men waiting for someone else to arrive and tell them what to say.

Declan glanced at his phone. The appointment reminder sat there like a dare.

10:30 tomorrow.

Walt cleared his throat—there it was, that cough again, quick and contained, like he didn't want to make it real by letting it linger.

"So," Walt said. "Tomorrow."

Declan nodded. "Tomorrow."

Walt looked away, fiddling with something on the counter—mail, a rubber band, a pen. His hands needed a job. His hands had always needed a job.

"It's nothing big," Walt said.

Declan felt his jaw tighten.

He almost said: *That's not a thing you get to decide alone.*

He wanted to say: *If it's nothing, why am I here?*

He nearly said: *I heard your voicemail and it sounded like a man standing at the edge of something.*

Instead he said, carefully, "Okay. Walk me through it."

Walt blinked, surprised—like Declan had used a tool Walt didn't know he owned.

"It's just a follow-up," Walt said. "They want to check a few things. Make sure everything's... fine."

Fine. Another lie people told to get through doorways.

Declan nodded. "Alright," he said. "We'll go. We'll do it. Then we'll get coffee or something."

Walt's mouth twitched—not a smile, but something like it. "Yeah," Walt said. "Coffee."

Declan looked around the kitchen—the quiet, the old cabinets, the small pile of mail, the mundane evidence of a life continuing as the body started writing different terms.

He thought, unexpectedly, of Theo falling asleep mid-story, and of Walt saying, *I was doing something here and you left.*

Declan felt something soften in him—not enough to fix anything, but enough to make him present.

"Dad," he said.

Walt looked up, wary, like a man bracing for weather.

Declan swallowed. Sequence. One thing. Then the next.

"I'm glad you called," Declan said.

Walt stared at him as if Declan had spoken in a foreign language. Then Walt nodded once, quickly, like accepting a payment he didn't want to be seen taking.

"Yeah," Walt said. "Me too."

A small silence followed.

Not a moat. Not a wall. Just a pause where neither man knew what to build next.

Declan's phone buzzed—Mitchell, probably. Or Lena. Or some reminder that water existed.

He didn't check it.

Not yet.

He stood there in his father's kitchen, holding the appointment in his mind like a card with sharp edges, and for once he didn't sprint ahead to catastrophe.

He let tomorrow be tomorrow.

He let now be now.

And in the quiet—among the refrigerator hum and the low murmur of the TV—Declan felt something rare settle in his body.

Not peace. Not triumph.

Just sequence.

Just the next right thing.

※

T he waiting room had its own liturgy.

Not hymns—nothing that generous—but a series of brief, disconnected sounds that formed a kind of choir for the living: coughs wrapped in tissue, paper shuffling, the plastic click of a clipboard, the clunk of a vending machine taking someone's money with casual contempt. Somewhere, a daytime television anchor smiled through an apocalypse, the captions running underneath like a second language nobody asked to learn.

Declan sat in a chair that had been designed by someone who believed comfort was a moral hazard. The vinyl stuck faintly to the backs of his thighs through his jeans. The fluorescent lights above were not bright so much as honest. They erased shadows. They made skin look like skin—thin, tired, real. They made time feel measurable.

Walt sat two chairs away, angled slightly as if distance counted as privacy.

He'd insisted on driving himself to the clinic, as if the act of turning a key could keep his body from betraying him. Declan had followed in his own car like a teenager tailing a parent, half resentful, half terrified. The ride had been quiet in that particular Burke way—radio off, talk minimized, both men pretending silence was neutrality and not a strategy.

Now Walt's hands rested on his thighs. Declan couldn't stop looking at them.

They were thinner than Declan remembered. The skin was dry, faintly shiny in spots, like it had been washed too many times. The knuckles looked prominent, not heroic—*exposed*. Walt's wedding ring sat a little looser than it should have, as if metal had questioned what it belonged to.

Walt cleared his throat.

Declan's stomach tightened immediately, because his mind had begun cataloging Walt's sounds the way it cataloged symptoms: cough, pause, breath. Evidence. Audio of decline. He hated that he did this. He hated that love in his body translated so quickly into surveillance.

"I hate these places," Walt said, voice pitched casual, like he was talking about traffic.

Declan almost smiled. Almost. "You mean the palace of health and optimism?"

Walt gave a short grunt that might have been a laugh. "It's like they designed it to make you confess."

Declan looked around. Posters on the walls: **Know Your Numbers. Early Detection Saves Lives. Talk to Your Doctor.** The slogans were cheery in the same way a warning label was cheery: polite, blunt, unavoidable. A rack of brochures displayed smiling faces that looked medically insured.

"Yeah," Declan said. "It's the church of compliance."

Walt's eyes flicked toward him. The faintest warning. *Don't get dramatic.*

Declan tried to slow down. Sequence. One thing, then the next. He pressed his tongue to the back of his teeth—an old trick to keep himself from spilling words just to fill the air. Walt did not do spill. Walt did not do air-filling. Walt did containment like it was citizenship.

Across the room, an elderly man coughed with the deep, wet persistence of someone who'd been bargaining with his lungs for years. A woman in a puffer jacket tapped her foot in a rhythm that sounded like impatience and prayer at the same time. A nurse walked past, shoes squeaking lightly, carrying a clipboard like scripture.

Declan watched Walt's chest rise and fall.

Measured. Controlled.

Like every breath was being counted.

Walt's posture was good—too good. A man sitting as if sitting itself were a performance review. Walt's shoulders were squared, his hands still, his jaw set in that familiar line that said: *I am fine. I am not a problem. I require nothing from anyone.*

Declan had spent a lifetime thinking of Walt as an icon: stern devotion, fixed jaw, a man built out of work and restraint. In the waiting room, Walt was a body. A body doing its best to appear unbothered. A body that had started making sounds it couldn't fully disguise.

It was unsettling. It was intimate.

A door opened near the hallway, and a woman stepped out wearing a bright smile and a lanyard. Not scrubs. Not a doctor. Something else. A volunteer vest—navy with a stitched logo. She held a small stack of pamphlets, and her expression was soft in a way that felt practiced.

She scanned the room the way certain people scanned a crowd: not looking for faces, but for openings.

Her eyes landed on Walt and Declan.

She approached with calm certainty, stopping close enough to feel like attention and not close enough to be refused without social friction.

"Good morning," she said. "How are we doing today?"

There it was. The phrase. The soft authority.

Declan felt the flash of recognition so sharply he almost laughed.

It was the same posture as Mr. Malloy's concern. *How're you holding up?* Concern as a data harvest. Tenderness repurposed into surveillance. The wrong kind of softness—softness that expected payment.

Walt looked up. His face did not change, but something in his eyes cooled, like a shade pulled down.

"We're fine," Walt said.

The woman's smile didn't dim. She nodded as if *fine* were merely the first layer of a deeper truth she was entitled to.

"I'm with the prayer team," she said gently, as if prayer were a service like valet parking. "Sometimes it helps to talk. You'd be surprised what people carry in places like this."

Declan's jaw tightened. It wasn't what she said. It was the assumption behind it: that confession was universally good, and that offering it was always safe. That intimacy could be requested on demand and nobody would be harmed by providing it.

Declan thought of Malloy's office—the half-closed door, the questions without questions, the pleasure of power wielded and denied. He thought of how vulnerability became currency in the wrong hands. He felt his mouth preparing, reflexively, to smooth things over—to say something polite, to carry the social burden, to make the room comfortable.

He looked at Walt, expecting him to do what Declan often did: smile politely, offer a small disclosure, build a bridge he didn't want to stand on.

Walt didn't.

"No thank you," Walt said. Polite. Firm. Final.

The woman blinked once, surprised, then recovered. She kept the smile on like a mask that had been glued.

"Of course," she said, a touch too bright. "If you change your mind, I'll be around. Just... remember you're not alone."

Walt nodded without gratitude.

The woman walked away, her smile already searching for a new target.

Declan felt something in his chest loosen—respect, unexpected and clean.

Walt, for all his flaws, could do boundaries in public without collapsing. Walt could refuse a forced intimacy. Walt could keep the institution at arm's length.

Declan realized—mildly sickened—that he envied his father for it.

Walt stared ahead as if the exchange hadn't happened. The waiting room resumed its liturgy. The vending machine took someone else's money. The TV anchor smiled through catastrophe. Declan watched a caption crawl by and thought, absurdly, that the captions were the truest part of the whole performance: language running beneath the surface, explaining what the face refused to admit.

Declan tried small talk, because small talk was their shared native tongue.

"Traffic wasn't bad," Declan said.

Walt snorted. "That's because no one wants to come here."

Declan almost smiled again. Walt's jokes were always defenses. A laugh that said: *don't make me feel.*

A commercial came on the TV: a smiling couple walking on a beach, medication name spoken with a voice that sounded like it had never been afraid. The man on the screen lifted a child into the air. The child laughed like nothing could happen. Declan's throat tightened at the ease of it. The lie of it.

He glanced at Walt's hands again. He wanted to ask the thing. The real thing. *Are you scared? What are they looking for? Why didn't you tell me sooner?*

He tried to begin with one honest sentence, something that didn't lunge.

"I'm glad you let me come," Declan said.

Walt's shoulders lifted slightly, then fell. A micro-shrug, as if gratitude were too slippery to hold.

"You didn't have to," Walt said.

Declan felt the old frustration rise. Walt's reflex was always to deny need. To make every offer optional so he wouldn't owe anyone tenderness in return.

"I know," Declan said. "But I wanted to."

Walt's eyes flicked over. A glance that was almost contact.

Then Walt looked away and said, "You take time off work for this?"

There it was. The deflection dressed as concern. The safest subject: labor. The easiest way to keep love from becoming visible.

"Yeah," Declan said. "It's fine."

Walt nodded. "Malloy give you any grief?"

Declan felt a quick pulse in his throat. The institutional father echoing in the same breath as his real father. Power without warmth.

"He doesn't know," Declan said. "And I'm not rushing to tell him."

Walt gave another grunt, approving. "Good. Don't give them anything."

Declan stared at his father. The irony almost made him laugh out loud.

Don't give them anything.

Walt's whole life had been built on not giving. Not giving weakness. Not giving fear. Not giving anyone the satisfaction of seeing him bend. Declan wanted to say: *You taught me this.* He almost said: *And it doesn't always work.*

Before he could, a nurse appeared in the doorway and called, "Walter Burke?"

Walt stood quickly, too quickly, and then steadied himself with a small pause that he tried to hide by adjusting his sweatshirt zipper.

Declan's stomach turned. The pause was nothing. The pause was everything.

"I'll be right back," Walt said, as if he were going to the restroom.

Declan nodded, because nodding was safer than speaking.

Walt disappeared down the hallway behind the nurse.

Declan was alone with the waiting room choir.

Cough. Paper shuffle. Vending machine clunk. The TV murmuring about weather somewhere that wasn't here.

Declan's wrist itched.

He looked down. The patch had bloomed a little brighter, as if his body were raising a hand: *Excuse me, yes, we are panicking.* His chest felt tight—not pain, not exactly, but that banded sensation like someone had wrapped a rubber strap around his ribs and pulled.

He took a slow breath. Then another. Sequence, he told himself.

Air in. Air out. No story.

His phone buzzed.

He glanced at it before he could stop himself.

Mr. Malloy — Just checking in. You around?

Declan stared at the screen.

It was incredible, the timing. The way institutions could smell vulnerability across distance. Malloy, with his half-closed door and his concern-as-control, reaching out like a hand that wanted information.

Declan's thumb hovered over reply.

A part of him wanted to appease. To be polite. To say, *Yes, sir. I'm here. I'm fine. I am compliant.*

Another part of him—a smaller part, newer—remembered what he'd done recently. The small rebellion. The clean sentence. The refusal to confess to a man who collected confessions.

Declan locked the phone and put it face-down on his thigh.

No response.

A boundary.

It felt both brave and ridiculous, like refusing a god by ignoring a text.

He exhaled slowly

The nurse's doorway opened again, and a different staff member walked out carrying forms. She called another name. A couple stood and followed her, bodies moving like they'd been rehearsing this. Declan watched their backs disappear and felt the strange envy of people whose fear had an assigned hallway.

He stared at the door Walt had gone through and tried not to narrate himself into catastrophe.

He pictured Walt in an exam room, shirt lifted, doctor listening with a stethoscope to the private music of his father's chest. He pictured Walt making a joke. Walt saying, *nothing big.* Walt smiling like control.

Declan's stomach churned.

He wondered, briefly, what it would feel like to have someone approach him in this room and demand confession again—to ask him to "share" like it was harmless. His mouth started forming the safe offer before he'd agreed to it. He tasted surrender like pennies.

Walt, he thought again, could refuse. Why couldn't Declan?

He heard footsteps.

Walt emerged from the hallway.

Declan stood instinctively, then stopped himself halfway, embarrassed by his own eagerness.

Walt walked with the same steady gait, but his face looked slightly rearranged—like a man who had heard a word he didn't want to carry and was trying to fit it into his pocket without anyone seeing the bulge.

"Everything okay?" Declan asked, voice too tight.

Walt waved it off immediately. "Yeah. Yeah. Nothing big."

Declan held Walt's eyes for a second. Waited.

Walt sighed—small, controlled.

"They want another test," Walt admitted. "Just to be sure. They're going to 'monitor.'" He made the word sound like something irritating, like a neighbor watching your lawn.

Declan felt his throat tighten. "Monitor what?"

Walt's mouth tightened too. He glanced around the room, as if walls had ears.

"My blood pressure's been up," Walt said. "And they want to tweak a medication. That's all."

That's all.

Walt's voice stayed casual, but a pause betrayed him—one fraction too long between sentences, like his body had cut in to say: *We're lying, but we're doing it kindly.*

Declan nodded, trying to keep his face neutral. "Okay," Declan said. "So… you're done for today?"

"Yeah," Walt said. "We can go."

Declan picked up his jacket, and as he did, he noticed a pamphlet half-slipped under the edge of a side table. One of those clinic brochures designed to be helpful without being intrusive.

Talking to Your Loved Ones About Your Health.

Declan stared at it and felt something rise that was half laughter, half grief.

The world was never subtle. The world was fluorescent and blunt and full of slogans.

He reached down and picked up the pamphlet. Walt saw him and raised an eyebrow. "What's that?"

"Homework," Declan said, trying for humor because humor was still his emergency exit.

Walt snorted, which might have been a laugh.

They walked out together into the hallway. The fluorescent light followed them like a judgment.

In the lobby, Walt paused at the doors.

"He didn't have to drive me," Walt said automatically. Reflex. Deny need.

Declan didn't argue. "I'm driving you," he said—clean, final. No apology.

Walt's jaw tightened, then loosened.

"Fine," Walt said, and the word was an acceptance disguised as irritation.

Outside, the air felt colder, realer. The parking lot smelled like exhaust and winter. Declan walked slightly behind Walt, watching his gait, watching the way his shoulders moved, noticing how careful he was trying not to be.

At Walt's car, Walt reached for his keys. Declan held out his hand, palm up.

Walt stared at him for a second, then dropped the keys into Declan's hand with a small, resigned motion.

It was a tiny thing.

It was intimacy in their language.

Declan slid the pamphlet into his jacket pocket like contraband. He didn't know if he'd read it. He didn't know if he'd laugh at it later or cry. But his body already knew, walking toward the driver's side with Walt beside him under a hard winter sky, that something had shifted.

It wasn't a cure. It wasn't a confession. \nBut the keys sat in Declan's palm, and Walt didn't reach for them again. \nTwo men under fluorescent truth, letting the institution hum while they tried—awkwardly, sincerely—not to disappear from each other.

And for Declan, who had made an art out of postponement, that counted as gospel.

⁂

The marker line bled when it got wet.

Declan stood at the sink rinsing his mug, watching black ink smear into a faint gray bruise along the ceramic. It wasn't dramatic—nothing in the kitchen ever was, not unless someone set it on fire—but the fading felt like a verdict. A ritual dissolving into its own evidence.

He turned the cup in his hands as if the angle might change the truth. The mark had been thick yesterday. It had looked decisive, adult, structural. Now it looked tired. Now it looked like something drawn by a man who needed a rule more than he wanted one.

Behind him, the house made its morning noises: a cupboard closing too hard, Theo's feet slapping down the hallway, Daisy's nails clicking like a patient metronome. A series of brief, disconnected sounds that meant: time is already moving. Keep up.

Declan set the mug on the counter, took the marker from the drawer, and uncapped it.

He hovered.

He could redraw the line exactly where it had been. Same inch and a half of silence. Same moat labeled "self-care." He could give himself the same old allowance and call it structure.

Instead, he drew the line lower.

Not much. A quarter inch. A petty act of bravery. A smaller republic.

He capped the marker and felt a tiny flare of shame—how childish it was to feel proud of ink. And then, beneath it, the usable part of the feeling: the recognition that a life was mostly built out of small decisions no one applauded.

Theo burst into the kitchen like a thrown object.

"Dad," he said, already loud. "Daisy looked at me like I was going to commit a crime."

Daisy, lying in the doorway, blinked slowly.

Correct.

Declan scratched behind her ear, and Daisy leaned into his hand with the calm of an animal who did not perform but still remained. Declan envied her that. How she could be present without narrating it. How she could set boundaries without announcing them. She was simply there, and her being-there was enough to change the temperature of a room.

Lena came in with her hair gathered back, face still partly asleep, competence already awake. She poured herself coffee, no marker line required. She did it the way she did most things: efficiently, without ceremony, without the need to sanctify.

She looked at the mug. Looked at the new mark. She didn't comment. She didn't have to. Lena's silence, unlike his, wasn't a weapon. It was an assessment tool.

"How was it?" she asked, and it was the kind of question that tried to sound casual and failed.

Declan felt his mind reach for story.

He had a whole version ready—the one where he sounded thoughtful and wounded, the one where the waiting room became a metaphor and the fluorescent light became a sermon. The one where he made his fear lyrical enough to be impressive. The one where he turned pain into language and then used the language as proof he'd handled it.

He opened his mouth.

Lena's hand lifted slightly—not stopping him rudely, not punishing him, just... guiding the conversation away from his instincts.

"Just tell me what happened," she said gently. "Not the whole... thing. What happened."

Declan swallowed.

Clean sentence.

Practice, not observation.

He leaned back against the counter and forced himself to speak like a man giving a report, not a performance.

"There's a follow-up," he said. "They adjusted a medication. They want to monitor his blood pressure. He says it's nothing big."

Lena's eyes narrowed, not in suspicion—recognition. She knew that phrase. She'd heard it in Declan's voice for years, and she'd heard it in Walt's voice now. A family heirloom: minimization passed down like furniture.

Declan continued before he could soften it. Before he could lace it with a joke. "He's scared," he said. "I'm scared."

The words sat there, plain and unadorned. No flourish. No joke. No cleverness to slide out through. Just the truth, like a plate set down quietly on a table.

Lena exhaled—slow, like she'd been holding her breath since the question left her mouth.

"Okay," she said. "Thank you."

Theo climbed onto a chair and started peeling a banana with militant focus. "We'll monitor," he said suddenly, parroting the phrase like it was a magic spell.

Declan froze.

Lena glanced at Theo, then at Declan, then away again, because watching your kid absorb adult language was like watching him put on a coat that didn't fit.

"What?" Theo asked around a mouthful of banana. "That's what the nurse on TV said."

Declan realized he didn't know where Theo had heard it—daytime TV in the background, a passing conversation, a commercial—because kids didn't need context. They absorbed power language the way sponges absorbed water. They learned minimization like it was manners. They learned the tone adults used when they were trying to keep the room from collapsing.

Declan crouched beside Theo's chair. The kitchen floor was cold through his socks. He could smell banana, coffee, and that faint detergent sweetness drifting in from the laundry room like the house itself was trying to reassure him: I am still doing my jobs.

"Hey," he said, keeping his voice steady. "Sometimes grown-ups say 'nothing big' because it helps them not feel scared."

Theo's eyes widened slightly, interested, the way they did when he suspected a hidden rule existed.

"But sometimes things are big," Declan said. "And we can still talk about them. Even when we're scared."

Theo considered this with the seriousness of a tiny philosopher.

"So... is Grampy big?" he asked.

Declan felt the urge to reassure—*No, no, it's fine, everything is fine, we're fine*—that cheap lie adults bought to calm themselves.

Clean sentence.

"Grampy has something we're watching," Declan said. "We're going to help him."

Theo nodded once, satisfied by the simple shape of truth. Then he said, "Okay. Can I have toast too?"

A child's mind: capable of gravity, then instantly back to carbohydrates. It was one of the few forms of wisdom Declan trusted.

Later, when Lena left for work and Theo's bus swallowed him, the house finally opened a small pocket of silence.

⁂

Not the marker kind. The accidental kind. The kind that didn't demand worship.

Declan stood in the kitchen and felt the itch in his body—less on his wrist now, more behind the ribs. A restlessness. The familiar thought drifted in like a soft salesman:

You could get high. You could slow down. You could stop feeling the edges of things.

He crossed to the cabinet where he kept the pen and paused with his hand on the door.

For once, he didn't treat the craving like a private shame. He named it like a fact.

"I want to disappear," he said aloud to the empty kitchen.

Daisy lifted her head from her bed in the doorway and stared at him as if he'd said something important, which, unfortunately, he had.

Declan took his hand off the cabinet.

Not a moral victory. Not a puritan stance. Just sequence.

"One thing," he muttered. "Then the next."

His phone buzzed.

Mr. Malloy.

Declan fixed on the name and felt the old reflex: answer quickly, be available, prove devotion. The institutional father's favorite sacrament.

He opened the message.

Need a quick chat. Where were you yesterday afternoon?

There it was—concern as control, dressed up in managerial tone. A confession request masquerading as logistics.

Declan's fingers hovered over the keyboard. The tempting response rose immediately: *Family health thing. Dad appointment. Hospital. I'm stressed.*

A confession. A throat offered.

Declan deleted it before he could send. He typed, slower.

I met my deadlines. I'll continue to. I was unavailable for a scheduled block and I'll make up the time as needed.

He hit send.

No details. No story. No softness he could later be punished for.

He felt his heart race anyway, because boundaries always felt like breaking a law the first time you tried them.

He set the phone down and forced his shoulders to loosen. The day continued. Laundry beeped. The dishwasher needed emptying. A permission slip lived on the table like an accusation.

Declan did not announce his intentions. He moved.

He folded clothes. He signed the form. He packed Theo's folder properly this time. He found the number for Walt's clinic, wrote it down, and put it where it couldn't be lost under a receipt. He set out Daisy's food and watched her eat with the calm focus of a creature whose needs did not come with shame.

Then, the real act: he opened his calendar.

He typed in the follow-up appointment as Walt had described it—day, time, location. He added a reminder for the day before. Another for the morning of.

He didn't ask Lena to do it.

He didn't tell her he was doing it. Not because he was hiding it. Because he was trying, for once, not to turn responsibility into a performance.

When Lena came home that evening, she paused in the doorway of the kitchen like she'd stepped into a room that had been rearranged while she was gone.

The counters were clear. Theo's folder was ready by the backpack. The laundry pile had been reduced from mountain to hill. The small tasks—the ones that were never "big," but somehow always mattered—had been handled.

The house felt... marginally less heavy.

※

Lena didn't smile. Not yet. She didn't swoon. She wasn't a character in a commercial about "helping out."

But her shoulders dropped a fraction, and Declan saw the effect more clearly than any compliment could have delivered.

"What's all this?" she asked, not suspicious, just startled.

Declan shrugged, trying to keep it simple. "Sequence," he said.

Lena set her keys down and leaned against the counter, watching him. Her eyes were tired, but there was something steadier in them too—something like cautious relief.

"I can't be the only adult in the room," she said.

Declan felt the urge to say something big. Something romantic. Something that would turn the moment into a speech and make him feel like the hero of his own repair.

He didn't.

He stepped closer, not touching her yet, closing the distance like a small, deliberate choice.

"You're not," he said. "I'm here."

And then—crucially—he acted like it.

He took Theo's backpack and checked it without being asked. He started dinner without narrating the sacrifice. He listened when Lena spoke instead of preparing his own defense while she talked. He answered Theo's questions without disappearing into his phone. He laughed when Theo made a stupid joke and didn't use the laugh as a trapdoor.

In the living room, Daisy stationed herself between rooms as if blessing the new shape of the evening with her body. Her presence made the house feel monitored in the best way—not surveilled, but held.

Later, when Theo fell asleep on the couch mid-story Declan felt the old flare begin—the wounded pride, the inherited anger at being "left."

He let it pass through him without obeying it.

He finished the page anyway, quietly, as if finishing mattered because it mattered—not because anyone was watching.

In the kitchen afterward, Declan rinsed the mug again. The line held, darker now, lower.

He set it on the drying rack and turned off the light.

Phone down.

Calendar set.

Dog breathing softly in the hallway.

One thing.

Then the next.

⁎⁎⁎

The morning he drew the line thinner, Declan felt betrayed by his own hand.

Same mug. Same marker. Same kitchen light that never flattered anyone—flat, practical, the kind that made even a clean counter look vaguely guilty. But the mark—his tiny domestic border wall—came out less authoritarian, more... humane. A modest line. A line with a conscience. The kind of line that would apologize if it bumped into you in a hallway.

He stared at it like it had been drawn by someone else.

The old line had been a moat. This new one was a politely worded suggestion.

He had meant to do it. That was the problem. He'd told himself he would. Lena's voice had been in the air for months, not nagging, not pleading—accurate: *Your silence isn't neutral.* And he'd been trying, in small increments, to reduce the tax his nervous system charged the household.

So: a thinner line. A little less space demanded from everyone. A little less power claimed in the name of "coping."

Growth, in theory.

In practice, it felt like dental work—necessary, expensive, and vaguely humiliating.

He capped the marker and set it down with the careful finality of a man putting away a weapon he was not sure he could live without. Then he poured the coffee and watched it bloom, that bitter smell that was both comfort and warning. The kettle hissed like a reprimand. The grounds swelled and darkened as if they were deciding to become something useful. He took the first sip too hot, because he liked pain in controlled doses. Controlled pain felt like proof he still had agency. Uncontrolled pain felt like the universe doing whatever it wanted with him.

He held the mug up and watched the coffee level slide down toward the mark.

The line, he reminded himself, was a symptom. Not a solution. It was the fever, not the cure.

From the doorway, Daisy appeared—big head, heavy eyelids, the slow, benevolent seriousness of a creature who had accepted that humans were fragile and still chosen to love them anyway. She blinked once, padded forward, and pressed her shoulder into his shin, establishing contact the way she always did: ballast.

This is where you are, her body said. *In this kitchen. In this morning. In this life you keep trying to postpone with rituals.*

Declan scratched behind her ear, because touching Daisy was the one kind of contact that didn't feel like a performance review.

"Morning," he said, even though the rule didn't apply to him speaking. Obviously. It would be absurd to create a system that inconvenienced the architect.

Daisy's tail thumped once against the cabinet—approval, or gravity.

From upstairs: a thud—Theo's foot missing a stair—and then the voice, already awake enough to demand the universe.

"Dad! I need you! It's urgent!"

Everything was urgent in Theo's world, which was funny until you realized it was also Declan's world, with different nouns. The office had simply taught him to say *urgent* with a calmer face.

Declan looked at the cup. The coffee was still above the line. In the old days, he would have waited. He would have pretended not to hear. He would have clung to silence like it was a right.

Instead he took another sip—faster than he wanted to—and called back, "I'm coming."

He said it like a sentence. Not a sigh. Not a martyr's announcement. Just: *I'm coming.*

It landed in him oddly—like a kindness to his own life.

He resented it immediately.

Because if he could do that—if he could cross the border early and survive—then the line had never been a law. It had been a preference dressed up as doctrine. And the doctrine had been built out of fear.

Upstairs, Theo was waiting at the top landing in dinosaur pajamas, one sock on, one sock missing, hair doing its usual impression of an electrical accident. He held up the single sock like evidence at trial.

"Dad," Theo said, solemn, "this is not allowed."

Declan blinked. He'd grown accustomed to Theo's sudden little proclamations—rules falling from his mouth as if the world came with subtitles—but something about the phrase still made Declan's skin prickle.

"What's not allowed?" Declan asked.

"This," Theo said, shaking the sock. "A sock without its brother. It's not allowed. It's not the rule."

Declan almost laughed, then didn't. Because the phrase wasn't cute anymore—it had started showing up everywhere, like a new kind of mildew. Not allowed. Not appropriate. Not permitted. Language that sounded moral but was really just the world's way of keeping people manageable.

Allowed by who, buddy? Declan wanted to ask. Allowed by which invisible committee of nervous adults?

Instead he crouched, because crouching was the only way to meet a small person without looming. He could feel his knees complain in the way they did now—quiet reminders that he wasn't twenty anymore, and time didn't care how young he still felt inside his head.

"Okay," Declan said. "What do we do when something's not allowed?"

Theo's face tightened with earnestness. "We tell. We follow the rules."

Declan felt something shift in his chest—pride and alarm doing their usual handshake. Theo was learning a moral vocabulary that sounded good and meant... compliance. A language of permission slips.

Declan reached for a better script, the way a man reaches for an extinguisher in a kitchen fire that isn't dramatic yet but might be.

"Sometimes," Declan said slowly, "allowed isn't always the same as kind."

Theo stared at him, trying to parse it. Kids could smell hypocrisy the way dogs smelled thunderstorms. If you lied, they didn't always call you out. They simply stored it and used it later.

"Ms. Ridley says we have to follow the rules," Theo replied. "Rules are the rules."

Declan nodded. "True," he said. "Rules help keep people safe."

Theo's eyes brightened. *Safe* was a concept Theo liked. Safe meant the world was in bounds.

"But," Declan continued, "if the rule is just 'because I said so'—if it doesn't protect anybody—then you can still choose kindness. You can still be gentle. You can still notice."

Theo considered this like he was weighing two snacks.

"So," Theo said carefully, "it's allowed to be kind even if it's not the rule."

Declan exhaled, relieved. "Exactly."

Theo held up the sock again. "Then I'm going to be kind to the sock," he declared, and draped it over Daisy's head like a tiny hat.

✳

Daisy didn't move. Daisy had the patience of an animal that had endured toddlers and capitalism. She stared at Declan as if to say: *This is your species. Do your best.*

Lena appeared at the top of the stairs, hair half-up, face already assembled. She looked at Daisy wearing a sock hat and didn't react, which meant she was either deeply evolved or too tired to fight any more symbolic wars before 7:30.

Declan glanced at her and felt that small internal flinch he always felt around her lately: the awareness that she could see him. Not his behavior, but his motives. His performances. His little disguises.

"You're up early," Lena said, eyes flicking to the mug in his hand.

"I adjusted the line," Declan said before he could stop himself.

It wasn't a confession, exactly, but it was close. It was offering evidence of growth like a man presenting a receipt.

Lena's mouth twitched. "Did you," she said. Not impressed. Just noting the weather.

Declan wanted praise. He hated that about himself. He wanted her to say: *good job.* He wanted it the way a tired employee wanted a supervisor to acknowledge he had a pulse.

Instead she asked, "Are you here?"

It wasn't philosophical. It was diagnostic.

Declan swallowed. "Yeah," he said. "I'm here."

Lena held his gaze for a second longer than comfortable—then nodded once and walked down the stairs.

It wasn't warm. It wasn't cold.

It was contact attempted.

The school parking lot was a small, polite war.

SUVs moved like slow sharks, all blinkers and entitlement. Parents performed the choreography of morning competence: sliding doors, backpacks swung onto shoulders, goodbyes shouted with the volume of people who wanted the world to witness their love. *How are you?*

floated through the air like a weaponized greeting—less a question than a test of whether you could still pretend.

Declan parked and immediately regretted being alive in public.

Theo bounced in his seat, already half out of his belt before Declan had stopped the engine. His excitement had a physical quality, like static: it filled the car, made everything feel louder.

"Remember," Lena said, turning toward Theo with her steady voice, "walk in the lot. Hold hands to cross."

Theo nodded solemnly, absorbing rules like scripture.

Declan opened his door and stepped out into the cold. The air had that mitten-season bite—not winter's full cruelty, but the warning edge that made you think about skin. The world touching you felt... personal. He pulled his collar up. The breath that left his mouth looked briefly visible, like proof he was still here.

He watched other parents. The way they smiled without looking. The way their laughter seemed preloaded, like an app that launched automatically. The way some of them performed casual outrage about traffic as if outrage were a hobby. Two parents stood by a minivan doing what Declan privately called the Polite Dance—smiling, nodding, saying things that sounded kind but functioned like small territorial claims.

"We should definitely do a playdate," one said.

"Yes, absolutely," the other replied, already backing away.

Declan felt the familiar urge: to hate everyone for it. To declare himself above it. To call it fake and therefore not real.

Then he recognized the urge as what it was: panic wearing sophistication.

He took Theo's hand, because it was the simplest, most honest thing available. Theo squeezed his fingers too hard, like he was testing the structural integrity of love.

As they walked toward the entrance, Theo pointed at a boy near the curb—Carter, likely, because there's always a Carter: small, loud, already practicing dominance.

"That's Carter," Theo whispered. "He broke the rule yesterday."

Declan looked down. "What rule?"

Theo's face tightened. "He ran on the playground when it wasn't allowed. And he took the red ball when it wasn't his turn."

Declan felt it—the moral radar forming, but tuned to authority rather than empathy.

"What did you do?" Declan asked.

Theo looked proud. "I told Ms. Ridley. Because we have to follow the rules."

Declan nodded, trying to keep his voice neutral. He didn't want to shame Theo for trusting adults. He also didn't want Theo to become the kind of person who outsourced his conscience to policy.

"Okay," Declan said. "When someone breaks a rule, it's okay to tell a grown-up if someone might get hurt."

Theo nodded, eager.

"But sometimes," Declan added, "the better first move is to check on the person. Like... 'Hey, are you okay?' Or 'Do you want to take turns?'"

Theo blinked. The script was unfamiliar.

"But Carter isn't allowed," Theo insisted.

Declan paused. The lot felt loud. The world felt like an audience. He could feel other parents around them—eyes, smiles, the subtle social pressure to be normal. Public life, where everything became a message whether you meant it or not.

"Buddy," Declan said softly, "allowed isn't always the same as kind. Sometimes kindness is doing the right thing even before a grown-up tells you."

Theo stared at him as if Declan had suggested the sky was negotiable.

Then Theo said, with the careful seriousness of a small person trying to get it right: "So I can be kind as an extra rule."

Declan smiled despite himself. "Yes," he said. "Kindness can be your extra rule."

Theo nodded once, satisfied, and then said, "Okay. I'm going to tell Ms. Ridley that kindness is my extra rule."

Declan laughed—quiet, helpless.

"Maybe don't," Lena said behind him, and her voice held that dry humor that kept Declan alive. "Let's keep the revolution small."

Theo giggled and ran—walked, technically—toward the door.

Declan watched him go and felt the familiar mix of pride and fear: pride that Theo cared, fear that caring would get him hurt. Fear that in a world that rewarded hardness, a soft kid would be treated like something to be corrected.

A mother near the entrance smiled at Declan, bright and practiced. "Big day?" she asked.

Declan recognized the phrase. It was small talk shaped like a probe. Big day meant: *are you stable enough to be socially useful?*

He could play. He could smile. He could say something safe.

Instead he tried, for once, to be a clean sentence in public.

"Just a day," Declan said.

The woman blinked, smile hitching for half a second—tiny glitch in the program.

Then she laughed lightly—too lightly—and said, "Well, aren't you zen."

Zen, Declan thought. That's one word for it.

He nodded, because he didn't have the energy to explain the difference between calm and restraint. He had learned the hard way: in public life, kindness got misread as weakness or ideology. If you didn't perform panic like everyone else, you either looked sanctimonious or broken.

He walked back to the car with Lena in silence.

"What was that?" Lena asked as they got in.

"What was what?"

"The 'just a day' thing."

Declan shrugged, already defensive. "It's true."

Lena started the engine. The car shuddered to life, the heater coughing warm air like a reluctant favor.

"It is true," she said. "It's also... a little like you refusing to speak the same language as the room."

Declan looked out the window. The line of cars creeping forward looked like a species migrating out of obligation.

"Maybe the room's language is stupid," he said.

Lena didn't argue. She just said, "Maybe. But when you stop speaking it, people think you're making a point. Even when you're just trying to survive."

Declan swallowed. He hated how right she was. He hated more that he hadn't known it already. Or maybe he had known, and just preferred the story where his awkwardness was integrity.

They were outside when Declan pulled into his driveway later that afternoon—of course they were. The Dribble and The Hip moved through the neighborhood like slow, inevitable seasons. You couldn't miss them. They were the reminder that time didn't hurry for anyone, and that the only people who acted like it did were the ones still pretending they had endless years.

The Hip was near the mailbox in thick mittens, adjusting a trash can's position like it had offended him. The Dribble stood beside him, scarf pulled up, smiling his too-big smile.

Declan stepped out of the car and felt the cold hit his face. Mitten season. The part of the year where the world asked you to cover yourself to remain tolerable.

"Hey there!" The Dribble called, cheerful as ever.

Declan forced his smile into place. It landed like a bruise.

"Hey," he said. "How you guys doing?"

The Hip shrugged. "Same," he said. "You know. Cold makes everything honest."

Declan nodded, pretending that sentence didn't hit him in the ribs.

The Dribble took a small step closer, lowering his voice as if delivering neighborhood intelligence.

"Your old man okay?" he asked.

Declan felt the words land hard and small at the same time—deceptively small, like a pebble that still broke glass. He managed a casual tone, the one he'd learned in offices: friendly, noncommittal, careful not to reveal too much.

"Yeah," he said. "Yeah, he's... he's doing some follow-up stuff. Doctor."

The Hip's face softened in a way Declan wasn't prepared for. "Haven't seen Walt lately," he said. "Tell him we said hey."

Declan nodded. "I will."

The Dribble smiled, but it wasn't the big practiced one; it was smaller now. "It goes fast," he said quietly, and this time it didn't sound like small talk. It sounded like a warning delivered gently.

Declan's throat tightened. He wanted to make a joke—something about time being a thief with a mortgage—but the joke wouldn't come. His humor depended on distance. This was too close.

Instead he just said, "Yeah."

The Hip patted the trash can lid once like a seal. "All you can do is keep showing up," he said. "Even when you don't feel like it."

Declan's smile twitched. "That's... terrible advice," he said automatically, because sarcasm was still his first language.

The Dribble chuckled. "It's the only kind we've got."

Declan nodded again. He felt Daisy behind the front door—he could always feel her, like the house's heartbeat waiting for him. He waved to them and walked toward his porch, the bruise-smile fading as soon

※

as he turned away.

Inside, Daisy met him with weight and steadiness, pressing her shoulder against his leg like she was re-centering him in his own body. Declan leaned down and let his hand rest on her head longer than necessary. The fur was warm. Real. No subtext. No approval process.

By mid-morning, Mitchell's email arrived like a gift wrapped in silk and barbed wire.

Subject: Quick ask (should be easy!)

Declan stared at the parenthetical—*should be easy!*—and felt his body react as if it were an insult. Mitchell's "happy" was a tone. It was praise used as packaging. It meant the next demand would arrive smiling.

The email was three paragraphs long, each one a little more "reasonable" than the last.

Could you...

Would you mind...

If it's not too much...

And then: *We need it by tomorrow morning.*

Tomorrow morning was a deadline designed by someone who believed time was a suggestion for other people.

Declan read it twice. He felt the old pattern rise: over-deliver, resent it, then quietly punish everyone around him with exhaustion. He was good at that. It was one of his special skills. It allowed him to appear generous while staying secretly enraged—an emotional business model he'd perfected over years.

He thought of Theo's new vocabulary—allowed, not allowed—and how easily a person could confuse rules with goodness. He thought of his own version: *if I can do it, I should. If I should, I must. If I must, I will. If I will, I will die.*

He sat back and put one hand on his mug. The marker line stared up at him. Thinner. Less dramatic. Still there.

He opened a reply draft and let his fingers hover.

This was where he normally softened. This was where he normally apologized for reality. This was where he normally wrote himself into a corner and called it professionalism.

Instead he tried to do what he'd been practicing: clean sentences.

No martyr tone. No apology. Just sequence.

He typed:

I can have that by Thursday. If you need it sooner, we'll need to reduce scope or add support.

He reread it and felt his pulse spike. The sentence had edges. It was kind, but not submissive. It offered options instead of offerings.

It also, his body already knew, would be interpreted.

Kindness in public life was never just kindness. It was a signal people decided to decode according to their favorite ideology. If he held the boundary, he'd be "difficult." If he didn't, he'd be "reliable" until he wasn't, and then he'd be "a disappointment."

He hit send before he could self-sabotage with extra words.

A minute later, Mitchell replied.

Thanks! Let's aim for Thursday then. Appreciate you being so thoughtful and collaborative :)

Declan looked at the smiley face and felt the weirdest thing: relief, followed immediately by irritation. Thoughtful and collaborative. In Mitchell's language, his boundary had become a personality trait. Not a reality. Not a constraint. A vibe.

He could already feel the next "ask" forming somewhere out in the ether, wrapped in that same praise.

He closed the email and forced himself to keep working. His wrist itched under his sleeve, a faint reminder that his body still wanted to turn every social risk into a physical emergency. He breathed anyway.

One thing.

Then the next.

The day held.

⁂

Malloy, of course, noticed.

The next morning brought a follow-up that looked harmless until you read it twice.

Subject: Level-setting

Burke—good note to Mitchell. Appreciate the initiative.

For alignment, please keep all client-facing commitments inside the approved scope and run exceptions through me first.

I've copied HR for visibility.

Declan stared at the line—*copied HR for visibility*—the way you stare at a camera you didn't know was in the room.

HR didn't need visibility. HR was visibility. HR was the institutional eye that never blinked and never forgot. The phrase *for visibility* was the polite frosting people used when they wanted to pretend surveillance was a service.

He reread the email. The compliment at the top was the sugar. The policy in the middle was the leash. The HR line at the bottom was the reminder that the leash could become a collar.

The clean sentence sat in his sent folder like a small, bright object. Here is what I can do. Here is what I cannot. Here are the options.

Declan realized, with a faint nausea, how rare it was for him to say a thing plainly and then stop talking. How often he flooded his own boundaries with explanations as if boundaries needed to be loved into legitimacy. Like truth required a romance to be allowed to exist.

He remembered Malloy's favorite move—concern as a confession trap—and felt something harden usefully inside him.

A clean sentence was a structure. It held up the day. It kept him from turning his life into a series of resentful bargains.

He wanted to tell Lena immediately, like a kid with a gold star—then he didn't. He let the beam hold without applause.

Instead he felt exposed.

Because clean sentences made you visible. And visibility, in his experience, invited consequences.

The conference room coffee smelled burnt, and the table had that sticky-clean sheen that never feels clean—just wiped-down, just managed. The office around him hummed: keyboards, printers, the low murmur of people weaponizing friendliness in tight little doses.

Malloy's email sat open on Declan's screen. He didn't reply. Replying would be participating in the theater. He could already hear the tone he'd be expected to use: agreeable, grateful, obedient.

Thank you for the guidance.

Guidance. As if Malloy were a wise monk and not a man who used policy like a knife.

Declan closed the email and pulled up his task list. He needed the list. The list was his version of prayer: if he could arrange reality into sequence, maybe reality would stop behaving like a trap door.

Malloy reacts with soft consequences

The consequence arrived in the form of a compliment.

Mr. Malloy stopped by Declan's desk around 2:10, hovering in the aisle like a policy change. He didn't sit. Malloy never sat with you unless he wanted to stage intimacy.

"Burke," he said, pleasant.

⁂

"Mr. Malloy."

Malloy smiled. "Heard Mitchell's very pleased," he said. "Nice work."

Declan didn't trust the word pleased. He didn't trust praise in Malloy's mouth. Praise was recruitment.

"Thanks," Declan said, keeping his face neutral.

Malloy leaned in slightly, lowering his voice to the tone he used when pretending to be human.

"You've got a good way with them," Malloy said. "Calm. Reasonable. Clients like that."

Declan heard the subtext: clients like that, so we can use you more. If they liked his calm, the company could sell it. If they could sell it, Malloy could manage it. If Malloy could manage it, Declan would be rewarded with more work and less room to breathe.

Malloy continued. "So I'm going to loop you into a new initiative," he said, casual as a man ordering dessert. "It's an opportunity. Visibility."

Visibility.

Declan almost laughed. Visibility was what you called a spotlight when you didn't want to admit it could burn.

"What kind of initiative?" Declan asked.

Malloy shrugged. "Just supporting a few teams. You know—helping. You're good at helping."

There it was. The leash. Good job, and now: here's more.

Declan felt his body tense, the old reflex: accept it. Be agreeable. Don't make waves. Waves were for people who could swim.

He thought of Theo again, earnest and small, learning rules as morality. He thought of himself at Theo's age—already deciding that compliance was safety, already learning the art of being "easy" so no one would be angry.

Allowed isn't always the same as kind, he reminded himself.

He looked at Malloy and practiced, silently, the new script: a boundary without theatrics.

Then he said, out loud, carefully: "I can help if we define scope. I'm at capacity with Mitchell and my current deadlines."

Malloy's smile stayed in place. But something in his eyes cooled—a degree. Not anger. Calculation. The slight shift of a man adjusting his strategy.

"Of course," Malloy said. "We'll keep it light."

Light, Declan thought, like a boulder if you call it a paperweight.

Malloy patted the edge of Declan's desk—ownership disguised as reassurance—and added, "Also, I really like what you're doing lately. Keep it up."

It sounded like encouragement.

It felt like surveillance.

Malloy walked away.

Declan watched him go and realized: Malloy's version of approval was making you regret earning it. He wanted you to crave the compliment and fear the cost. He wanted your nervous system to start doing the company's management for free.

Declan's wrist itched under his cuff. He rolled it once, subtle. The rash was a petty thing. But it was loyal. It showed up whenever power did.

He forced himself back into work and kept his responses clean. No apology. No performance. Just sequence. A small internal rebellion he couldn't hang on a wall.

When Declan walked in, the house smelled like dinner and crayons and the faint detergent sweetness of someone doing laundry behind the scenes. Warmth without an agenda. Imperfect, lived-in warmth— the opposite of fluorescent cleanliness.

Daisy met him in the entryway, huge and calm, tail moving once— recognition, not performance. She didn't greet him like a fan. She greeted him like a witness.

Theo barreled in from the living room with the volume of a person

※

who still believed volume could secure love.

"Dad! Guess what! Carter did something not allowed today but then he said sorry and that was allowed!"

Declan laughed once, despite himself. "That's… complicated," he said.

Theo nodded, as if that was the point. "Yeah. Life is complicated."

From the kitchen, Lena's voice: "Shoes off, Theo."

Theo obeyed with the solemnity of someone submitting paperwork.

Declan stepped into the kitchen and saw Lena at the counter, not frantic, not soft—assembled. The kind of presence that didn't ask for applause but deserved it anyway. The kitchen light was warmer than the office light, softer at the edges. It made the world feel a little less like a report.

She looked up at him, and instead of asking about work, or Mitchell, or Malloy, she asked the same question she'd asked this morning.

"Are you here?" she said.

Declan felt the question land in his body like a hand on his sternum.

He wanted to say yes the way people said yes in polite conversations—quick, automatic, meaningless.

Instead he tried to tell the truth without panic. "I'm trying," he said.

Lena watched him for a second, then nodded once, like that counted as something. Like the attempt mattered.

Theo wandered in and climbed onto a chair, already narrating his day in rule-language.

"Ms. Ridley said we're not allowed to—"

Declan cut in gently. "Hey," he said. "Tell me what happened, but try this: instead of 'allowed,' tell me what was kind. Or what wasn't."

Theo blinked. Confusion, then effort. He looked upward the way kids do when they're trying to find the right drawer in their brain.

"Okay," Theo said slowly. "Carter took the red ball. That wasn't kind. And then I yelled. That wasn't kind either."

Declan felt something shift—Theo's moral radar sharpening, a hair. Lena's eyes flicked to Declan. Not praise. Not gratitude. Just... noticing. That quiet acknowledgment that said: you're building something.

Declan's phone buzzed in his pocket—work trying to follow him home in nicer packaging. The buzz felt like a hand reaching into his life without asking.

He didn't check it.

Lena watched him not check it. Then she said, quietly, "Thank you."

Two words. A beam in place.

Declan exhaled.

Then Lena stepped closer, not touching him yet, but near enough to be contact.

"Can you stay with us tonight?" she asked.

Not stay in the house. Stay as a person.

Declan swallowed. He felt how much meaning lived inside that request, how carefully she was asking. Like she was offering him an opening and also showing him the edge.

"I can," he said.

He meant it. And he hated, faintly, how much weight it carried—like he'd been withholding so long that presence itself had become a favor.

After dinner, Theo sat on the living room floor building something out of blocks—towers, bridges, little collapses he repaired without ceremony. Daisy lay nearby, head on her paws, eyes open, monitoring the room like an employee with perfect attendance. The TV was off. The house wasn't trying to entertain them. It was just being.

Declan sat on the couch, trying to stay inside his own body. Trying to be here. His mind kept reaching for the old exits—phone, weed, the soft numbness of distraction—but he held the line, the thinner line, the one that wasn't a law but a choice.

Theo's tower fell for the third time. He stared at it, face tightening.

⁎
⁎⁎

Declan braced for the rulebook: someone's not allowed, someone broke the rule, someone must be told.

Instead Theo looked at the scattered blocks and said, softly, almost to himself, "It's okay."

Declan blinked.

Theo gathered the pieces slowly. Not angry. Not performative. Just... patient in the way small children sometimes are when they aren't being watched for correctness. It was the kind of patience Declan couldn't access without chemical assistance, which was depressing, and also instructive.

Then Theo stood up, walked over to Declan, and held out a block—a small blue one shaped like part of a bridge.

"This is for you," Theo said.

Declan took it, confused. "Why?"

Theo shrugged. "Because you looked tired today."

The sentence hit Declan like a clean, unexpected kindness.

Theo didn't say: because it's allowed. He didn't say: because Ms. Ridley said. He didn't say: because the rule is.

He said: you looked tired.

A noticing. A mercy.

Declan felt pride rise in him—sharp, bright.

And fear right behind it—because if Theo could notice, he could also be hurt by what he noticed. Caring made you porous. Caring made you available to the world's bluntness. Declan had spent his adulthood trying to seal himself for that exact reason.

Lena came into the room and saw the block in Declan's hand. She didn't smile big. She didn't make it a moment for social media. She looked at Theo, then at Declan, and her face softened by a degree that mattered.

Theo returned to his blocks, humming, building his bridge again.

Declan sat there holding the blue block like it was proof of something he hadn't earned and didn't want to squander.

The world kept rewarding panic in nicer packaging—emails with smiley faces, compliments that became leashes, concern that wanted confession.

But here, on the living room floor, his son had done a quiet kind thing without being told.

Declan looked at the thinner marker line on his mug sitting on the coffee table. A symptom, yes.

But also—if he kept practicing—less a moat, and more a bridge.

And in mitten season, when everything in the world asked you to cover yourself to remain tolerable, Theo had offered him something small and uncovered:

Not compliance.

Not permission.

Just kindness.

Declan felt the ache of it—pride and fear braided together—and for once he didn't try to narrate it into something safer. He sat there. Present. Holding the block. Listening to the house breathe.

The email arrived at 6:12 p.m., which felt intentional, as if the message had been waiting for the moment a household's defenses went soft—pots cooling on the stove, bathwater running, a child's attention splintering into a dozen small wants.

Subject: FAMILY NIGHT + COMMUNITY SUPPORT (All Welcome!)

The sender line was the school, technically. The logo sat in the corner like a seal on a polite summons. A flyer was attached—bright colors, clip-art balloons, a smiling cartoon family holding hands as if their hands were the only thing holding them.

Declan read it twice without taking it in. Then he read it a third time and felt the pressure beneath the cheer. The message had that faint, practiced warmth of institutional friendliness: *We're excited to invite our families... we're so grateful... we hope to see you there...*

He could already see the cafeteria: the long folding tables, the paper tablecloths, the coffee that tasted like hot plastic. The gleaming tile floors that always looked freshly mopped and never, ever felt clean.

Lena stood at the counter peeling the backing off a strip of crescent-roll dough like she was unspooling bandage tape. Theo was on the rug, building a tower that leaned with the swagger of something expecting to fall.

"What's that face?" Lena said.

Declan had been looking at the screen long enough that it had begun to feel like a small light in a dark room—too bright, too close.

"Family night," he said, and tried to make it sound neutral. He failed. The word came out with an edge he hadn't meant to sharpen.

Theo's head snapped up. "Family night?"

"It's at your school," Lena told him. "There's food. Games. A fundraiser."

Theo's eyes went wide in the uncomplicated way children still have. "Can we go?"

Declan watched the tower sway. He watched Theo's hands hover, careful, ready to correct the lean. The kid had a gift for steadiness. Declan felt something twist in his chest—pride, fear, both.

"We can," Lena said, already committing them with the same tone she used when she scheduled dentist appointments. "It'll be good."

Declan's body made a quiet refusal before his mouth could. He felt his shoulders tighten as if bracing for a shove.

"It's not optional," he said, half to himself.

Lena paused. She didn't look at him at first, which was her way of not escalating—like touching a live wire with the back of your hand before you grabbed it.

"It's optional," she said. "Theo wants to go."

Theo's tower fell with a soft, blunt collapse. He didn't cry. He rebuilt.

Declan fixed on the email again. The phrase *community support* sat there like a hand on the back of his neck.

He could have refused. He could have written a brief apology, feigned illness, claimed a scheduling conflict. But the pressure wasn't in the words. The pressure was in what would come after—quiet questions, sideways looks, that tiny adjustment people made in their faces when they decided you were one of those parents.

One of those families.

He pictured Malloy's office again, the fluorescent hum, the way Malloy listened like a man taking inventory. *How are we doing today?* Concern shaped like a form.

Declan put the phone down like it might bite.

"Fine," he said. "We'll go."

Theo whooped as if Declan had promised him a trip to the moon.

Lena's eyes softened, but he saw the carefulness underneath it. She knew him. She knew the cost of that fine.

The next evening, the school's parking lot was full in that helpless way that made Declan think of crowded beaches: everyone arriving to relax, everyone immediately stressed.

Cars crawled. Headlights swept across faces. Doors opened and shut with muted impatience. He saw familiar parents—people he'd nodded to at pickup, people whose names he didn't know but whose lives were outlined in the little details: the stickers on their bumpers, the coffee cups wedged in their consoles, the way they leaned into their kids as if bracing them against the world.

Theo bounced in the back seat, seatbelt clicking as he shifted, a human metronome of excitement.

"Do they have pizza?" he asked.

"They probably have pizza," Lena said.

Declan's throat felt dry. "They'll have something."

They found a spot near the far fence. Declan parked and sat for a beat with his hands on the wheel as if he needed permission to release it. The interior of the car still smelled like home—dog, kid, winter coats—but through the glass he could see the bright mouth of the school, inviting and fluorescent, swallowing families in batches.

Lena glanced at him. "You okay?"

The question was gentle, but it landed like a probe.

"I'm fine," he said.

Theo was already unbuckling. "Come on."

Inside, the air was warmed by too many bodies and the smell of reheated food. A banner hung crooked above the entrance: **WELCOME FAMILIES!** The exclamation point looked like a small, inevitable shout.

People clustered in loose rings of conversation. The smiling started immediately. Declan had forgotten how much smiling there was at school events—smiling as greeting, smiling as shield, smiling as proof you belonged.

Everyone was smiling the way people smiled when they wanted to be seen smiling.

It made his skin itch.

He caught himself doing it too: corners of his mouth lifted, eyebrows raised, chin tipped up. A performance he'd learned before he'd learned to read. His face had been trained for approval.

"Hey!" someone said, too loudly.

A mother in a beige coat approached with her son—one of Theo's classmates. Declan knew her face like his body already knew the shape of a room he'd entered twice. He did not know her name.

"Hi," Lena said, bright and normal.

Declan said it too, his voice careful not to sound careful.

"How's everyone doing?" the woman asked, and Declan felt the question settle in his stomach.

The phrase was everywhere in this building, like a slogan, like a password.

It's amazing what you can make people produce if you keep the air warm and call it support.

Theo sprinted toward a table of cupcakes before anyone could stop him.

Near the gym doors, a volunteer had set up a cotton candy machine. The clear bowl spun with loud patience, and the air around it smelled like hot sugar—bright, fake, irresistible. A paper cone rotated in a stranger's hand as pink floss gathered from nothing, accumulating into a cloud.

It looked like abundance. It dissolved the second you put it on your tongue. It left your fingers sticky, and somehow you were the one apologizing for the mess.

Lena called after him—"Theo, wait!"—in that tone parents used when they'd already accepted they weren't in control, but wanted the world to believe they were trying.

The mother laughed. "Kids, right?"

Declan gave a laugh that matched, an imitation of agreement.

Small talk came at him like cotton—soft, smothering, impossible to breathe through once it settled. Questions about work. Questions about the weather. Questions about whether they liked the new principal. Nothing sharp. Nothing illegal. Nothing that mattered.

Declan answered in polite fragments, watching his own mouth move. He felt trapped inside it, as if his body had been loaned to someone who knew the lines.

A man with a volunteer shirt walked past, offering raffle tickets. The shirt said **COMMUNITY SUPPORT TEAM** in bold letters. The words looked clean. That was the problem. Everything looked clean. Like fluorescent light—bright, precise, draining.

A table near the gym doors held pamphlets. Declan saw a rack of brochures and felt his scalp tighten. The colors were pastel, the fonts friendly, the language soft: *Parenting Support. Family Wellness. Community Care.*

He did not touch them. He did not want ink from those pages on his skin.

Lena's hand found the small of his back—a quiet, anchoring pressure. "Let's get Theo food," she said.

Theo returned with frosting on his lip like a small crime. "They have cupcakes," he announced, as if the world had been saved.

Declan forced a smile and handed him a napkin. Theo wiped his mouth, then looked past Declan's shoulder and waved

"Mr. B!" Theo shouted.

Declan turned.

A man approached wearing a lanyard and a cardigan that said *I am safe* in a language Declan distrusted. His hair was neat. His eyes were steady. His smile was that confident tenderness you saw in people who had decided their kindness was a credential.

The lanyard read: **COMMUNITY CHAPLAIN / PRAYER TEAM VOLUNTEER.**

Declan's body reacted before his mind caught up. A cold tightening, like a seatbelt locking.

"Declan, right?" the man said, using Declan's first name like they were already acquainted. "I'm Mark. I've seen you at drop-off."

"Hi," Declan managed.

Mark nodded at Lena, smile widening slightly. "And you must be Lena."

Lena's eyes flicked to Declan—one fast glance, a question without words. *Do you know him?*

Declan did not. He hated that Mark knew their names anyway. He hated the casual intimacy of it, the way familiarity could be manufactured by mere observation.

Mark crouched to Theo's level, which looked like kindness until

Declan saw the practiced ease of it. "Hey, buddy. You having a good time?"

Theo beamed. "Yeah. There's cupcakes."

Mark chuckled like cupcakes were a holy discovery. "That's the spirit."

Then Mark stood, turning the full beam of his attention on Declan and Lena. He spoke gently, like a nurse. Like a counselor. Like a man trained to make people feel seen while he measured them.

"How are we doing today?" Mark asked.

It was the exact phrase, delivered with the exact tone: soft authority dressed as care.

Declan heard Malloy inside it. Malloy's office. Malloy's pen. Malloy's little nods that were not nods but checks in boxes.

Declan's mouth went dry. His brain reached for a polite answer, then another, then another. There were so many ways to respond to a question like that and none of them felt safe.

"We're good," Lena said first, her voice bright enough to be acceptable, but not so bright it looked like desperation.

Mark held the smile. "Good, good. These events can be such a blessing. Family, community... it's important."

"Sure," Declan said, and immediately regretted the flatness of it.

Mark didn't react. He absorbed it and went on, unbothered. "We're so grateful to support families. To be here for you."

Declan felt the phrase *be here for you* slide across his skin like oil. It wasn't the words. It was the ownership beneath them, the way they implied proximity without permission.

Theo tugged Lena's sleeve. "Can I go play?"

"Stay where we can see you," Lena said. Theo ran anyway, already testing the boundary.

Mark watched him go with a soft expression, then returned his attention to Declan. "Kids pick up on so much. They need stability.

※
※※

They need—"

"Consistency," Declan said, surprising himself.

Mark's smile sharpened in approval. "Yes. Exactly. Consistency."

The word hung between them, clean and bright.

Declan's jaw tightened. He felt the trap forming—not a sudden snapping thing, but a slow closing, like a door eased shut until you realized the room had no handle on your side.

Across the cafeteria, another parent laughed too loudly. A cluster of dads clapped a man on the shoulder. Someone called someone else "buddy" with an edge of judgment hidden in the friendliness.

Declan had the sensation of being watched from every direction, not in a paranoid way, but in the normal way communities watched: to know where you fit, to decide how to treat you.

Surveillance disguised as belonging.

At a nearby table, a woman with a clipboard spoke to another mother, her voice casual, bright.

"My religion says I should always show up for the kids," she said, smiling like it was a personal quirk. "Even when I'm exhausted."

Declan heard it and felt nothing. That line was fine. People had beliefs. People had needs. People had little private maps that helped them navigate.

Then the woman continued, lowering her voice as if sharing a secret. "And my religion says you can't let your family get too—" she searched for the word, found it—"isolated. It's not healthy."

The other mother nodded like this was wisdom instead of judgment in a cardigan.

Declan felt the switch flip in his chest.

He didn't argue. He didn't look at them. He felt his body settle into a quieter kind of alertness, the way a dog's ears lift when something in the woods moves wrong.

Mark's voice drifted in again, still warm. "You know, we've got a prayer team here tonight. Nothing formal. Just... support. If anyone needs it."

Declan watched Mark's hands as he spoke—open palms, a posture of harmlessness. It looked honest. That was the trick: honesty as theater.

Lena's eyes had gone slightly distant, her expression smoothing into polite stillness. Declan recognized it. It was the look she got when someone tried to touch a part of her she hadn't offered.

Mark turned to Lena, voice gentling even more. "How's your heart, Lena? You holding up?"

The phrase *your heart* made Declan's stomach turn. It was intimate without permission.

Lena's mouth lifted. "We're fine."

Mark nodded, but it didn't end there. "Of course. Of course. But you know... parenting is heavy. Marriage is heavy. Sometimes we carry things we don't have to carry alone."

Declan's fingers curled around his plastic plate. He felt the cheap fork bending slightly under his grip.

Mark continued, as if he'd been given an invitation. "If you ever need prayer... if there's anything you're struggling with... we're here. No judgment."

No judgment, Declan thought, was what people said when they were about to judge you.

Theo sprinted back, breathless, cheeks flushed. "Dad," he said, and then, in the exact tone Declan had heard from teachers, from administrators, from adults who loved control, Theo added: "That's not appropriate."

Declan blinked. "What?"

Theo pointed across the room, where a boy was pretending to sword-fight with a balloon animal. The boy's father was laughing. The boy's mother looked tired.

Theo repeated, not mean, not smug—just copied. "That's not

※

appropriate."

Lena's face changed—something tight behind her eyes. Declan felt the cold clarity of it: Theo was absorbing the world's polite forms of control. Not the cruelty of shouting. Not the ugliness of fists. The clean, socially acceptable language that made correction sound like care.

"Who said that?" Declan asked.

Theo shrugged, already bored with the question. "I heard it."

Declan looked around, trying to locate where it had come from. He saw Mark watching Theo with a gentle expression that did not reach his eyes.

The fluorescent light hummed overhead. The room gleamed. Everything looked like help. Everything felt like pressure.

Mark's attention returned to Declan, as if Theo's little phrase had been a cue. "Kids mirror what they see," Mark said. "It's why family culture matters so much."

Declan could feel himself being guided toward a ledge. Toward confession. Toward some small admission that could be turned into a case file, a prayer request, a conversation later framed as concern.

Mark smiled. "How have things been at home?"

There it was. Not a direct question, but an opening—a warm door.

Declan's mind flashed: Malloy, leaning forward, pen poised. *Tell me more about that.*

Declan felt the old reflexive guilt—if you refused to share, you looked guarded; if you shared, you were vulnerable; if you shared the wrong thing, you were guilty. There was no clean exit except the one people punished you for taking.

Mark waited, patient as a net.

Lena's hand found Declan's again, her fingers squeezing once, small and sharp. A warning, or a lifeline. Maybe both.

Declan inhaled. He tasted cafeteria air—grease, sugar, bleach.

And then he said it. The clean sentence, simple as a shut door: "We're good, thank you. If we need help, we'll ask."

No story. No defensiveness. No invitation.

Mark's smile held. It didn't drop, but Declan saw the flicker behind it—the faint recalibration. The polite disappointment of a man denied access.

"Of course," Mark said smoothly. "Absolutely. I love that. Strong boundaries. That's healthy."

Declan heard the subtle twist: strong boundaries as compliment, but also as observation. As something to note.

Mark's eyes moved to Lena. "And you, Lena? You feel supported?"

Lena's smile sharpened a fraction. "We're fine."

Mark nodded again, still warm, still confident. "Well. I'm glad you came. It matters. Showing up matters."

He touched Theo's shoulder lightly as he passed, a gesture too familiar for a stranger, and walked away to greet another family with the same practiced tenderness.

Declan felt the room breathe again, but his body didn't unclench.

He'd refused. Cleanly. And still the guilt rose in him like nausea.

Refusing confession was treated like arrogance.

He watched Mark across the cafeteria, moving from parent to parent, his lanyard swinging like a small badge of sanctioned access.

Theo ran off again, the moment already forgotten by him. Declan envied that.

Lena leaned close. "You did good," she murmured.

Declan didn't answer. Praise in that room felt risky too—as if a compliment could be overheard and repurposed.

He wanted to leave. He wanted to go home, shut the door, and feel the air of his own living room, imperfect and honest.

Instead he stood under fluorescent light and pretended this was normal.

They stayed longer than Declan wanted because Theo was happy, because Lena insisted with that quiet determination that meant she was trying to hold something together. Declan drifted through conversations like a man walking through a shallow pool, always aware of what was touching him, never able to dry off.

He heard more of it—religion used as a soft club, wellness used as a leash.

"God just wants what's best for your family," someone said to someone else, smiling.

"Sometimes the hard choices are the loving ones," a father murmured, hand on his son's shoulder like a restraining bar.

Declan watched the way people corrected their children without raising their voices. The way they used gentle language to do sharp things. The way their faces stayed calm as they tightened control.

He watched Theo move through the room, absorbing the rhythms, the phrases, the acceptable tones. Theo's face remained open, bright. But Declan felt the subtle shift in the air around him, as if the boy was learning how to live under fluorescent light.

When they finally left, Theo protested in that dramatic way children have when they're forced back into time. "Just five more minutes."

"Tomorrow," Lena said, and Theo groaned like it was a tragedy.

Declan walked them to the car with the relief of a man leaving a hospital. Outside, the night air felt like water poured over skin.

Inside the car, Theo fell quiet almost immediately, the way children do when the stimulus stops and their bodies remember fatigue. He hummed softly, eyes half-lidded.

Declan started the engine. The parking lot lights cast everything in a harsh white glow.

Lena buckled her seatbelt, then turned toward him. "You got weird," she said.

Declan laughed once, no humor in it. "I got weird."

"What was that?" Lena asked. Not accusing. Curious. Worried.

Declan kept his eyes on the windshield. He watched a family cross in front of the car, the father's hand on the child's shoulder steering him like a shopping cart.

"They were fishing," Declan said.

Lena exhaled. "Declan."

"His body already knew our names," Declan said. "He didn't know us. He just knew."

"He's... friendly," Lena said, but the word sounded thin.

"He's trained," Declan replied. "He's not just being nice. He's collecting. It's a system."

Lena's jaw tightened. "Not everyone is Malloy."

Declan gripped the wheel. He felt the old panic trying to ignite—heat rising behind the ribs, the impulse to flee, to vanish.

He swallowed it down. He spoke carefully.

"Enough of them are," he said.

Lena stared at him for a beat. Then she looked out the window, watching the parking lot recede, the fluorescent glow fading behind them.

Theo's voice came from the back seat, small and sleepy. "Dad?"

"Yeah, buddy?"

Theo yawned. "Can we have cupcakes again sometime?"

Declan's chest loosened a fraction. "Yeah," he said softly. "We can."

Lena's hand found his knee briefly, a grounding touch. Not agreement, exactly. A reminder: you are here, you are not alone.

They drove home in the quiet.

But the quiet wasn't peace. It was aftershock.

At home, the house greeted them with its familiar imperfections: shoes by the door, a dish in the sink, the faint smell of laundry detergent and dog.

Daisy appeared from the hallway, tail thumping hard enough to sound like a drum. She pressed her head into Theo's stomach, demanding attention like it was a moral law.

"Daisy!" Theo giggled, suddenly awake again, his hands in her fur. Daisy accepted his affection as tribute, not as confession.

Lena shepherded Theo toward the bathroom. "Teeth," she called. "Then bed."

Theo protested weakly and obeyed anyway, Daisy following as if appointed guardian.

Declan stood in the kitchen, the room dimmer than the school, warmer. The light over the stove was soft, imperfect. He could breathe.

Still, the residue from the event clung to him. He felt it on his skin, in his mouth. The performative warmth. The smiling surveillance. The gentle extraction.

His body wanted to dull it.

He opened the cabinet where the weed was kept—out of Theo's reach, out of sight, like a compromise with himself. The jar sat there, quiet. A small, dependable door out of his own mind.

He touched it and felt the instant promise: disappear.

Lena entered the kitchen behind him without sound. Declan didn't turn, but he felt her presence like a change in air pressure.

"You're going for it," she said.

It wasn't accusation. It was observation. The kind that made him feel more naked than anger ever did.

Declan kept his hand on the jar. He stared at the label, the handwriting, the date.

"I want to disappear," he said.

The sentence landed heavy in the small room.

Lena didn't speak right away. She moved closer, not touching him yet. "Is it because of tonight?" she asked.

"It's because of... all of it," Declan said, and he heard how close that sounded to confession. He hated it. He wanted to keep everything sealed. But the pressure was there, pressing, pressing.

Lena's voice stayed calm. "He didn't have to disappear," she said.

Declan's throat tightened. "I know."

He felt the choice like a fork in a road. If he used, the edge would blur. The residue would soften. The fluorescent hum in his head would quiet.

But he'd been trying—quietly, imperfectly—to make deliberate choices instead of reflexes. To live in the discomfort without running from it.

He took his hand off the jar. Closed the cabinet.

Lena's shoulders loosened, slightly. She hadn't asked him not to. She'd watched him choose.

Declan leaned forward, palms on the counter, eyes shut for a moment.

"I hate that I can't just—" he began, and stopped, because he didn't have words for it. Because words turned into openings, and openings turned into hooks.

Lena stepped closer and touched his back, the same spot she'd touched at the school—an anchor. "You can," she said softly. "Not tonight. But you can."

Declan swallowed hard. He nodded once.

From the hallway, Theo's voice drifted down, sing-song, telling Daisy she was "a big fluffy cloud." Daisy's nails clicked on the floor in steady, satisfied rhythm.

Declan listened to it, the ordinary sound of home.

Later, after Theo was in bed and the house had settled into its nighttime hush, Declan sat on the couch with a glass of water he didn't want and a mind that refused to stop turning.

Lena folded laundry with small, efficient motions, a quiet ritual of keeping the world from falling apart.

Declan stared at the dark television screen as if it might reflect something back to him. The room felt safe, but his body still carried the cafeteria's brightness, the scrutiny, the way Mark's voice had slid under his skin.

Lena glanced at him. "You're still there," she said.

Declan exhaled. "I know."

"You think he's going to... what?" Lena asked. "Show up at our house?"

Declan almost laughed. "No. Not like that. Not yet."

"Not yet," Lena repeated, the phrase turning sour as she said it.

Declan nodded. "It's never immediate. It's the follow-up. The 'helpful' check-in. The call. The 'just making sure you're okay.'"

Lena folded a shirt with too much force. "So what do we do?"

Declan's mouth tightened. He thought of his clean sentence. He thought of Mark's smile flickering and recalibrating, not angry, not offended—adjusting strategy.

"We keep it simple," Declan said. "We don't give them anything."

Lena's eyes narrowed slightly, not in disagreement—more like she was measuring the weight of that plan. "Not everyone is hunting," she said, but the conviction wasn't as strong now.

Declan looked at her. He spoke quietly, the way you speak when you don't want to wake children or demons.

"Enough are," he said again. "Enough that it matters."

Lena set the folded laundry down and sat beside him. Her shoulder pressed against his.

"We can go to school events," she said, steady, "and still not let them in."

Declan's chest loosened slightly at the *we* in her sentence. He leaned back into the couch. "I want to believe that."

Lena's hand found his, fingers lacing through his. "Then believe it," she said. "And if you're wrong, we deal with that when it happens. Not before."

Declan let his head tip back, eyes closed. He wanted to live in that moment—her warmth, the quiet, the safety of a house where no one demanded confession.

From the hallway, Daisy appeared, padding into the living room like she owned it. She stopped in the doorway between the living room and the hall and sat down—squarely in the threshold, as if posted there by a sane god.

Declan watched her.

Daisy didn't look at him with questions. She didn't ask how his heart was. She didn't offer support in exchange for access. She simply sat, present, steady, her body a warm fact.

Animals didn't demand confession.

They demanded consistency.

Declan stared at her, feeling something unclench in him that had nothing to do with the school, nothing to do with Mark, nothing to do with Malloy. Something older. Something simpler.

He reached out and Daisy rose, crossing the room to place her head on his knee with the blunt honesty of love.

Declan rested his hand on her skull, feeling the weight of her, the reality of her.

Behind them, the world could smile and harvest and shine bright as fluorescent light.

Here, in the dim room of his own house, Daisy's steady breathing made a verdict of sorts:

He didn't have to confess to be real.

You have to be the same person in every room.

⁂

Declan saw it before he was ready to see it.

Performance Check-In — 10:30 a.m.

The calendar entry sat there like a verdict rendered in advance. A clean block of time, a polite font, the kind of corporate inevitability that pretended it was neutral. Declan stared at it and felt his body answer first—jaw tight, wrists prickling, a faint heat along his neck that wasn't a rash and wasn't nothing.

His skin believed in Malloy.

That was the part that made him angrier than the meeting itself.

He closed the laptop. Opened it again. The entry still sat there. He wasn't superstitious, but he'd understand why people became that way: if you could convince yourself that rearranging objects changed outcomes, you could pretend you weren't powerless.

A truck groaned past outside, and the building responded with its usual little tremors—HVAC exhale, a door shutting down the hall, distant laughter that sounded like someone trying to prove they were unafraid. His office chair squeaked when he shifted, a cheap sound for an expensive anxiety.

He stood, walked to the kitchen, filled a glass with water, drank too fast. The cold hit his teeth like punishment. He stared at the sink, at the clean plates Lena had stacked to dry the night before, and tried to borrow the simple honesty of dishwater and ceramic.

But his mind kept pulling him back to fluorescent rooms.

The school. The lanyard. *How are we doing today?*

And now: Malloy. Warm voice, controlled concern, the gentle invitation to empty himself into a folder.

Declan checked the time. He had ninety minutes to pretend he was fine.

His inbox chimed.

Mitchell.

Of course.

The subject line was bright enough to be a joke.

Quick ask

Declan opened it and felt the familiar squeeze behind his ribs. Mitchell's tone was always buoyant, always friendly, always framed as a small favor that carried the weight of a deadline.

Hey man—could you reorganize the deliverable structure? Leadership wants it more "narrative." I know it's annoying but it'll make us look good. Appreciate you.

Declan read the word *narrative* and felt something cold settle in him. Narrative was what they asked for when they didn't want facts. Narrative was what they demanded when they wanted a story they could own—something pliable, something that could be lifted and reused without the person who built it.

Structure costs time, he thought.

Time costs approval.

He could do the minimum—reshuffle headers, add a few connecting sentences, hope no one noticed the weakness underneath. Or he could do it properly: make it clean, defensible, unambiguous. Mitchell would look better. The team would look better. Malloy would have fewer excuses.

Declan's fingers hovered above the keyboard.

He chose structure anyway.

The choice didn't feel noble. It felt like habit and triage: make it sturdy so it can't be used against you. Make it so clear no one can "misunderstand." Clarity was a kind of armor—heavy, but reliable.

The cost arrived immediately: minutes evaporating, the calendar inching closer, his heart rate rising with every tab he opened. He heard his own breath in the small quiet between keystrokes. He could feel sweat gather along his spine beneath his shirt, the body's private commentary on the day.

He worked fast and clean, the way he'd learned to work when the room didn't feel safe: no wasted movement, no extra flourish, no evidence of emotion. He stitched the document into a shape that would survive interrogation. He wrote transitions that sounded human without confessing anything human. He turned raw data into something "narrative," which is to say: something palatable to people who wanted comfort more than truth.

When he sent it back, he wrote only:

Done. Structured per request. Let me know if you need anything else.

Mitchell replied within two minutes.

You're a lifesaver

Declan didn't feel saved.

He checked the time again. 10:12.

His phone buzzed—Kyle.

Declan's stomach tightened. Kyle didn't call for nothing. Kyle called when the wind was shifting and he wanted to make sure you knew which way to lean.

Declan answered. "Yeah?"

Kyle's voice came through with its usual mildness, that careful friendliness people used when they wanted to be liked while doing something unkind.

"Hey, man. Quick thing. Malloy's in a good mood today," Kyle said, as if that were weather. "Just... you know. He likes people who are team players."

Declan heard the translation immediately: Be compliant. Be liked. Be safe.

He waited long enough that Kyle filled the silence with a little laugh. "Not saying you're not. Just... you know how he is."

Declan felt the old reflex—appease, reassure, perform humility. He watched it rise in him like a trained animal looking for a treat.

And then, unexpectedly, he didn't feed it.

"Noted," Declan said.

Kyle paused. A small, confused pause, like a man who'd expected a different script.

"Right," Kyle said. "Cool. Just wanted to give you a heads up."

Declan ended the call without adding anything else. No explanation. No smile in his voice.

He sat still at his desk and listened to the building's noises: HVAC breath, distant laughter, keyboards like rain. The ordinary soundtrack of people pretending their lives weren't being traded in small units of obedience.

10:28.

He stood. Straightened his shirt. Picked up his notebook though he didn't need it—an object to hold, a prop to keep his hands from giving him away. He made his way to Malloy's office with the calm gait of a man going into a dentist appointment he couldn't reschedule.

Malloy's door was open.

Warm light spilled out—not warm in color, but warm in invitation. Malloy sat at his desk with a mug and a smile that looked almost sincere. That was the problem. Warm was worse. Warm meant he wanted something soft.

"Declan," Malloy said. "Come on in."

Declan stepped inside. The room had the same tidy sterility as always: framed motivational prints, clean surfaces, a faint scent of

✳

peppermint that tried too hard to suggest health. Even the chair had a kind of polite firmness to it—supportive, yes, but only in the way a brace supported a limb you weren't supposed to use.

Malloy gestured to the chair. Declan sat.

Malloy didn't open with metrics. He didn't open with tasks. He opened with the exact kind of question that sounded humane and functioned like a keyring.

"How are you holding up?"

Declan felt his skin react again—jaw, wrists, that faint heat. His body wanted to confess so the pressure would stop, the way a kettle whistles because it wants release. He could feel his tongue preparing the usual offerings: *busy, but okay. hanging in there. doing my best.* A series of phrases that let someone else decide what they meant.

Malloy leaned forward slightly, voice gentle. "Anything going on I should know about? Anything impacting you?"

There it was. The invitation to give him soft spots. To offer up the parts of Declan that could be managed.

Declan could have lied. He could have said: All good. He could have performed cheer. But cheer was also a confession, in its own way—proof he was willing to play.

So he offered neither cheer nor secrets.

He met Malloy's eyes and kept his voice steady.

"I'm meeting deadlines," Declan said. "Mitchell's stabilized. If there are performance concerns, I'd like them in specific terms."

Malloy blinked once. A small surprise. The room seemed to recalibrate around it.

Specific terms.

Malloy's smile held, but it thinned at the edges. "No concerns," he said quickly. "You're doing great."

Declan nodded, neutral. He didn't smile. He didn't thank him. Praise without substance was a leash.

Malloy continued, as if he needed to regain control of the conversation's shape. "Just... watch the tone."

Declan felt the word land like a soft slap.

Tone. Obedience with plausible deniability.

He let the silence sit. He didn't rush to patch it. He kept his voice level and his hands still—no pleading, no performance.

"What tone, specifically?" Declan asked.

Malloy's smile froze. Not fully—Malloy was practiced—but enough that Declan saw the hesitation. The man had expected tone to work as a vague warning: a fog you couldn't grab. A weapon you couldn't point back.

Malloy shifted in his chair. "You know," he said, laughing lightly, "just... sometimes you can come across a little—"

"—What?" Declan asked, still calm. "Direct? Dismissive? Curt?"

Malloy's eyes flicked, assessing. He didn't like being offered options. Options narrowed the field. Options forced definitions.

"I don't want to over analyze," Malloy said, and Declan almost smiled because it was such a perfect evasion. Over analyze was another word for *make me be honest.*

Declan nodded once, as if agreeing. "I'd just like to correct anything that's actually a problem. If you can point to a specific example, I can adjust."

Malloy sat back. His hands moved slightly on the desk, fingers touching the mug, then the pen, then nothing. A man looking for a lever that wasn't there.

"Well," Malloy said, voice still warm but no longer intimate, "overall you're a strong contributor. Reliable. We value that."

Corporate fog. Retreat language.

Declan waited.

Malloy cleared his throat, reasserting the formal frame. "Let's talk goals for the quarter."

※
※※

They did. Not long. Not dramatic. Malloy listed broad objectives, Declan acknowledged them, asked a few clarifying questions that made the objectives concrete. Concrete was what Malloy didn't like. Concrete meant accountability ran both ways.

When the meeting ended, Malloy stood and offered a handshake with the same gentle smile he gave everyone—warmth as brand consistency.

Declan stood too. Shook Malloy's hand. Kept his expression polite and blank.

As Declan reached the door, Malloy added, lightly: "And Declan—good talk. I appreciate your professionalism."

Declan paused long enough to make the words matter.

"Thanks," he said. Then he left.

In the hallway, his knees felt faintly unreliable, like his legs had been holding him up on borrowed patience. His pulse thrummed in his throat. He wanted to lean against the wall, close his eyes, let his body finish panicking now that it was allowed to.

But he didn't.

He walked back to his desk, sat down, opened his email, and did the next thing. That was the victory. Small. Real. No fireworks. No confession given. No throat offered.

Just intact.

At home, later, the house met him with its usual mild chaos: Theo's backpack slumped by the door like a collapsed animal, a permission slip on the counter, Daisy's tail thumping the baseboard like applause she didn't mean. The air smelled like onions softening in a pan and something sweet underneath—clean laundry, or shampoo, or the faint ghost of crayons ground into carpet.

Lena looked up from the kitchen, where she was rinsing a pot. Her gaze swept him the way it always did now—quick inventory, quiet hope.

"How was it?" she asked, careful.

Declan set his keys down. Hung his coat. The ordinary motions felt like proof of something.

"Fine," he said.

Lena waited, expecting the story. He could see it in her face—the instinct to brace, to prepare, to meet him where he was.

But Declan didn't narrate his victory. He didn't ask for applause. He didn't fully trust it yet. He knew how quickly a "good day" could be reinterpreted as attitude. He knew how institutions punished people for learning.

He moved into the evening like a man who intended to remain present.

He picked up Theo's backpack. "Where's the form?" he called.

"On the counter," Lena said, and something in her voice shifted—surprise, maybe, or relief.

Declan found the form, read it, signed it. Put it back in the folder. He rinsed a dish, then another. The hot water steamed his hands. The small heat felt honest—earned, direct, not curated. He checked the fridge for what needed to be cooked, not because he was hungry but because the act of checking felt like returning to the world.

Lena watched him like she was listening to the air.

"You're... here," she said finally.

Declan glanced over. "Yeah," he said.

The words were plain. But Lena's shoulders softened as if she'd been holding weight that wasn't entirely hers.

Theo wandered in, rubbing his eyes. He took one look at Declan and stopped, studying him with that unnerving child-perception that always seemed to bypass the obvious and land on the truth.

"Is Dad in trouble?" Theo asked.

Lena's head snapped slightly, surprised by the bluntness.

Declan didn't minimize it. He didn't lie. He didn't make it funny.

He treated Theo like a person.

"I had a hard conversation," Declan said. "I did okay."

Theo frowned, thinking. Then he tilted his head and delivered the line with the exact cadence of a movie he'd watched too many times.

"New territory, Bucko?"

Declan laughed—an actual laugh, startled out of him. It came out warmer than he expected, and it hurt a little too, because it meant something.

"Yeah," Declan said, smiling at his son. "New territory."

Theo nodded as if that settled it. He wandered toward Daisy, who immediately demanded tribute. Theo scratched behind her ears with solemn devotion.

Declan watched them and felt the ache underneath the moment: Theo was watching him learn. Watching him try. Watching him become the kind of adult who didn't fold.

Lena stepped closer, her voice low. "What happened?" she asked.

Declan shook his head gently. "I didn't give him anything," he said. "He wanted a story. I gave him facts."

Lena held his gaze. "And?"

"And he didn't like it," Declan said. "But he couldn't do much with it."

Lena's mouth lifted slightly. Not a smile of victory. A smile of recognition.

The air in the room felt lighter. Not because life had become easy, but because it had become less lonely.

Winter light slanted in without warmth, making the dust in the air look intentional.

Later, when the dishes were done and Theo was asleep, Declan stood in the hallway staring at his phone as if it were a small animal he didn't trust.

Walt.

The call he'd been avoiding didn't feel like avoidance in his head. It felt like caution. It felt like not wanting to disturb something fragile. But he was starting to see how avoidance worked: it dressed itself up as wisdom, then ate your calendar alive.

Declan walked into the living room. The lamp cast a warm pool of light on the side table. Daisy lay on the rug, breathing steadily, a creature who didn't need explanations.

Declan picked up his phone and opened the reminders app.

He didn't call yet. Not as a performance. Not as a grand gesture.

He chose a time—tomorrow, after work, before Theo's bedtime, when there would be no convenient chaos to hide behind. He set the reminder. He labeled it simply:

Call Walt.

No adjectives. No apologies.

Then he placed the phone on the entry table where he would see it the moment he walked in. Where avoidance couldn't pretend it was accidental.

He stood there for a beat, feeling the quiet.

Structure, it hit him, wasn't theater.

Structure was love—the kind that didn't smile for anyone, the kind that showed up on time, the kind that didn't ask permission to be real.

In the other room, Lena shifted in bed. A soft sound, half-sleep, half-sigh.

Declan turned off the lamp, leaving the reminder waiting in the darkness like a small, faithful lantern.

And for once, the pressure didn't feel like fate.

It felt like sequence.

⁎⁎⁎

The reminder hit his phone at 7:12 a.m.
Walt — follow-up appointment.
No emojis. No softened language. Just the name and the function, blunt as a stamp. Declan stared at it until the screen dimmed, then tapped it awake again, like repetition might change the meaning.

It didn't.

The marker line surfaced in his mind the way old tools do—an old vice in an old drawer. He pictured the thick black stroke Malloy had made once, drawing a boundary around Declan's time as if time belonged to whoever wrote hardest. Declan felt the ghost of that pressure in his wrists, but he didn't do the old thing—didn't spin it into prophecy.

He breathed once, slow, and named it without drama.

Fear.

In the kitchen, Lena moved quietly, already dressed, hair pulled back, coffee poured. Not bustling. Not managing. Just present in a way that made the room feel less like a test. The morning light was thin and winter-clean, making everything look slightly sharper than it needed to: the edge of the countertop, the paper pile on the table, the faint smear of peanut butter on Theo's plate from yesterday.

"You're taking him?" she asked.

Declan nodded. "Yeah."

"And after," she said, not a question, more like a simple bracket placed around the day, "you come back here."

Declan looked at her. It was the gentlest form of coordination: partnership that didn't pretend to be permission.

"Yeah," he said again. "I'll come back."

He ate toast he couldn't taste. He checked his wallet twice. He pocketed his phone and didn't try to joke about any of it. His stomach felt hollow in that particular way it did when he was bracing—like the body clearing space for impact.

Daisy watched from the doorway, half awake, her enormous head resting on her paws. Her eyes followed him with quiet accuracy, the animal version of: *I see you.*

Declan stopped long enough to scratch behind her ear. Daisy leaned into it, unimpressed by human schedules.

Walt was waiting on the porch when Declan pulled up, jacket zipped, hands in his pockets like he was trying to keep himself from floating away. His posture said he was fine. His face said something else—tight around the mouth, eyes a little too alert. A man trying to look like a man, not a body.

"Look at this," Walt said as Declan got out. "Free chauffeur service. Must be nice to be important."

Declan smiled—not because it was funny, but because it was the only way Walt knew to lift the weight without admitting it existed.

"How's work?" Walt added, the question tossed casually, like a cigarette flicked toward the curb.

Declan heard what it meant.

Don't look at me too closely.

Don't make this a thing.

"It's work," Declan said, plain. "I'm doing what I can."

Walt grunted approvingly, as if simplicity were a virtue. Then he climbed into the passenger seat with more care than he wanted to

⁎⁎⁎

show, adjusting himself like the seatbelt mattered more than it did. His breath hitched once—small, quick—then he smoothed it out with a throat-clear that tried to sound normal.

Declan started the car. His hands settled on the wheel with a strange seriousness, like an oath he hadn't spoken aloud.

They drove mostly in silence—two men pretending it was traffic, that the red lights weren't counting anything down.

When Walt did talk, it was in small observations: a new building going up, a pothole the town still hadn't fixed, the way the morning sun made the windshield impossible. Ordinary language. Safe language.

Declan didn't fight it. He didn't fill the gaps with reassurance. He kept the car moving, kept the heat steady, kept his eyes where they needed to be.

Sequence. Not myth.

The clinic parking lot had that institutional smell even outside— exhaust mixed with cold air and the faint chemical aftertaste of a building that cleaned itself too often. Declan parked. Walt lingered a second before opening his door, like he wanted to delay the moment without admitting it.

Inside, the waiting room was a familiar kind of purgatory: chairs bolted down, a TV murmuring about weather no one believed, a magazine rack stocked with optimism and dental hygiene. A vending machine clunked somewhere, swallowing someone's bills with the confidence of a small predator.

Coughs. Paper shuffles. Chair creaks.

Brief, disconnected sounds—like a choir made of impatience and lungs. Declan had heard these noises before and treated them like a message aimed at him personally.

Today, he heard them as time talking.

He felt his body reflex anyway: a tight chest, a faint itch at his wrist where his watchband sat. The old alarm system, eager and stupid. He didn't spiral. He didn't indulge it.

Fear, he named again. Just fear.

Walt sat with his arms folded, staring at a wall poster explaining blood pressure as if it were a foreign policy issue. He nodded once at a nurse who passed, like he was making a point about being civilized. His foot tapped once, then stopped, as if he caught himself doing it and decided the body didn't get to vote.

Declan watched a woman across the room twist a tissue into a rope in her hands. An older man stared at the TV without blinking. A child swung his legs, shoes knocking the chair frame with a rhythm that sounded like boredom and dread braided together.

Then Declan saw a familiar shape in the corner: a person with a lanyard and a practiced softness. Not the exact same face from the school night or the fundraiser, but the same breed of presence—a cousin-version. In hospitals they called it patient liaison or spiritual care or something similarly gentle.

The person walked over with that confident tenderness, the smile designed to be seen.

"How are we doing today?" they asked, the plural doing a lot of work.

Declan felt the old irritation flare—data harvest disguised as care, confession as currency. He could almost hear the filing cabinet in the question, the little labeled folder opening with a soft, polite hiss.

He didn't feed it.

"We're alright," he said. "Thanks."

Clean. Closed. No story.

The liaison's smile flickered, recalibrated, and they shifted their attention to Walt. "And you, sir? How are you holding up?"

Walt looked at them the way he looked at salesmen on his doorstep. "I'm here," he said. "That's how I'm doing."

Polite. Firm. No openings.

⁂

The liaison hesitated, tried one more gentle hock. "If there's anything you'd like to talk about—any worries—we're available."

Walt's gaze stayed neutral. "I appreciate it," he said, which in his dialect meant: You will not be needed.

The liaison retreated.

Declan watched them go and felt something odd rise in him—respect, sharp and reluctant. Walt could refuse intimacy without turning it into a story. Walt could keep a boundary without apologizing for having one.

Declan filed it away like a tool.

A door opened. A name was called.

"Walter Haslam?"

Walt stood too quickly, then masked the small stiffness with a shrug, like his body was simply being dramatic. Declan stood with him.

"Want me in there?" Declan asked quietly.

Walt paused, just long enough for a crack of truth to show. "Yeah," he said, then immediately added, "Just so you can hear it the first time. They talk fast."

Walt said it like logistics, but his pause said the rest.

Declan nodded. "Okay."

The exam room was bright in the specific way hospitals are bright: fluorescent truth that made everyone look slightly guilty. The paper on the table crinkled when Walt sat, a sound that made Declan think of packaging—something you opened to reveal what you'd bought, or what you couldn't return.

A nurse came in and moved through the ritual with cheerful competence: blood pressure cuff, thermometer, questions delivered like checkboxes.

"Pressure's a bit elevated today," she said, as if reporting a temperature. She wrote it down without drama. Numbers, neutral. Walt nodded like it was weather.

Declan watched Walt's jaw tighten anyway.

The doctor came in with a tablet, the kind of person whose calm could feel like a threat if you didn't trust the system. He spoke in a tone meant to reassure—measured, even, careful not to alarm—and that carefulness itself was a kind of alarm.

They talked about a follow-up test. About a medication adjustment. About "monitoring." About an "elevated number" that sounded small until you listened to it properly.

Declan listened properly.

He watched Walt nod at the phrases designed to be soothing: *We'll keep an eye on it. Probably nothing. Let's be cautious.*

Declan saw the math of minimization. Words that shrank the problem so the room could keep moving.

The doctor looked at Walt. "Any symptoms? Chest pain, dizziness, shortness of breath?"

Walt shook his head quickly. "No, no. I'm fine."

Declan didn't contradict him. Not here. Not like a kid tattling. But he noticed the speed of Walt's denial and how his knee bounced once beneath the paper-draped table, then stopped as if he'd caught himself.

The doctor looked at Declan then, not unkindly. "You drove him, huh?"

Declan nodded.

"Good," the doctor said. "Support matters."

Support. Another word that could mean affection or compliance. Today, Declan heard it as simple: show up.

They scheduled the test. Printed the instructions. Walt folded the paperwork with care, as if neatness could control outcomes. He tucked the papers into his jacket pocket like contraband.

In the hallway after, Walt's shoulders loosened a fraction, like leaving the room counted as victory.

Declan didn't pretend it was.

⁂

In the parking lot, the cold air hit them cleanly. Walt stood by the car, keys in his hand though Declan had driven. A reflex: something to hold that meant he still had agency.

"Alright," Walt said briskly. "That wasn't so bad."

Declan watched him. "Mm-hmm."

Walt opened the passenger door, then paused, one hand on the roof of the car. He stared across the lot at nothing in particular. The crack came quietly, almost by accident—one real thing slipping out because the mask shifted wrong.

"I don't want to be a burden," Walt said.

Not a speech. Not a plea. Just a sentence that landed heavy and plain.

Declan felt the old instinct to soothe—to swat it away with reassurance, to fix the feeling by denying it.

He didn't.

"I know," Declan said.

Walt looked at him sharply, as if expecting a lie and finding respect instead. He swallowed, nodded once, and got into the car.

Declan closed the door gently, like it mattered.

Walt wouldn't accept big help. Declan already knew that. If Declan offered to come over every day, to manage the appointments, to "take care of everything," Walt would react like someone had tried to repossess his dignity.

So Declan offered care in a dialect Walt could live with.

"Pharmacy drive-thru," Declan said as he got in. "You need the new meds."

Walt grunted. "I can get it."

"I'm already here," Declan said. "I'm going that way."

Walt's eyes narrowed—an old man's radar for pity. Declan kept his tone flat, practical. No heroism. No sympathy face. Just logistics.

They went to the pharmacy. Declan handed over the insurance

card before Walt could argue. Walt muttered about prices, about how everything was a scam now. Declan didn't debate it. He watched the pharmacist's gloved hands slide a paper bag across the counter like a small fate.

On the way back, Declan pulled into a grocery store lot.

Walt looked over. "What's this?"

"You're low on food," Declan said. "I saw the fridge last time."

Walt exhaled, annoyed. Then, after a beat: "Just a few things."

It was permission, disguised as conditions.

Inside the store, Walt moved slowly but insisted on pushing the cart. Declan didn't fight him. The wheels squeaked faintly, the sound of friction—something continuing anyway.

Declan grabbed what was needed—oatmeal, bananas, eggs, soup, the kind of groceries that quietly admit you're being watched by time. Walt added coffee, because pride had limits, but not that one.

At checkout, Walt tried to pay.

Declan stopped him with a small motion of his hand, not theatrical. "I've got it."

Walt's jaw tightened. "Declan—"

Declan met his eyes. "It's groceries. Not a eulogy."

Walt's mouth twitched, almost a smile. He let it happen.

That was intimacy in their dialect: tasks instead of feelings. Receipts instead of speeches.

Back at Walt's house, Declan carried the bags in and replaced a lightbulb in the hallway that had been out for weeks. Walt stood beneath it when it came on, squinting like the brightness was rude.

"Look at that," Walt said. "Modern miracles."

Declan smiled. "Try not to get blinded."

Walt snorted. It was the closest thing to gratitude he'd offer without feeling exposed.

Declan didn't ask for more.

※

He left when he was supposed to leave—before care could turn into occupation.

Sequence, again.

At home, Lena was at the table with paperwork spread out: Theo's school forms, a bill, the calendar open like a map. Not in a frantic way—the household's quiet administration.

Declan walked in and didn't hover. He didn't delay. He didn't hide behind small talk.

"There's a follow-up test," he said.

Lena looked up, attentive.

"He's tired," Declan added. He hesitated, then said the sentence he wouldn't have said a few chapters ago, back when he needed to dress fear in sarcasm or silence.

"He's scared. I'm scared."

Lena didn't pounce on it. Didn't demand the narrative. Didn't try to turn it into a sermon about coping.

She made space.

"Okay," she said softly. "Thank you for saying it."

Declan sat down. His shoulders lowered without him asking them to.

Lena slid the calendar toward him. "Do you want to put the test in?" she asked.

Not: Did you remember? Not: I'll handle it. Just an invitation to share the load without making him a child.

Declan nodded. "Yeah."

He wrote the appointment in. Carefully. Legibly. Like it mattered. Like it was real.

Theo came in mid-writing, carrying a toy superhero with one arm missing.

"Dad," Theo said, solemn. "Grandpa's gonna be okay because… we'll monitor."

He said *monitor* like it was a gadget. Like it was a secret weapon. Like it meant control.

Declan looked at him, then at Lena, who watched with quiet steadiness.

"Monitoring means paying attention," Declan said, gentle. "It means we don't pretend we didn't see something. We can pay attention together."

Theo's eyes widened. "Like a team."

"Like a team," Declan agreed.

Daisy wandered into the doorway and sat between rooms as if she'd been assigned the post by a sane god, her presence a small verdict: calm, consistent, unbothered by speeches.

Declan finished writing the appointment. Then he didn't set the calendar down and hope someone else would remember.

He opened his phone. Pulled up the clinic portal. Confirmed the time. Set the next reminder himself. Chosen time, chosen place. No accidental avoidance.

Sequence chosen.

And when the phone chimed its small confirmation, Declan didn't feel heroic.

He felt connected.

※

The ping landed like weather.

Not the obvious kind—the kind you could dress for. This was the tiny, modern kind: a vibration in the pocket that changed the temperature in a room without moving any air.

Declan was standing at the counter trying to make sense of a permission slip Theo had smuggled home in the bottom of his backpack like contraband. The paper was crumpled at the corners, soft from being touched too many times, as if responsibility itself had oils. There was dried glue along one edge where it had once been taped to something and then ripped free. The ink from the school's logo had bled slightly, that cheap printer bleed that made everything feel provisional.

He smoothed it with his palm anyway, the way he always tried to smooth things: flatten the evidence, make the day lie down.

His phone buzzed again.

Group chat.

He didn't even have to look to know what kind of thread it was. The neighborhood one. The work-adjacent one. The "guys" one that was never officially "guys," but always somehow arrived with a tone: camaraderie as cover, joking as a laundering machine. A place where people got to say what they meant, as long as they pretended they didn't.

He tapped the screen.

A video loaded.

A woman crossing a street—tight dress, unaware, filmed from behind. The camera lingered with the lazy confidence of entitlement. Someone had added text across the bottom in a font meant to be cute:

GOD'S MASTERPIECE 🔥

Another message beneath it:

My religion says I can't look away

Then the rest: laughing emojis, a "relax," a GIF of someone fainting, the ritual offering of men pretending to be harmless while they consumed a person. The comments arrived in the familiar cadence of people congratulating one another for not being ashamed.

Declan felt something rise in him—fast and clean. Not sadness. Not confusion. Anger. Righteous and electric, the kind that made him feel tall. The kind that made his spine straighten as if his body had been waiting for a chance to be correct.

He could already feel his thumbs reaching for the perfect sentence. The moral grenade. The one that would detonate across the thread with a satisfying bright flash: *Here is why you're wrong. Here is what you're doing. Here is the part of you that you refuse to see.*

He started typing.

This is predatory. You're filming strangers without consent and calling it religion like that absolves you. You're not funny; you're—

He stopped. Deleted. Drafted again.

You're using "religion" as a joke to excuse objectification, and it's embarrassing.

Delete.

If you think filming women like prey is normal, you need help.

Delete.

His heart was doing that thing it did when he got to be right: speeding up as if the body mistook moral clarity for survival. He could

⁂

taste adrenaline—metallic, like pennies—at the back of his throat. The house around him felt too bright, too exposed, as if even the kitchen light could see the argument forming.

He was still staring at the screen when Theo drifted into the kitchen, socks half on, hair doing its morning protest. The kid moved with the soft drag of someone still half made of sleep, rubbing his eyes as if friction could erase whatever he didn't want to face in the day.

"Dad?" Theo said, voice soft. "What's wrong?"

Declan blinked. "Nothing."

Theo narrowed his eyes the way kids did when they sensed the adult lie—the one adults told because they didn't want to admit they had weather too.

"It's not nothing," Theo said. "You're making your angry face."

Declan almost laughed. "I don't have an angry face."

Theo pointed at him. "That one."

Declan lowered the phone like hiding it made it less real. But Theo's eyes had already flicked to the screen. Theo was collecting language the way he collected rocks—shiny words, strange words, things you held because they felt important when you didn't know why.

Theo read the bold text out loud, slow, sounding each syllable like he was stepping across it.

"God's... masterpiece."

Declan felt his stomach tighten. "Yeah."

Theo frowned. "Is that like... a compliment?"

It was a simple question. It was also a trap, because it demanded a simple answer in a world built to make cruelty look playful.

Declan's mind started sprinting ahead, staging a lecture, building a scaffold of explanation about consent and objectification and how men learned to look without seeing and how jokes were often weapons with smiley faces. He could feel the speech assembling itself—smart, righteous, airtight.

But Theo was standing there in dinosaur pajamas, waiting. Eight years old—young enough that moral truth still fit in a sentence without footnotes. Young enough to believe adults said what they meant.

Declan swallowed.

"It's not a compliment," he said. "It's... people being gross."

Theo's face scrunched. "Why?"

Declan exhaled, slow. The coffee he'd poured earlier had cooled in the mug, forgotten. The kitchen smelled faintly of toast and dish soap and Daisy's warm fur, that clean-unclean smell of a big dog who lived in the house like furniture with a heartbeat.

"Because they're acting like she's not a person," Declan said. "Like she's... just something to look at."

Theo stared at the phone again and then at Declan, as if comparing the world on the screen to the world in the kitchen. "That's inappropriate," he said—pronouncing it carefully, like a word he wanted to be sure he used correctly.

Declan felt something in him shift. Not pride. Not relief. Responsibility.

Theo wasn't listening to Declan's arguments. Theo was learning Declan's reflexes.

Declan looked back down at the thread. New messages had arrived— more emojis, more "lol," more casual hunger. The thread moved with the easy confidence of people who expected no consequence beyond someone else being "too sensitive."

He could still throw the grenade.

He could still perform moral violence in the name of justice.

He could still win.

His thumbs hovered.

Then he remembered Lena in the kitchen months ago, saying: *Don't say the pretty line.* Don't perform. Don't make your righteousness into another way to leave the room.

⁂

He thought of Maloy's office, the way power smiled while it rearranged the air.

He thought of Theo's small face watching him now, collecting the shape of his father's response.

Declan typed a sentence.

Not a sermon. Not a dunk.

A boundary.

Don't share videos/photos of people like that. Not funny.

He hit send before he could add the extra paragraph his ego wanted. Before he could climb onto the stage and perform his own goodness.

For one second, the thread went still.

Then the responses came, predictable as gravity.

Relax.

It's a joke.

My religion says I can't be offended

Wow, sensitive much?

And then the one that made Declan's jaw tighten:

If he didn't like it, don't look. Freedom, brother.

Freedom, brother.

A phrase that meant: I want the freedom to do what I want without the cost of seeing myself. A phrase that pretended consent was a switch you could flip by looking away.

Declan felt his hands shake slightly. That old itch for battle flared again—the desire to reply, to dismantle, to press the argument until someone conceded or the chat burned down. He could already feel the old pleasure of righteous escalation: the way conflict made him feel awake, the way it gave his nervous system a job.

The phone buzzed with a private ping.

Kyle.

Not a neighbor Kyle—work Kyle, the polite-angry one, the man who wore calm like armor.

Careful.

Malloy doesn't like waves.

Declan looked at the message.

It wasn't advice. It was an invocation of law. The office religion: you're allowed to have principles as long as they don't interrupt the hierarchy.

Declan glanced at Theo, who was watching him with the plain curiosity of someone who hadn't yet learned to pretend not to notice tension.

Theo said, "Did you make them stop?"

Declan swallowed. "Probably not."

Theo nodded slowly, taking that in. "But you said it."

"Yes," Declan said. "I said it."

Theo looked down at his own hands, then back up. "Is it hard to say it?"

Declan felt a laugh try to rise and die in his throat. "Yeah," he admitted. "It's hard."

Theo accepted that with a solemnity that made Declan's chest hurt. Then Theo said, casually, as if offering a snack, "Do you want to read my book now?"

Declan blinked again. The bridge book. The one Theo always chose. The one about connection disguised as bedtime. It was morning, not night, but Theo didn't care about the clock. Theo cared about the idea: *stay with me.*

Declan stared at his phone. The thread still flickered with comments. Someone had pasted another GIF. A man cheering. Another man wiping tears of laughter. The usual performance of men reassuring one another they were harmless.

His thumbs itched.

Then he put the phone face-down on the counter like a man placing a weapon out of reach.

⁂

"Yeah," he said to Theo. "Let's read."

Theo climbed onto a chair with the exaggerated effort of a child who believed furniture was mountains. He slid the book across the table like a contract.

Declan opened it and started reading.

A river. A bridge. Boards laid one by one.

He read slowly, trying to keep his voice steady. He could still feel the adrenaline in his system, the moral heat burning behind his ribs. It felt unfair that doing the right thing didn't calm him. It felt unfair that his body still wanted the fight, still wanted the spectacle, still wanted to be seen.

Theo leaned against him, head resting on Declan's upper arm. His small body did what it always did: made Declan's nervous system argue with itself. The part of him that wanted to be elsewhere softened under contact. The part of him that wanted to fight remained, restless.

The phone buzzed again. He ignored it.

After the book, Theo slid off his chair and wandered toward the living room, already forgetting the chat in the way children forgot adult poison. Daisy followed him, nails clicking softly like punctuation, a steady rhythm that said the house was still the house.

Declan stood at the counter, staring at the face-down phone.

He picked it up.

The thread had moved on. Someone had posted a meme about taxes. Another had posted a photo of a grill. A man's dog. The usual pivot: cruelty addressed, then immediately buried under normalcy, like a stain wiped with a damp paper towel.

But Kyle's message remained, sitting there like a warning label.

Careful. Malloy doesn't like waves.

Declan felt his skin prickle.

He wanted to reply to Kyle—*Malloy can eat my whole ass*—but he could already see how that would go, too. Private backlash. Reputation management. The subtle punishment of being labeled "emotional." The slow tightening of the room's oxygen.

The office loved morality when it was decorative. The office hated it when it was structural.

He slid his phone into his pocket and tried to move through the day like a person.

By late afternoon, he still felt charged—like the argument hadn't ended, paused. He drove home with his jaw clenched and his shoulders lifted. He didn't notice he was doing it until he pulled into the driveway and felt his hands ache from gripping the steering wheel like it was steering his whole life.

Inside, the house smelled like dinner and laundry and Theo's unstoppable ability to turn crackers into geography.

Lena looked up from the kitchen when he walked in. Her eyes moved over his face the way Daisy's did—reading weather, not words.

"You did something," Lena said.

Declan blinked. "What?"

"You're lit up," she replied. "Like you're holding a match."

Declan almost smiled at that. Almost. "Group chat."

Lena's mouth tightened. "What now?"

Declan took his phone out and showed her the thread. Not to recruit her to his side. Just… to let her see the world he'd been handed. To let her understand why he felt like he'd walked through smoke.

Lena scanned it quickly. Her expression didn't become dramatic. It became tired in a way that had weight.

"Jesus," she said softly.

"He's not in it," Declan said before he could stop himself. The joke—the reflexive line.

Lena looked at him. A pause. The air sharpened.

"I said something," Declan added quickly. "I didn't just—let it happen."

***

"I know," Lena said. "I can tell. You're vibrating."

Declan felt a flare of defensive pride. *I did the right thing.* He could feel his body wanting credit the way it wanted caffeine.

He said, "I kept it clean."

Lena nodded. "Good."

He waited for praise and felt ashamed for waiting.

He tried to get ahead of it—tried to manage her reaction the way he managed clients, the way he managed Malloy: offer the right words, steer the conversation into a safe lane.

"It's just—" Declan began. "I can't stand that stuff. It's—"

Lena cut in gently. "I know you can't stand it."

Declan paused.

Lena's voice stayed calm. That was the cruel mercy of it: calm meant she was saying something real, not something thrown.

"You're not here yet," she said. "You're still in the thread."

Declan's jaw tightened. "I am here."

Lena didn't argue. She just looked at him, steady. "Your body isn't."

Declan felt the old pattern rise: explain yourself, make it a court case, narrate your stress like evidence. Turn the moment into an argument he could win, because winning felt safer than being known.

He started to do it.

"Kyle messaged me privately. He basically threatened me with Malloy—"

Lena lifted a hand. Not to silence him. To slow him.

"Declan," she said. "I don't want the whole transcript."

He stopped.

She softened just slightly. "I want you."

The sentence landed in him—tender, terrifying. Because "want you" required more than being correct. It required being reachable.

Declan felt his nervous system look for the nearest exit.

Weed.

Not because he was a cartoon stoner. Because his brain ran at an illegal speed and weed could slow it down. It could take the edge off the fight still buzzing in his blood.

He moved toward his bag without thinking. Muscle memory.

Lena watched him do it.

She didn't make it dramatic. She didn't yell. She didn't accuse.

She said, evenly, "If you do that right now, it will feel like you leave me with the aftermath."

Declan froze with his hand half in the zipper.

Lena continued, still calm. "You do the conflict outside, you do the boundary, you do the right thing—then you come home and you disappear. And I'm left holding the residue."

Declan's throat tightened. He felt the reflex to defend himself. *I need to decompress. I'm trying not to explode. You don't know what it's like in my head.*

Instead he did something that felt unfamiliar and therefore dangerous.

He let the truth come out without decoration.

"I want to disappear," he said.

The room went quiet, not like punishment—like a held breath.

Lena's eyes changed. Not pity. Not triumph. Recognition.

"Yeah," she said softly. "I know."

Declan pulled his hand out of the bag, zipped it closed like sealing away a tool he didn't trust himself with.

He stood there, feeling exposed. Unarmored. Not righteous.

Theo wandered in from the living room holding a pencil and a piece of paper. "Mom," he said, "I need you to help me spell 'volcano.'"

Lena opened her mouth, reflexive, ready to handle it, because she always did.

Declan heard himself speak first.

"I've got it," he said.

✳

Lena looked at him. A flicker of surprise. Not because she doubted his competence—because she doubted his presence.

Declan sat at the table with Theo and the paper. Theo perched on the chair like an impatient professor.

"How do you spell volcano?" Theo asked.

Declan leaned over. "V-O-L-C-A-N-O."

Theo wrote it carefully, tongue sticking out in concentration.

Then Theo paused and said, without looking up, "Dad?"

"Yeah?"

Theo asked, as casually as if asking for water, "If someone is mean in a joke, is it still a joke?"

Declan's chest tightened. The question was a small hand reaching into the exact place he'd been scorched.

He could answer like a man trying to be impressive. He could build a lecture, a TED Talk, a sermon about humor and power and cruelty.

Instead he gave Theo what Theo had asked for: clarity.

"No," Declan said. "It's not."

Theo nodded once, satisfied, then returned to his volcano as if morality could be settled like spelling.

Declan glanced up and saw Lena watching.

Her shoulders dropped—a fraction, like someone exhaling without permission.

Declan felt something in him loosen too, a small internal reordering.

Not triumph. Not a moral victory.

Contact.

He stood up, walked to the sink, and started doing dishes without announcing it. No performance. No "look at me being good." Just hands moving, unglamorous, the warm water returning him to his own skin.

Lena didn't stop him. She moved beside him and started wiping down the counter, their motions overlapping in quiet domestic choreography—the kind that only happened when the room wasn't full of hidden knives.

The phone buzzed in Declan's pocket again.

His thumbs twitched with the old hunger: Check it. Answer. Fix. Win.

He didn't.

He left it where it was—a small, living itch.

Theo finished his volcano and held it up. "Look."

Declan smiled. "That's a really good volcano."

Theo beamed. "It's going to erupt."

Lena said, "Of course it is."

Theo grinned and ran back to the living room to build an eruption out of couch cushions and imagination.

Declan stood at the sink, hands wet, and felt the lingering moral heat in his blood cooling into something usable.

He pulled the phone out, looked at the screen, and saw the thread still alive—someone had replied to his boundary hours late:

Damn, Burke. Didn't know you were the joke police.

Another message beneath:

My religion says I can't be policed

Declan stared at it.

His thumbs wanted to answer. Wanted to slice clean. Wanted to win.

He could already feel the old pleasure of righteous anger rising—the substitute tenderness, the drug that made him feel powerful.

Instead, he turned the phone over, face-down again, like a deliberate choice.

He walked into the living room, sat beside Theo, and picked up the book Theo had left on the floor—another bridge, another crossing.

Theo looked up. "Story?"

Declan nodded. "Story."

※

He opened the book and began reading.

His thumbs still itched for battle. His hands stayed on the page—doing something gentler, something real.

In the kitchen behind him, Lena kept moving, quieter now. The house held itself together with small repairs. Daisy lay near Theo's feet, eyes open, monitoring as if she'd been hired by the universe to keep them from drifting too far apart.

Declan read on, letting the story do what stories did: build a structure where the river ran.

And for once, he didn't choose spectacle.

He chose contact.

※

The kitchen was still half-asleep. The kind of quiet that made sound feel rude.

Declan stood at the counter in socks, shoulder blades slightly hunched, performing the morning like it was a contract he could satisfy with the right sequence: grinder lid off, beans poured, lid on, pulse, pulse, pulse. The kettle clicked into its small electric insistence. The mug waited, clean and blank, as if it hadn't already heard him think through the day three times in bed.

Behind him, Daisy's nails made their soft metronome against the hardwood. She paced once, twice, then settled in her usual spot as if guarding the doorway from anything that might try to enter without permission.

Lena moved in the periphery—quiet, competent, barefoot. She was rinsing something, then not, then leaning against the sink like she was watching the weather. Her hair was gathered back in the quick twist she used when she had things to do and didn't want any strand of herself getting snagged.

Her jaw worked once, a small grind of restraint. She pressed her thumb into the inside of her wrist, hard enough to leave a crescent, and then let the hand fall—resetting herself before the day could ask for more.

Theo had not yet detonated the morning. That alone felt like a gift

※

with strings attached.

Declan checked the phone without touching it. The screen was dark. No new notifications. No accidental red badges. No fresh demands dressed up as information. The line between him and the rest of the world was, for the moment, faint—barely there. If he could keep the ritual intact, he could keep the day intact.

He poured the grounds into the filter. The kettle reached a boil and shut off with a sigh that sounded almost human.

He started the pour—slow, clockwise, a thin stream darkening into bloom, a small, controllable storm. The smell rose—bitter, promising, the closest thing to assurance he trusted before 8 a.m.

He lifted the mug for the first sip.

The phone rang.

Not the polite vibration of a text. Not a little chime that asked for entry. A ring was a knock you couldn't ignore. A ring was a hand reaching through the door.

Declan froze, mug halfway to his mouth, and felt the invasion travel up his spine. The coffee trembled slightly in the cup, a dark surface rippling as if it had its own nerves.

It rang again, louder by repetition.

Lena's head turned. Daisy's ears lifted.

Declan set the mug down carefully—as if any sudden motion might cause the call to become worse—and picked up the phone.

Unknown number.

His thumb hovered. In his mind, delay unfurled like a blanket: *If I don't answer, it isn't real yet.*

It rang again.

He answered.

"Hello?"

A pause, then a voice that was not Walt's—worse in the way it didn't belong to their story.

"Is this Declan Burke?"

His name in a stranger's mouth landed like a physical thing. His stomach dropped with the clean certainty of a trapdoor.

"This is," he said, and hated how steady he sounded, as if steadiness could buy safety.

"Mr. Burke, hi—my name is—" she said her name quickly, the way people did when they believed names were paperwork, "—I'm calling from the clinic."

Clinic was a word that tried to sound harmless. It wore beige. It held magazines no one touched. It implied waiting and forms and cheerful posters about prevention.

Declan's free hand gripped the edge of the counter. He looked down at the coffee bloom—dark, expanding, inevitable—and felt a strange anger at how perfectly it kept going.

"Okay," he said. "What's going on?"

"I'm calling regarding your father," the voice said. The way she said *your father* was practiced—careful not to sound dramatic, careful not to sound dismissive. Professional balance, as if balance could keep a body from falling.

Declan turned on speaker without asking. It wasn't bravery; it was a tactic. If he had to hear this, he wanted Lena in the room with him. He wanted proof later that it happened the way it happened, not the way panic edited it.

The sound that spilled into the kitchen wasn't a human story. It was a corridor.

A low hum. A distant PA announcement warped by distance into syllables without meaning. Paper rustling. Someone coughing somewhere down the hall with the wet, casual certainty of a body that did not care who was listening. A cart wheel squeaked—one of those small indignities that had outlived everyone who ever cursed it.

Declan heard mortality the way he heard office printers: relentless, indifferent, always doing its job.

"Your father missed his appointment this morning," the nurse said. "We—he was scheduled for—" a small shuffling, "—a follow-up. He didn't arrive, and we weren't able to reach him on the number we have."

Declan kept his face neutral because his face was where panic liked to perform.

"He missed it," he repeated, not as a question but as an anchor.

"Yes." Another sound: a pen clicking, or perhaps a badge being adjusted. "And there's also a change in some of his recent results. It's not... I don't want to alarm you, but it's important that he come in as soon as possible."

Not catastrophic, his mind tried to label it, like a folder. Just urgent.

But urgency was its own kind of catastrophe. Urgency reordered the day without permission.

"What change?" Declan asked.

"I can't go into full detail over the phone," she said, and he heard the line she was following, the boundary she wasn't allowed to cross. "But the doctor would like to see him. Ideally today. If not today, then tomorrow morning at the latest."

Declan fixed on the coffee dripping through like time refusing to stop for him.

"Okay," he said. "He's... he's not answering his phone. I can go to his house."

There was another pause. In the background, the PA crackled and died. Somewhere, a door opened and closed with the soft finality of a decision.

"Thank you," the nurse said, and her tone softened by one degree—enough to be human. "If you do reach him, please ask him to call us. Or you can call back and we can schedule—"

"Yeah," Declan said. "I'll take care of it."

He ended the call without the nicety of a goodbye. The moment the speaker went silent, the kitchen felt like it had swallowed a different kind of quiet—thicker, heavier, almost loud.

Lena was already moving.

"What did they say?" she asked, not frantic. The question had weight, but her voice didn't add any.

Declan set the phone down like it might ring again out of spite.

"He missed an appointment," he said. "And there's a change in his results. They want him in today."

Lena's jaw tightened once. Not fear, exactly—more like focus arriving. She didn't ask for the story. She didn't ask him to reassure her. She asked, with her whole stance, what needed doing.

"Okay," she said.

Declan exhaled. His chest felt narrow. He looked at Daisy, who was sitting now, watching him with the solemn patience of an animal who understood thresholds.

Theo's feet padded into the kitchen. He appeared in the doorway in pajama pants and a too-big shirt, rubbing one eye like he was erasing sleep with friction.

"Dad?" he said, and then, seeing the shapes on their faces, went quiet.

Declan forced his voice to remain the same size.

"Buddy," he said. "We're going to have a busy morning, okay?"

Theo nodded too quickly—eager, already trying to be helpful before anyone asked.

Declan checked the time. The day's schedule—his clean grid of tasks—fell apart in his mind like paper soaked through.

He didn't let himself stand there and mourn it.

He stepped into the other room, opened his laptop on the table, and pulled up the work chat before his courage could evaporate.

There was a message waiting from Malloy—of course there was.

A check-in about the Mitchell deliverables. A question that pretended to be a question but was a reminder of ownership. Declan could almost hear Malloy's voice in the punctuation, warm and managerial.

Declan didn't type the whole truth. He didn't type clinic or results or today like a blade.

He typed a clean sentence under fire.

I have a family medical situation. I'll be out for a few hours. Mitchell deliverables will be met by end of day; I'll send an update by 3 p.m.

He read it twice. No apology. No drama. No offering of the throat. He hit send.

The typing bubble appeared on Malloy's end almost immediately, like Malloy had been sitting with his fingers poised, waiting for Declan to try to be human so he could correct the tone.

Malloy's reply came in.

Hope everything is ok. Please make sure coverage is in place and that this doesn't slip. Also, try to give more notice next time.

Declan felt something flare—hot, brief.

More notice. As if medical need issued calendars.

He typed back before he could talk himself into politeness.

Coverage is in place. Deliverables will not slip. That's the plan.

He sent it and closed the laptop, not because the work disappeared but because the conversation did. A door shut, an interior boundary asserted.

When he turned back, Lena was already on her phone.

"I'm calling the school," she said. "We'll need someone to pick Theo up if this goes long. Or I can—"

"I can get him," Declan said automatically.

Lena gave him a look that wasn't a challenge—a check.

"Declan," she said gently, like a reminder he could accept. "We can split this."

He heard his own old reflex—control through taking everything on, control through pretending there's time to decide later.

Reality had called first.

He nodded once. "Okay."

They stood in the kitchen like two adults finally agreeing to stop being lonely in the same house.

"Here's what we do," Lena said. No heroics. Just teamwork. "You go to Walt's. I'll get Theo dressed and drop him at school if we can. I'll pack snacks in case you're stuck somewhere. And I'll call the clinic back to get details we're allowed to have."

Declan grabbed his keys, then stopped.

"What about the pharmacy?" he asked. He didn't even know if there was one yet—he just heard *results* and his mind raced ahead to prescriptions, to pick-ups, to waiting lines beneath fluorescent lights.

"We don't know there's a pharmacy yet," Lena said, and the clarity of her sentence steadied him. "One thing at a time."

He nodded again. Sequence over speed.

He called Walt. The line rang.

Once.

Twice.

Three times.

Declan stared at the screen as if he could will an answer.

Voicemail.

He didn't hang up and try again like a teenager. He didn't leave a dramatic message to be proven right later.

He left something simple. Something that wasn't a performance.

"Dad," he said, voice low, controlled. "It's Declan. Call me. I'm coming over. The clinic called. We need you to go in today. Call me."

He ended the call.

Theo came into the kitchen with his sneakers in hand and a serious expression that didn't belong to someone his age.

"I can put my shoes on," he said. It wasn't bragging; it was an offer.

✻

Lena looked at him and softened without collapsing.

"Thank you, love," she said. "Yes, please."

Theo sat on the floor and worked his sneakers on with a level of concentration that made Declan's throat tighten. Theo's fingers fumbled the laces, then tried again. Daisy walked over, nosed Theo's elbow, then sat beside him like a companion assigned.

Theo patted Daisy's head once. "Good girl," he said in a voice that sounded like Declan's.

Role swap beginning, quiet as a tide.

Declan watched his son repeat adult phrases, attempt adult tasks, become strangely calm—as if the house had taught him that emergencies were weather and the best you could do was put on a coat.

Declan crouched beside Theo.

"Hey," he said. "You're doing great."

Theo looked up. "Is Grandpa okay?"

Declan didn't lie big. He also didn't pour fear into a child like it was honesty.

"We're going to check on him," Declan said. "And make sure he goes where he needs to go."

Theo nodded, absorbing the plan like a small soldier.

Declan stood. The keys felt heavy in his hand. The day—the other day, the one he'd been building—was gone. In its place was a narrow corridor of tasks that demanded doing in the present tense.

He moved toward the door.

Lena was at the threshold already, steady. Not stoic—steady. She held Theo's backpack strap in one hand, her phone in the other. Daisy stood between them, looking out as if the outside had personally offended her.

Declan paused with his hand on the knob.

He didn't sprint mentally ahead. He didn't rehearse every worst outcome like a ritual offering.

He chose action without theater.

One thing. Then the next.

He opened the door. Cold air rushed in. Daisy stepped forward, then looked back at him for permission.

Declan nodded once.

Theo watched from behind Lena's leg, calm in the way children get when they realize the adults are trying, finally, to be adults.

Declan stepped out, shut the door gently behind him, and went.

⁂

Declan turned onto Walt's street and felt the familiar suburban geometry clamp around him: the same curb lines, the same tasteful mailboxes, the same lawns clipped into quiet obedience. Nothing here looked urgent. That was the trick. Urgency didn't change siding or porch posts. It moved in.

Walt's driveway appeared like it always did—two hairline cracks running up the concrete, parallel as old arguments. Declan pulled in without ceremony. No dramatic pause, no steering-wheel stare. He shut off the engine. The ticking heat of the car settling felt indecently normal.

The house sat back with a stubborn posture. Shutters that needed paint. A porch light that flickered when it felt like it. Steps worn in the center. A storm door that never latched. The lawn wasn't overgrown—unloved. Maintained the way you maintain a sentence he didn't believe in anymore: enough to pass, never enough to change.

Declan stepped out and took it in the way you take in a face you've known too long to see. A biography in deferred maintenance. A life built around not needing anyone.

He carried a pharmacy bag in one hand and a paper grocery sack in the other—bananas, bread, soup, peanut butter. Sick-house staples. He hated that his body already knew. Hated more that he didn't.

Before he reached the steps, the front door opened.

Walt stood in the frame like he'd been waiting so he could control the moment, already wearing the version of himself that didn't ask for anything.

"Well, look who's here," Walt said, bright and defensive. "You bring the marching band too or just the federal government?"

Declan didn't smile. Not because humor was gone, but because humor was a barricade and he was done negotiating with barricades.

"They called," Declan said.

Walt waved a hand, shooing the sentence away. "They call everybody. That's how they keep the lights on."

Declan lifted the grocery sack slightly, like a receipt.

"I'm coming in," he said.

Walt's eyes flicked to the bags, then back to Declan's face. Irritation flashed—pure, almost youthful—the reflex of a man who still believed he could refuse by making it unpleasant.

Then Walt did the thing he'd always done: made room and turned compliance into choice.

"Fine," he said. "But if you start rearranging my kitchen like it's a TV show, I'm calling the police."

Declan walked inside as if the argument had already been settled by reality.

The house smelled the same—coffee that had sat too long, dust warmed by forced air, the faint medicinal edge of something kept out of sight. The living room looked preserved, not lived in. Remote in its trough on the recliner arm. Magazines stacked like a leaning tower of deferred interest. Calendar on the wall with dates crossed off in Walt's heavy hand, as if time could be managed by marking it.

Declan set the bags on the counter and turned.

Walt was behind him, trying to appear casual. It almost worked until Declan noticed the pauses: the small delay as Walt shifted weight, the way he stood like he was listening for his own balance to report in.

※

His hands were thinner. Not fragile—Walt had always been bone and tendon—but thinner in a way that made his ring look like it belonged to someone else. The skin at his knuckles had a faint paper quality.

Declan clocked it all without comment.

The body was the plot now. There was no skipping ahead.

Walt caught him looking and moved immediately to reroute it.

"You getting sleep?" Walt said. "You look like hell."

Declan nodded once. "Not much."

Walt leaned into the insult like an old joke. "That's parenthood. You're learning."

Declan didn't take the bait. "They said you missed your appointment."

Walt shrugged. "Didn't miss it. I rescheduled it in my head."

Declan waited. Silence was sometimes the only language Walt respected.

Walt exhaled slowly, controlled, the way you breathe when he didn't want anyone to notice you're counting.

"I didn't feel like going," Walt said, clipped at the end, as if annoyed by the fact of having said it.

"They want you in today," Declan said.

Walt's jaw tightened. "They always want me in. They want me in, they want blood, they want to poke me, they want to talk to me like I'm a toddler who wandered off."

Declan didn't argue about attitude. He stayed on task.

"Eat something," he said, sliding the grocery sack forward.

Walt snorted. "Now you're my mother."

Declan set the pharmacy bag beside the groceries. "I'm your son."

Something flickered across Walt's face—recognition of a truth he didn't like being reminded of. He covered it immediately.

"Great," Walt said. "Then you can do that thing you do—fix three random things in my house and pretend it isn't emotional."

Declan looked at him. "Okay."

Walt blinked, thrown for half a second. He'd expected a protest. An argument. A speech.

Declan moved through the house like a man doing inventory. Porch light first. Smoke detector chirping with a low-battery complaint Walt had trained himself to ignore. Cabinet door that stuck because the hinge had loosened and the screw had been turning in place for months.

He changed a bulb. He swapped the battery. He tightened the hinge with the screwdriver from the junk drawer—the same junk drawer as always, full of rubber bands that had died and pens that didn't write.

He found the prescription organizer on the kitchen table and filled it with careful attention, hating how quickly he'd learned the pattern. Morning, noon, night. Like feeding a machine that ran on pills and stubbornness.

Task by task. Intimacy by clipboard.

Walt hovered in the doorway, refusing "help" as a concept but accepting it when it wore the costume of chores—each one small enough to pretend it didn't count.

Then the doorbell rang.

Walt stiffened like he'd been caught doing something private in front of a mirror.

Declan opened the door.

Mrs. Hargrove from two houses down stood on the porch holding a foil-wrapped loaf. She smiled the way people smiled when they wanted to be seen smiling.

"Oh, Declan," she said, eyes widening just enough to advertise concern. "We heard—well, we didn't hear it directly, but you know. People talk. How's Walt doing?"

Behind her, the street looked empty and ordinary. Yet Declan felt observed, as if the neighborhood had become a room with too many windows.

"We're handling it," Declan said.

Mrs. Hargrove's smile tightened. "We've got folks praying," she added quickly, and the words landed with weight that wasn't comfort. Surveillance dressed as virtue.

Walt appeared behind Declan, too close, tension radiating.

"I'm not dead," Walt called out, too loud, too cheerful. "Unless you know something I don't."

Mrs. Hargrove laughed—high, obligated. "Oh, Walt, don't you say that. We just care."

Declan heard Malloy in the cadence: concern as a harvest. Care that wanted a report.

"Thank you," Declan said, taking the loaf without letting it become a conversation. "We appreciate it."

Mrs. Hargrove hesitated, hungry for a detail she could carry home like a prize.

Declan didn't feed her.

When the door closed, Walt's breath came out sharp.

"I hate this," Walt said. "The neighborhood hospice committee."

"They mean well," Declan said, automatically.

"No," Walt said, sharp. Then softer, almost to himself: "They mean to watch."

Declan didn't correct him. Some truths didn't need correction. They needed holding—quietly, without turning them into a sermon.

Declan's phone buzzed on the counter.

Lena: Theo with me. Dropping him at school now. I called the clinic—doctor wants Walt in today. Can you get him there? I can meet you if needed.

Declan read it twice. Not because it was complicated, but because it was steady. Lena's invisible scaffolding: logistics without martyrdom, care without narration.

He typed back: Yes. I'll take him. Keep Theo normal. I'll update after.

Walt watched him text.

"Lena running the war room?" Walt said, attempting lightness.

"She's handling Theo," Declan said. "So you and I can handle you."

Walt opened his mouth for a joke and closed it. The joke didn't fit.

A minute later the front door opened again—Lena must have doubled back for something, or Theo had forgotten his folder. Theo stepped in with his backpack on, sneakers tied wrong but tied, face unusually serious.

He saw Walt and stopped.

"Hi, Grandpa," Theo said.

Walt's face softened one millimeter. One. Enough for Declan to notice, not enough for Walt to tolerate.

"Well, hello," Walt said, reaching for humor like a coat. "You here to lecture me about vitamins?"

Theo shook his head. He walked closer and held out a small plastic dinosaur—a scuffed triceratops with blunted horns.

"You can have him," Theo said. "He's strong."

Declan felt his throat tighten. Theo was offering strength like a tool. Like a charm. Like he'd learned——that emergencies could be negotiated with objects.

Walt stared at the dinosaur, then took it carefully, as if it might crack.

"Strong, huh?" Walt said, voice quieter.

Theo nodded. "I can be good."

Walt's eyes flicked up to Declan and away. Emotion tried to enter. Walt blocked it with a grin.

"Don't be too good," he said. "You'll ruin your reputation."

Theo didn't laugh, but he looked relieved. The script had returned: help quietly; don't make it emotional.

Lena stood behind Theo, one hand on Theo's shoulder, the other already holding her phone.

"I have to get him to school," she said to Declan, then to Walt, "Hi, Walt."

"Lena," Walt said, and managed something that resembled gratitude without using the word.

Declan watched them—no speeches, no declarations—bodies coordinating in a shared direction. This was what functioning looked like. The unglamorous competence of people choosing to be a team.

Lena bent to Theo. "Okay, love. Time."

Theo looked at Walt. "Bye."

Walt lifted the dinosaur slightly. "I'll keep him on duty."

Theo nodded, satisfied, and left with Lena as if leaving was part of the plan and not a betrayal.

When the door closed, the house went still again.

Walt set the dinosaur on the table like a paperweight on a document he didn't want to sign.

"Don't rearrange your life for this," Walt said suddenly, almost angry. The sentence came out too fast, like it had been waiting behind his teeth. "You've got a kid. You've got work. You've got—" he waved at the air, at the shape of Declan's life, "—you've got your stuff."

Declan looked at him. Walt's eyes were bright, but not with tears—more like irritation at being seen.

"I hate being monitored," Walt added, quieter. "Feels like everyone's waiting."

Waiting for the ending, he didn't say. But the word sat in the room anyway.

Declan let it hang there. He didn't rush in with comfort. Comfort could feel like condescension when a man was trying to remain himself.

"It's not rearranging," Declan said. Clean. Even. "It's showing up."

Walt's mouth tightened. He looked toward the living room, toward the preserved objects, as if the furniture might rescue him.

Declan picked up his keys. "Coat. Shoes. We're going."

Walt didn't move for a moment. Then he sighed—older than his jokes.

"Fine," he said. "But if they poke me, I'm—yeah. I'm poking them back."

Declan nodded as if this were a reasonable medical policy.

They left together. Walt insisted on locking the door himself, fingers slower on the key than he wanted them to be. In the driveway the cold air hit his face and he paused, long enough to recalibrate.

Declan didn't offer an arm. He offered time.

Walt walked to the car. Declan opened the passenger door. Walt sat carefully, as if negotiating with his body. He buckled the seatbelt without looking at Declan.

Declan started the engine and pulled out.

In the rearview mirror, the house shrank: porch, stubborn door, the biography of deferred maintenance receding into neat suburban distance.

At the end of the driveway, Declan glanced back.

Walt stood in the doorway.

Not waving. Not calling out. Just standing there too long, like he didn't want to be seen needing—but also didn't want to go back inside alone.

Declan drove away and felt a thought settle, calm and grim, like a truth he could no longer postpone:

Avoidance isn't neutral.

It's a kind of abandonment with good manners.

※

The first thing Declan saw when he opened his laptop was not work.

It was a calendar invite.

Quick Sync — 15 minutes
Organizer: Malloy Mercer
Attendees: Declan Burke, Kyle Noland

No agenda. No context. Just the bright, clean euphemism of urgency with a smile stapled to it.

Declan looked at the subject line the way you stare at a note on your windshield—small, polite, and unmistakably meant to move you. The kind of language that pretended to be harmless because it was written in corporate baby-talk instead of blood.

His inbox refreshed. More messages stacked in, all of them wearing their own soft masks: *Circling back. Touching base. Friendly reminder.* The euphemism was the knife. Everyone knew it. Everyone pretended they didn't.

He clicked open Mitchell's thread before he clicked anything else. He'd learned to do that the way you check the stove after you leave the house: not because you forgot, but because forgetting had consequences.

Mitchell had replied overnight.

Appreciate the structure. This is the first time I've understood the next steps without needing a call.

Two things: can you standardize this format for the full workstream? Also, can you send me a "weekly status cadence" template so I can mirror it on my end?

Declan read it twice, the way you reread praise when you don't trust it. The structure worked. Mitchell, impossible Mitchell, had responded to a system like it was a rope thrown over deep water.

And now he wanted more rope.

Declan felt the labor show itself, plain and unromantic. Kindness as infrastructure wasn't a vibe; it was time. It was building something sturdy enough that other people could stand on it without noticing the person holding the beams.

He drafted a reply—short, clear, deliverable-minded. He could do that. He'd built an entire personality around doing that.

Then his calendar pinged again, as if the machine had to remind him who had priority.

Quick Sync — starting in 12 minutes.

Declan's chest tightened—not panic, not fear. Recognition. The same recognition he'd had in Walt's kitchen when the smoke detector chirped: this sound will not stop until you answer it, and it will not care what it costs you.

He stood, made coffee, and drank it too fast. A ritual shortened into a function. He listened to the house: the muted clack of Lena's mug in the sink, Theo's small footsteps upstairs, Daisy's nails on the floor as she repositioned herself—not following, not leading, simply making sure no one was alone by accident.

When he sat down again, Daisy settled in the doorway between the kitchen and the hall, a warm, watchful mass. Like a bouncer for feelings.

Declan clicked into the meeting.

Malloy appeared first, centered in his frame with the calm efficiency

⁂

of a man who believed stress was a failure of character. Kyle joined seconds later, camera on, posture upright, expression carefully neutral—the face you wore when you wanted to look concerned without being contaminated by concern.

"Morning," Malloy said. "Thanks for hopping on."

Declan didn't correct the word *hopping*. He wasn't a rabbit.

"Morning," he said.

Kyle nodded, then smiled faintly, as if they were three people who happened to share a meeting instead of two people being watched by a third.

Malloy folded his hands. "So. Quick check-in. Where were you yesterday afternoon?"

The question landed cleanly, like a paperweight. Not accusatory in tone. Accusatory in function.

Declan kept his face steady. He had learned something over the last week: the institution didn't need your guilt. It needed your details.

"I had a family medical situation," Declan said. "I notified you I'd be out for a block of hours. The Mitchell deliverables were met by end of day."

Malloy nodded slowly, the way people nodded when they were turning your words into a record.

"Right," Malloy said. "And is this... ongoing?"

There it was. The appetite. Not for empathy—for timeline.

Declan heard the hidden question underneath it: *How long will your private life inconvenience us?* He also heard the second, more dangerous one: *How much can we use later?*

Kyle leaned in slightly, offering his face as help.

"People are noticing," Kyle said gently. "Just looking out. There's been... chatter. Perception stuff. You know how it is."

Perception. The old language. The word that meant: We're not discussing reality. We're discussing optics.

Declan felt something harden, not in anger—something steadier. A spine.

"I'm not available for speculation," Declan said, still calm. "If there's a performance concern, name it."

A beat.

Malloy blinked once, as if Declan had spoken in a dialect he didn't expect.

"No, no," Malloy said quickly, smiling with managerial warmth. "No performance concern. We just want to ensure you have what you need."

Declan watched him do it—the pivot from interrogation to care. The same hand, different glove.

"What I need," Declan said, "is to keep work scoped to work. I'll meet my commitments. If there's any impact to timelines, you'll know in advance. For now: no adjustment is required."

Kyle's smile tightened. He looked briefly down and back up—the micro-movement of someone who'd been denied a role.

Malloy nodded again. "Okay. Okay. Appreciate that."

Then Malloy's tone changed by a degree—still friendly, now administrative.

"One more thing," he said. "We're going to redistribute a portion of the Mitchell comms. Just to create coverage. Kyle will be included on the thread and handle interim updates if you're unavailable."

Kyle's expression went blankly pleased. Not triumphant—disciplined. He'd auditioned for loyalty and been cast.

Declan understood the move instantly. It wasn't coverage. It was a leash. A way to make his absence visible, his autonomy permeable.

"Understood," Declan said.

Malloy smiled wider, relieved the friction had been swallowed.

"And we'll send a quick recap," Malloy added, as if this were a gift.

A report about the report.

※

The call ended with the usual polite choreography—thanks, talk soon, appreciate you. The kind of language that left no fingerprints.

Declan sat still for a moment, staring at his own reflection in the black rectangle of the monitor. He felt the consequence arrive the way weather arrives: not dramatic, inevitable.

Polite punishment.

Administrative cruelty.

He opened the email recap when it arrived two minutes later.

Action items:

- Add Kyle to Mitchell comms for coverage and visibility
- Declan to provide weekly status cadence template by EOD
- Declan to flag any anticipated absences in advance

Visibility. Coverage. Cadence. Words that sounded like professionalism and operated like surveillance.

He went back to Mitchell's email and replied with the template, because the work still mattered, and because Mitchell—oddly—had become a moral counterweight. Someone who responded to clarity like it was oxygen. Someone who punished vagueness with chaos and rewarded structure with cooperation.

Declan sent the file and wrote:

Happy to standardize—here's a version you can reuse. I'll keep it consistent.

Then he did what he always did. He worked.

Hours passed in clean blocks: messages, revisions, a call that he kept crisp. Kyle chimed in on the thread with enough helpfulness to be applauded, enough presence to make Declan's absence a story. Kyle's sentences were always a hair too polished, like a man wiping down a counter while you watched—performing cleanliness, advertising control.

Declan watched it happen without flinching. Flinching would be giving it drama. He didn't have extra drama to donate.

By late afternoon, he closed his laptop and sat quietly for a moment, feeling the day's weight in his wrists and eyes. He wasn't sad. He was depleted in the way a battery was depleted—still functional, dimmer.

When he walked through the front door, he didn't announce the day as a tragedy. He didn't unload it onto Lena like a sack of wet cement.

Lena was at the kitchen counter, shoulders tense but moving, a meal happening by force of will. Theo's voice drifted from the living room, narrating something to Daisy as if she were a co-conspirator. Daisy lay with her head up, listening to two rooms at once.

Declan set his bag down.

He looked at Lena and asked one useful question.

"What needs doing right now?"

Lena exhaled—not a sigh, more like a release. She didn't thank him. She didn't perform relief. She answered like an adult who had decided not to be lonely in the same house.

"The forms," she said. "And Theo's lunch for tomorrow. And... can you call the clinic back? They left another message."

Declan nodded. "Okay."

He washed his hands. He made Theo's lunch. He sat at the table with the forms and filled in the boxes the way you fill in boxes when you'd rather be anywhere else. He called the clinic back and took notes in a steady voice, not offering explanations, not asking for permission to be a son.

All of it unglamorous. All of it real.

At some point, Daisy stood and moved to the threshold between the living room and kitchen, body angled so she could see both spaces. Not anxious. Just present. As if she'd appointed herself the house's quiet monitor—not of performance, but of people.

Declan noticed and felt something soften in him—not sentiment, something truer.

The dog did what he kept calling "calm."

She didn't theorize it. She didn't optimize it.

She stayed.

And Declan, watching her, understood with a strange clarity that staying was not passive. It was a choice. It was work. It was the only kind of report that mattered.

⁂

The text arrived the way kindness often arrived now—bright, uninvited, and impossible to ignore without looking like the villain.

Hi Declan—this is Marjorie Lasky from St. Brigid's Community Care.

We've been thinking about your dad. I'm checking in. We're here for your family.

Could I stop by today? Even five minutes.

Declan read it once. Then again, slower, as if the second pass might reveal the hook.

It was warm. It was reasonable. It was the kind of message you were supposed to be grateful for.

And it was porous.

He didn't answer right away. He set his phone down on the counter like it was hot. The coffee machine hissed in its small, predictable way. The marker line inside his mug—today's reduced ritual, the last thin inch of control—stared back at him like a rule he hadn't agreed to but had followed anyway.

Outside, the sky had that winter brightness that didn't warm anything—blue and sharp, as if the sun was ornamental. The window glass was cold when he leaned near it, and he caught his own reflection: unshaven, eyes too alert. He looked like a man bracing for impact in a room where nothing was falling.

Lena came in from the hallway with her hair still damp, moving with that morning economy that meant she'd already done three things without announcing any of them. She had Theo's lunchbox in one hand and a folded permission slip in the other, as if the household produced papers the way trees produced leaves.

"Who's that?" she asked, nodding at the phone.

Declan didn't pick it up. "Church," he said. "Community care."

Lena made a face that wasn't disdain, exactly—more like recognition. The look you give a flyer taped to your door handle.

"What do they want?" she asked.

Declan exhaled through his nose. "Help."

"Mm," Lena said, and the sound carried a whole syllabus.

Upstairs, Theo was narrating something to Daisy—his voice doing its bright, earnest thing, as if the world could be kept safe through commentary. Daisy's tail thumped once against the wall: her standard acknowledgment, her version of *I'm here*.

Declan fixed on the text again.

Could I stop by today?

His mind did what it always did with these questions: it began building a courtroom. Evidence, arguments, the perfect phrasing. He could already feel his tongue forming a polite refusal that would also be a performance of gratitude—an offering to soften the boundary so it wouldn't count as one.

He didn't want to do that anymore. He didn't want to give away the clean part.

He typed back before he could overthink it.

Thanks, Marjorie. We're okay. We're keeping things private right now.

A moment passed. Then the typing bubbles appeared—those little three dots that turned a polite boundary into a live negotiation.

Of course, honey. Totally understand.
We want to make sure you're supported.
How is Walt doing?

There it was. *Really.* The word people used to make curiosity sound like virtue.

Declan felt a familiar nausea bloom behind his ribs. Not because he was ashamed—because he recognized the mechanism. The same mechanism as Malloy's *ongoing?* The same soft, careful questions that converted your life into a file.

He didn't reply.

The doorbell rang.

Not urgent. Not aggressive. The gentle, hopeful press of someone who believed they were doing the right thing.

Lena's eyes met his for half a second. No discussion. No "should we." Just a quiet, shared calculation. The kind couples learned when they'd had to keep a child safe in public spaces: quick assessment, unified front.

Declan went to the door.

Marjorie stood on the stoop holding a covered casserole dish like it was evidence of moral character. She was in her late fifties, hair set, scarf knotted neatly, smile practiced into something almost permanent. Behind her—visible, significant—a minivan idled at the curb as if she might be collecting returns.

"Declan!" she said, voice pitched high with affection they hadn't earned. "Oh, sweetheart."

She leaned in slightly, the first move of a hug that assumed consent.

Declan stepped out instead, keeping the threshold between them. Not hostile. Just placed. The cold air hit his cheeks and made the moment feel clearer, less domestic, less negotiable.

"Hi," he said. "Thanks for dropping something off."

Her smile brightened at the word *thanks.* Gratitude was the currency

※
✱✱

she dealt in.

"We've all been praying," she said, and lifted the dish a fraction, as if prayer needed a prop. "I wanted you to have something he didn't have to think about."

"That's kind," Declan said. He took the casserole and held it with both hands. It was warm through the foil. He felt the heat like a small accusation: *See? We care.*

Marjorie's gaze slid past him into the house, searching for the story inside.

"How's Lena holding up?" she asked, already peering. "And little Theo... I can't imagine. And Walt—sweet Walt. What's really going on with Walt?"

Declan kept his face neutral. He could almost hear Malloy's voice: *Just a quick check-in.* The same cadence, different uniform.

"We're handling it," Declan said.

Marjorie tilted her head with sympathetic intensity. "Well, of course. But you know... sometimes people think they have to be strong alone. And that's when the enemy gets in."

Declan's jaw tightened. *Enemy.* The melodrama of it. Like illness was a moral event, like suffering was a door you left unlocked.

From behind him, Theo padded into the hallway, drawn by the doorbell like a magnet. Daisy followed, positioning herself in the angle between the kitchen and the entry—her silent habit of monitoring.

Theo came to Declan's side and looked up at Marjorie with wide, polite eyes. Then, as if reading from a script he didn't know he'd memorized, he said, clearly:

"That's not appropriate."

Declan froze.

Theo's voice was so adult, so borrowed, that it felt like a ventriloquist act. Declan saw, in a flash, all the small deflections that had become household habits: *Nothing big. We're fine. Don't worry.* The way they'd tried to keep Theo safe by making reality smaller than it was.

Marjorie blinked, smile wobbling at the edges. "Oh!" she said, laugh too quick. "Well, aren't you the little gentleman."

Theo nodded once, solemn. "We don't talk about that."

Declan felt something split in him—rage and tenderness, both looking for the same exit.

Walt's boundaries, it hit him, were an inheritance. Not genetics. Training.

Marjorie recovered, turning back to Declan with a softer face that had a faint steel underneath it. "It's just that people worry," she said. "We want to make sure you're surrendering it to God."

The word *surrender* landed wrong—like compliance dressed up as holiness. Like the only kind of faith that counted was the kind that made you easier to manage.

Declan held the casserole, felt its weight, and chose a sentence the way you choose a tool: simple, correct, not decorative.

"Thank you," he said. "We're handling it privately."

Marjorie's smile tightened. "But privacy can isolate," she said, still sweet. "And sometimes families don't realize they're drowning until—"

"I'm not going to discuss Walt's health," Declan said, evenly.

The air shifted.

Not dramatic. Just a subtle cooling, like a thermostat had been adjusted.

Marjorie's eyes narrowed a fraction. The mask didn't fall off so much as rotate—same face, different function.

"We're only trying to help," she said, voice still gentle but now edged with the faintest reprimand. "People feel shut out."

Declan didn't bite. He didn't justify. He didn't explain. Explanations were the slippery slope into confession.

"If you want to help," he said, "meals are concrete. Or rides to appointments. That's what we can accept."

※

Marjorie blinked again, as if the lack of emotional spectacle disappointed her. Help, she wanted, was a doorway. Declan was offering her a delivery window.

Behind him, Lena appeared in the hallway. She didn't step forward like a shield. She simply existed there—steady, present, an adult in the room who didn't need to perform alliance.

"Hi, Marjorie," Lena said calmly.

Marjorie's smile flared, relieved to have another audience. "Oh, Lena. Dear. I was just—"

"We appreciate the food," Lena said, polite as a closing statement. "Thank you for thinking of us."

Marjorie looked between them, measuring. Two people. No cracks.

She tried again, softer. "Tell Walt we love him," she said. "And we're here. If he'd just... open up. Sometimes people need to—"

Declan interrupted gently, which was its own kind of aggression. "We will," he said. "Thanks for coming by."

He closed the door without apology. Not slammed—finished.

Marjorie's smile held for one last second, and then, like a curtain slipping, her expression sharpened into something faintly disappointed.

"Alright," she said, too brightly. "Well. We'll keep you in prayer."

The minivan at the curb rolled forward as she walked to it.

Declan watched her go, casserole still warm in his hands, and felt the adrenaline spike that came after resisting a polite invasion. His nervous system wanted release. He wanted a rant. He wanted to step outside and smoke until the day blurred at the edges.

Instead he walked to the sink.

He set the casserole down. He picked up his coffee mug. The marker line inside it—his daily measure—had already begun to fade, the black ink bleeding into the porcelain like doctrine being revised by water.

He turned on the faucet.

The sound of running water filled the kitchen, steady and indifferent.

It grounded him the way nothing else did. A task with an end. A boundary you could see.

Theo hovered beside him, still solemn, as if he'd done something important and wasn't sure if it was wrong.

Declan rinsed the mug, watching the ink dissolve.

"Hey," he said quietly to Theo.

Theo looked up. "Was she being nosy?"

Declan almost laughed—Theo's little New England bluntness, the tiny jab of humor that made the world bearable. But it wasn't funny, not really.

"She was trying to help," Declan said. "And also… yes. A little nosy."

Theo considered this, then asked the question that always arrived like a pin finding a balloon.

"Is Grandpa gonna die?"

Declan's throat tightened. The confessional he refused at the door was now sitting at his sink in dinosaur pajamas, eyes honest as headlights.

He didn't flinch away. He didn't minimize.

"Grandpa's sick," Declan said. "We don't know what happens yet. Sometimes things are big. We can talk about big things without panicking."

Theo nodded slowly, absorbing it like a new rule.

"Okay," he said. Then, after a beat: "Can Daisy come with us if we have to go fast?"

Daisy lifted her head at her name, ears perked, as if volunteering.

Declan looked at her—this animal who didn't ask questions, didn't demand explanations, didn't harvest details. She stayed close enough to matter.

"We'll figure it out," Declan said to Theo. "One thing at a time."

Theo leaned in and pressed his forehead briefly to Declan's arm, then stepped back like it hadn't happened.

⁎⁎⁎

Declan turned the phone face-down on the counter.

The water kept running.

The marker line vanished completely.

And Declan stood there in the clean, ordinary noise of the kitchen, surprised by how much refusing to confess felt like rebellion—how, in a world built to extract you, saying no could be its own quiet kind of care.

※

The mug was still damp from yesterday. Declan held it under the faucet and watched the inside of it—what had been a crisp black marker line now softened into a gray bruise, as if the porcelain had learned what bodies learned: nothing stays sharp for long.

He dried it with the corner of a dish towel. The marker sat on the counter like an instrument waiting for a verdict.

He drew the line again out of habit—then stopped halfway through, tip hovering. The old line had been a moat: *this much coffee, this much space, this much me before the world reaches in.* A private superstition dressed up as self-care.

He lowered his hand.

He didn't draw it.

He poured the coffee until it was—what it was. Warm. Too much. Maybe not enough. Not measured. Not defended. The smell rose like a small forgiveness, bitter and familiar, the kind of comfort that didn't pretend to solve anything.

Behind him, the house had already started without his permission.

Theo was loud in the way only seven-year-olds could be—full-volume narration, a running broadcast of the immediate. He was building something out of blocks and declaring it a "security tower," which meant he'd been listening again. Lena moved through the kitchen with the quiet, competent speed that made Declan feel both grateful and slightly ashamed; she could do three things at once without naming any of them. Daisy stationed herself between the kitchen and the hallway, her body angled like a union rep for everyone's nervous system: *I'm here. I'm watching. Nobody collapses alone.*

Declan didn't ask for ten minutes.

He chose one thing—one—and did it.

The folder.

The one that had become their household's new sacred object: Walt's forms, appointment summaries, prescription lists, the awkward stack of institutional paper that turned a person into a case. Declan slid it into a tote bag, added a pen, added the pharmacy receipt, added the sticky note Lena had written last night: **Ask about dosage change.**

He clipped Theo's lunchbox shut. The click felt like an accomplishment. He tucked an extra granola bar into the side pocket the way you tuck a spare tire into a trunk: not dramatic, just acknowledging the world's tendency to surprise you.

He turned, coffee in hand—and his phone rang.

Not a text. Not a notification he could swipe away and pretend didn't count.

A ring. A demand.

He stared at the screen:

WALT.

For a second his body tried its old move—delay as control. Let it go to voicemail. Let it become a message. Let it be later. Let it be safe.

Then he answered because the house was already moving and postponement no longer matched the moment.

"Hey, Dad," he said, voice plain, not warmed up. "I'm here."

On the other end: breath, faint static, a room tone. Then Walt's voice—too casual to be casual.

"Morning," Walt said. "They want me in today."

Declan's stomach tightened. "Who's *they*."

"The clinic," Walt said. Then, quickly: "It's nothing. Just... follow-up. They bumped it up."

The phrase *bumped it up* landed like a shove.

Declan glanced at Lena. She didn't ask questions. She read his face like it was a headline.

"Okay," Declan said into the phone. "What time?"

"Eleven."

"It's nine," Declan said, already counting minutes like a man counting steps across ice. "Can you drive?"

A pause—small, loaded.

"I can," Walt said. "I just—"

"I'll drive," Declan said. Not sharp. Not pleading. Not negotiable. "I'm leaving in ten."

Walt exhaled, a sound that was almost a joke and almost not. "You didn't need to—"

Declan didn't argue the need. He didn't litigate dignity. He simply moved the day into sequence.

"I'll be there," he said. "Hold tight."

He ended the call and turned the phone face-down on the counter the way you put down a tool you might want to misuse.

Lena was already at the fridge, already scanning what could be made into dinner later, already doing the invisible math of a household.

"I can do school," she said. Not heroically. Factually.

Declan grabbed the tote bag, keys, jacket. "Can you text me Theo's pickup info if things shift?"

"I will," Lena said.

Theo—sensing something in the speed of adults—quieted. He watched Declan with a strangely careful face, as if he'd learned that sometimes the air changed before anyone explained why.

※

"Are you going somewhere fast?" Theo asked.

Declan crouched, zipped Theo's coat with fingers that felt too big and too clumsy for the job. The zipper snagged once; he steadied it, tried again. "Yes," he said. "But not scary-fast. Just... schedule-fast."

Theo nodded as if the pattern snapped into focus—the difference between panic and motion.

Daisy's tail tapped the floor once, then she followed Declan to the door. He scratched the top of her head—brief, grounding—and she stayed, watching him go like a sentry who didn't get to ride along.

Walt's driveway looked the same as it always had: suburban geometry, concrete, winter-pale grass. But today it carried a different weight, like a familiar song played in a minor key.

Walt came out before Declan could knock, already performing.

"You're early," Walt said, smiling as if this were a favor Declan had done for himself.

Declan didn't correct him. He took Walt's tote bag—lighter than it should've been—and guided him toward the passenger side as if they'd agreed on this years ago.

"I'm fine," Walt said, getting in. "You didn't have to drop everything."

Declan started the car. "I didn't," he said. "I moved things around. That's what people do."

Walt's mouth twitched, unhappy with the word *people*. He wanted to be an exception. He wanted to be the father who didn't need.

As Declan backed out, he clocked Walt's hands: one on his thigh, the other gripping the door handle like it was a rail on a moving train. Not fear exactly. Control pretending it was comfort.

They did small talk because it was the only bridge they knew how to walk without falling through.

Traffic. Construction. Someone's terrible merge.

"How's work," Walt asked, the old reflex: redirect to competence.

Declan felt the institutional shadow move across his mind—Malloy's *Quick Sync,* Kyle's watchful concern, the constant appetite for explanation.

He didn't feed it.

"It's work," he said. "I'm managing it."

Walt nodded like that meant good, like that meant everything.

The clinic parking lot was already full. Declan found a spot far from the entrance because far spots were the only honest ones left in this world: walk it out; don't pretend it's easy.

Walt moved slower than he thought he was moving. That was the thing Declan couldn't get used to—how the body revised itself without telling the mind.

Inside, the fluorescent lights made everything look guilty.

The waiting room sounds rose in their indifferent choir: coughs, the soft tear of a receipt, the clunk of a vending machine swallowing coins, the distant beep of a machine nobody wanted to need. Daytime television murmured from a wall-mounted screen, a bright, cruel comedy in which everyone's worst problem was a misunderstanding.

Declan's wrist itched—the old stress flare. His chest tightened as if the air had thickened.

He named it silently.

This is my body trying to sprint ahead.

He didn't obey it.

He sat. He breathed. He took out the folder. He checked the forms. He became sequence.

A woman in a pale cardigan approached, smiling in the careful way of professionals who weren't paid to be blunt. Her lanyard read **Volunteer Services** and her eyes were the soft, practiced kind that

⁂

said: *I'm safe until I'm not.*

"Good morning," she said. "How are we doing today?"

Declan felt the question's shape. Not curiosity. Intake.

"Fine," Walt said quickly, too quickly. "Just here for a follow-up."

"And how are you holding up?" the woman asked, turning the warmth toward Declan like a lamp.

Declan could hear Malloy in it. The same cadence dressed in gentler clothes: confess so I can file you.

The volunteer's smile widened slightly, as if inviting a performance. "Any fears we want to name? Sometimes it helps to bring things into the light."

Walt's posture stiffened. Politeness became armor. He was about to do the old routine—joke, deflect, pretend.

Declan spoke first, calm enough to sound like he wasn't making a decision.

"Thanks," he said. "We're not doing that. If you want to help, we need space."

The volunteer blinked. The smile held, then tightened by a millimeter—the mask slipping enough to show the underside: mild judgment, mild surprise, the faint offense of being refused.

"Of course," she said. "We just... want everyone to feel supported."

"We do," Declan said.

He didn't explain. He didn't soften it into apology. He didn't argue theology or policy or feelings.

He held the line like it was a door he didn't need to open.

The volunteer walked away, still smiling, now toward someone more pliable.

Walt watched Declan with a look that was almost irritation—almost gratitude—almost respect. Something in him loosened, minute and reluctant.

"You didn't have to be..." Walt began.

Declan kept his eyes on the folder. "I wasn't anything," he said. "I was clear."

Walt swallowed, and the swallow looked harder than it should've been.

When they called Walt's name, the nurse's voice had the same tired precision as all institutional voices: kind, efficient, refusing the weight of what it carried.

Walt stood too fast. Declan's hand hovered near his elbow—not touching, not babying, prepared.

Walt glanced at him, annoyed at the existence of help.

Declan didn't argue. He simply walked alongside.

The appointment was a blur of small measurements and soft phrases that were designed to land gently while still being true.

They didn't come out with a cinematic answer. They came out with the kind of reality that changed everything through paperwork:

a medication adjustment, "just to be safe,"

a new monitoring schedule,

another scan, sooner than planned,

a phrase like *rule out* that sounded polite and meant *we're not sure yet*.

Walt tried his reflex the moment they were back in the car.

"Nothing big," he said, staring out the windshield as if the parking lot could absorb it.

Declan didn't let minimization drive.

He turned the key, let the engine settle, and looked at Walt.

"Okay," Declan said. "Then we handle it. What's next?"

Walt exhaled, the air leaving him like surrender without the word.

"I've got to pick up the new prescription," Walt said. "And—" He hesitated, which was rare. "They want me back next week. Same time."

※
※※

Declan nodded, already mapping the week into parts that could hold this.

"I'll put it in the calendar," he said.

Walt's face tightened. "I don't want you rearranging—"

"It's not rearranging," Declan said, gentle but firm. "It's showing up. There's a difference."

Walt stared at his hands as if they were strangers.

"Can you—" Walt began, then stopped. The request got stuck on pride.

Declan waited without rushing him.

Walt swallowed. "Can you take me to the pharmacy," he said, like it was a confession.

Declan felt the moment for what it was: not logistics not errands—contact. Real-time.

"Yeah," Declan said, easy. "That's the plan."

Walt didn't joke it away. He simply nodded.

It wasn't a hug. It wasn't a speech. It was the smallest acceptance, and it landed like an emotional climax precisely because it didn't ask to be noticed.

Back home, the house was mid-day messy: coats on chairs, a cereal bowl abandoned like a thought that had wandered off. Lena stood at the counter slicing apples, the kind of unglamorous labor that fed a family and never made the highlight reel.

"How was it?" she asked, and her tone made it a real question without turning it into an interrogation.

Declan started to narrate the day the way his nervous system wanted to—fast, angry, defensive. Then he stopped. He felt the old urge to perform his own stress, to make it impressive enough to justify it.

He didn't.

He gave the clean report. The beam set in place.

"There's a follow-up," he said. "Medication change. Another scan. He's scared."

He paused, then added the part that mattered most because it was the part he'd usually hide.

"I'm scared," he said. "Here's what we're doing."

Lena didn't gasp. She didn't turn it into a speech. She nodded, like a person receiving information they could act on.

"What do you need from me?" she asked.

Declan's throat tightened again—this time from relief.

"Just... keep doing what you're doing," he said. "And I'll do the pharmacy and the calendar and the rides. We'll split it."

Lena slid a plate toward him. "Eat," she said, which was its own kind of love.

Theo came in from the living room clutching a toy dinosaur like it was a briefing document.

"We'll monitor," Theo announced, solemn. He'd overheard something—maybe on the drive, maybe in a whispered exchange. He was trying to be helpful in the only way kids knew: repeating adult words like they were spells.

Declan smiled despite himself.

Theo watched the smile like it was permission.

Declan crouched to Theo's level. "Yeah," he said. "We will."

Theo frowned. "Is monitoring like... watching him all the time?"

"It's watching enough," Declan said. "Not spying. Not panicking. Just paying attention."

Theo considered this, then asked, "If it's big, do we have to cry?"

Declan laughed quietly—one short, real sound that didn't try to escape the moment.

"No," he said. "You can cry if you want. But big doesn't mean hopeless. Big means we talk and we do the next thing."

※

Theo nodded, satisfied by the existence of a plan.

Daisy walked over and leaned her shoulder gently into Declan's leg, as if casting a vote for steadiness.

Night arrived with its usual small humiliations: the tug-of-war over pajamas, the negotiation of teeth, the endless request for one more of everything.

Theo fell asleep mid-story the way he always did—mouth slightly open, eyelids surrendering without ceremony. Declan felt the old spark of irritation rise—*I'm reading to nobody,* the petty, exhausted thought.

Then it dissolved into tenderness as quickly as it came.

This was the practice now: finishing without martyrdom. Continuing without theater.

He finished the chapter anyway—quietly, like a man learning to keep promises to himself in small units.

He closed the book.

He looked at his phone.

Walt's name was there with a timestamp from today—proof not of resolution, but of contact. Real-time. Not myth. Not voicemail. Not the private problem of a man disappearing with good manners.

Daisy lay in the hallway outside Theo's room, a dark shape against the wood floor, keeping watch without being asked.

Declan stood there for a moment, listening to the house breathe.

Not perfect. Not healed. Not resolved.

Stabilized.

He didn't sprint mentally ahead. He didn't build a catastrophe in his head to feel prepared for it.

He chose the only speed that mattered.

One thing.

Then the next.

⁂

The email arrived like weather—no thunder, pressure.
    Quick touch-base
    30 minutes
No agenda.

Declan read it once, then again, as if a second pass might reveal the hidden knife. His body reacted before his mind did: jaw tightening, wrist itching, a small, stupid flare in his chest like the beginning of a panic that wanted credit for being early.

He noticed it.

This is my system trying to sprint.

He didn't obey.

In the kitchen, the mug waited. The marker sat beside it. Declan poured coffee without drawing the line. The coffee rose too high, kissed the rim, dared him to turn it into a lesson.

He didn't.

Warm. Imperfect. Shared.

Theo was already talking—something about a dinosaur having a job and being "in trouble" for eating a mailbox. Lena moved through the morning like a person who had decided not to turn competence into a confession.

Daisy stood in her usual place, between rooms, ears half-up, keeping an eye on the human ritual of making everything urgent.

Declan packed lunch, signed a form, zipped a coat. One thing. Then the next.

By the time he stepped into the office, his body had downgraded the alarm from emergency to discomfort. It was still there, but it wasn't driving.

At the printer, Kyle appeared like a barometer—small talk with a forecast.

"Heard Malloy's been talking you up," Kyle said, loading paper like he was feeding a machine that couldn't be satisfied. The words were meant to sound like praise. They landed like warning.

Declan kept his eyes on the printer screen. "Okay."

Kyle smirked, trying to pull him into the usual ritual of nervous gratitude. "Just... don't make waves. He likes loyal."

Kyle lowered his voice. "I'm still trying to get out from under my last write-up. So—yeah. Loyal."

Declan heard the trap cleanly now: silence dressed as safety. Compliance wearing a suit.

He nodded once, the kind of nod that meant *I heard you* but not *I agree.*

At his desk, an email from Mitchell waited—short, clear, unusually respectful:

Mitchell:

Structure worked. Deliverables on track. Thanks for keeping it stable.

It hit Declan with a strange ache. Not pride exactly. More like the quiet cost of being useful in a world that charged interest.

He didn't screenshot it. He didn't re-read it for validation.

He filed it.

Moved on.

At ten-thirty, the calendar reminder blinked. Malloy's name. The word *touch-base.* The empty agenda.

Declan walked down the hallway with his shoulders set as if he were

⁎⁎⁎

carrying something heavy that couldn't be seen.

Malloy's office door was half-closed in the managerial way that suggested privacy while still promising surveillance. The perfect suit. The perfect desk. The kind of calm that came from never having to explain yourself to anyone who could hurt you.

Malloy lifted his gaze with his practiced concern-face, the one he wore for exits and funerals and quarterly numbers.

"Declan," he said warmly. "Come in. Sit."

Declan sat. He kept his hands still on his knees. He didn't fidget. He didn't offer any body-language bribes.

Malloy tilted his head, voice syrup-soft. "How are you holding up?"

There it was. Concern as intake. The confessional disguised as care.

Declan didn't bite. "I'm meeting deadlines," he said.

Malloy smiled as if Declan had made a joke. "Of course. That's exactly why I wanted to talk."

He opened a folder that didn't need opening. He did it anyway because props helped him believe his own performance.

"I've been looking at bandwidth and… opportunities." *Growth* meant more hours. *Opportunity* meant less sleep. The words were gift-wrapped theft. "There's a chance here for you to step into more visibility. Leadership track."

Declan waited. He'd learned not to fill silence like it was a weakness.

Malloy continued, enthusiasm carefully measured. "A bigger portfolio. Higher-level stakeholders. More strategic. It's… a promotion, in spirit." He smiled, as if spirit could pay a mortgage. "And we'd like you to take on Kyle's overflow for a bit. Just temporarily, until we stabilize."

Declan heard the math in his head: more work, same resources, a title bump without time, visibility as exposure. And under it, the older truth: *stabilize* never ended. It just found a new excuse.

Malloy leaned forward, voice dropping into intimacy. "I think you deserve it. But I want to make sure you're in a good place for it. Just be honest with me."

The words were soft. The mechanism was sharp.

Declan could almost see the future leverage in Malloy's mind: If Declan admits strain, then Declan becomes manageable. If Declan offers a family detail, then Declan becomes adjustable. If Declan confesses, Malloy can file him.

Declan didn't moralize. He didn't mention Walt. He didn't weaponize trauma. He didn't beg for compassion.

He gave Malloy what the system claimed to want but rarely tolerated: clarity.

"I can take Mitchell," Declan said, voice even, "and keep him stable. I can take X and keep it moving. I can't take Z without support."

Malloy's smile flickered—one millimeter.

Declan continued, still calm. "If support isn't available, I'm declining Z."

Then he stopped.

The old him would've explained. This time he didn't. He offered the clean sentence and let it stand.

For a moment, Malloy seemed genuinely surprised—not at the words, but at the absence of blood. There was nothing to collect.

Malloy's smile returned, thinner now. "I'm surprised," he said softly, as if Declan had disappointed him personally. "I thought you were a team player."

Declan didn't flinch. He didn't argue the definition of team. He didn't try to win Malloy back.

"I'm meeting deadlines," he said again. Same sentence. Same calm. "I'll continue to. That's the plan."

Malloy's eyes hardened politely. The corporate dagger moved under the table.

※
※※

"Noted," Malloy said.

He slid the folder—still meaningless—slightly to the side, as if closing a file on a person.

"We'll proceed accordingly," Malloy added. "I'll need you on a tighter schedule this month. Less... flexibility."

Declan nodded. "That's workable," he said. "With Mitchell stable and X covered."

Malloy waited for Declan to apologize for not being easy.

Declan didn't.

Malloy's smile became official again—end-of-meeting smile. "Thanks for your time."

Declan stood. "Thanks," he said, and left as if he belonged to himself.

In the hallway, his wrist itched once, then stopped. His chest loosened in the way it did after you stopped holding your breath for a person who didn't deserve your oxygen.

At the corner near the elevators, Kyle caught him like a predator hoping for either bragging or collapse.

"Well?" Kyle asked, bright with false casual. "You get the big news?"

Declan looked at him, not unkindly. "I set terms," he said.

Kyle blinked. His face shifted through a few expressions—confusion, irritation, a flash of something like envy.

"You can do that?" Kyle asked, not entirely mocking.

Declan shrugged slightly. "You can be clear," he said. "People might not like it."

Kyle's mouth tightened. He wanted the old script where Declan either performed loyalty or performed gratitude. Terms made the air different. Terms made the room less owned.

"Right," Kyle said, and walked away like he'd bumped into a wall that didn't apologize.

Declan returned to his desk and did what he'd promised: competence. Not martyrdom. Not theater.

He updated Mitchell. He moved the timeline. He documented what needed documenting and refused to document his own nervous system.

When the day ended, he left without the sickly ritual of one more email to prove *I'm good*.

In the car, he didn't replay Malloy's tone. He didn't write imaginary rebuttals. He didn't give the office extra real estate in his head.

Sequence.

Home smelled like real life: garlic, detergent, crayons. Lena was at the counter, assembling dinner with the same unannounced steadiness she'd carried for weeks. Theo sat at the table coloring, tongue out in concentration. Daisy lay between the kitchen and the hallway like a quiet verdict: *Here is where we live.*

Declan didn't narrate his day like a battlefield report.

He washed his hands.

He started laundry.

He checked the calendar for Walt's follow-up and confirmed the pharmacy pickup time. He signed Theo's folder form. He set the tote bag by the door.

Lena looked at him once and understood without speeches: the house felt lighter because Declan hadn't dragged the office home like a wet coat.

At bedtime, Theo asked the question that landed like a pebble dropped into deep water.

"Dad," he said, eyes serious in the dark, "is it allowed to say no to your boss?"

Declan paused. The old him would've made it a lesson, a speech, a moral—something grand enough to cover his own fear.

Instead he gave Theo the better script. The one that didn't require pretending.

"It's allowed to be clear," Declan said. "Sometimes people don't like it. We do it anyway."

Theo considered this, then nodded as if he'd been handed a tool.

Later, when the house quieted and Lena fell asleep with her hand on the edge of the blanket like she was still holding the day in place, Declan opened his laptop.

An email draft sat there—half-written, instinctive, automatic. An apology to Malloy. The old reflex: *I'm sorry for making things hard. I'm sorry I'm not easier. I'm sorry my life exists.*

Declan read it once.

He saw himself in it like an old photograph: younger, hungry, compliant, confusing self-erasure with professionalism.

He deleted it.

He set one calendar reminder—Walt's next appointment—and another for the Mitchell call. He closed the laptop. He put the phone down.

In the hallway, Daisy settled between rooms, ears flicking once as if approving the silence that was peace, not avoidance.

Declan stood there for a second, feeling the quiet not as an emptiness, but as a boundary holding.

He went to bed.

And the last thought he let himself have—simple, unpoetic, true—was the sentence he'd earned the hard way:

"I met my deadlines. I'll continue to."

About the Author

Kevin Haslam is a Rhode Island–based writer and multidisciplinary artist with a soft spot for New England atmosphere and sharp little human truths. He's the author of *The Quiet Parts* and *Salinger in the Rye*—an Amazon bestseller in American Literature Criticism—and he writes literary fiction that's equal parts lyric and bite. A recovering rockstar (yes, really—The Parker Star Band), he still believes in rhythm, big feelings, and making something out of noise. He's also the co-founder of Yoonie Co., an independent creative studio producing original work across writing, visual art, and music.

You can connect with me on:
🌐 https://houseofhas.com

Also by Kevin Haslam

The Quiet Parts: Short Stories
A collection of literary short stories set in Rhode Island and the nearby edges of New England, where daily life quietly intensifies under pressure. In clinics, apartments, bars, and back rooms, people navigate bureaucracy, grief, addiction, love, and the hard arithmetic of survival. With lyrical precision and emotional restraint, these stories explore what we carry without saying—how power moves through ordinary moments, how tenderness persists, and how silence can be both refuge and verdict.

You Forgot About Me:

A cycle of five interconnected stories unfolding over the final six months of World War II, moving from the Hürtgen Forest into wards, trains, and hometown streets where "home" feels like a rumor. Captain Norman Watt—composer turned infantry officer—can't reconcile leadership with slaughter, and his refusal to harden becomes its own liability.

As the fighting recedes, the damage doesn't: a nurse tries to salvage what war has unscrewed from the human spirit; an officer's mind turns the world into a phonograph of repetition; a battle-fatigued witness writes like a man trying to scatter proof into the wind; and a disfigured veteran returns to a Kentucky that has learned to profit without bleeding.

Dedicated to the men who fought in the Battle of Hürtgen Forest, this collection doesn't argue motives. It examines the cost—what's carried back in the quiet, and what the quiet carries forward.